STRUCK
from the
RECORD

Also by K.A. Linde

Avoiding Series

Avoiding Commitment (#1)
Avoiding Responsibility (#2)
Avoiding Intimacy (#2.5)
Avoiding Decisions (#1.5)
Avoiding Temptation (#3)

Record Series

Off the Record
On the Record
For the Record
Struck from the Record

Take Me Duet

Take Me for Granted
Take Me with You

All That Glitters Series

Diamonds
Gold
Emeralds
Platinum

Ascension Series

The Affiliate

Stand-Alone

Following Me

STRUCK *from the* RECORD

RECORD SERIES BOOK 4

K.A. LINDE

"**B**oys! Come help your father!" Marilyn called. She was standing at the top of the stairs that led from the pool of their Hilton Head home down to the beach.

Clay Maxwell looked to his older brother, Brady, for confirmation that they could ignore their mother and keep hanging out at the beach. They always came down here for the Fourth of July celebration with the Atwood family, but a couple of days ago, they had finally made friends with a group of kids nearby. Clay was even more excited because some of them were his own age. One of the girls was pretty, too.

While it was fun, hanging out with Brady and Chris Atwood, Brady's best friend, all summer, they would treat him like a baby even though they were only three years older. Clay would turn thirteen next month and he'd already dated and dumped a number of girls in his grade. He *wasn't* a baby.

"Coming, Mom!" Brady yelled back.

Clay slumped his shoulders. *Why did Brady always do the right thing? For once, couldn't he just ignore our mother and pretend like he hadn't heard her?*

"Let's go, Clay," he demanded, all high and mighty.

Brady, the perfect.

Clay rolled his eyes. "I'll be there in a minute."

Brady fixed him with one of his best death stares. Clay snorted and turned away. Brady could just stare at his back for all he cared. *I'd be there in a minute! Just like I'd said. Geez!*

"You should probably go," the girl in front of him said. She smiled sweetly.

She was better than pretty, he decided.

She had the biggest blue eyes ever, her hair was almost platinum in the bright afternoon sun, and her sun-kissed skin looked hot in her skimpy blue bikini. A soft layer of sand clung to her from playing in the water and messing around on the surf all afternoon.

"Yeah," he agreed.

"Maybe I'll see you later?" she asked hopefully. Her cheeks turned crimson, and she looked away.

Clay stood a little taller, unconsciously mimicking the way Brady would talk to girls he met on the beach. "Definitely. We're here the rest of the week."

"Okay!" Her face brightened.

"Clay!" Brady yelled. "Don't make Mom repeat herself."

"Jesus, I'm coming!" he yelled back. Clay groaned. "He's so annoying."

She giggled. "I'm an only child. I think it might be nice to have someone nag me."

"It's not. Trust me."

"I'll take your word for it. See you later, Clay."

"Bye, Andrea." He nodded his head and then jogged after Brady and Chris, who were waiting impatiently a few feet away.

"Look, I'm coming," he said. He spread his arms wide to indicate he was heading toward them.

"About time," Brady said.

When Clay reached them, Brady immediately pulled him into a headlock. He roughly rubbed Clay's hair with his fist.

"Brady!" he cried, trying to get loose. "Let go!"

Clay punched him in the stomach as hard as he could, but he might as well have been fighting with a brick wall. Even at sixteen, Brady played an endless amount of basketball and worked out relentlessly when he wasn't studying. He was solid and much bigger than his gangly younger brother who hadn't grown into his body yet.

In fact, they had always been night and day in looks as well as personality. Brady was tall with dark brown hair and even darker eyes. He looked just like their father. Clay, on the other hand, resembled his mother's picturesque beauty with dark blond hair that lightened under the summer sun and blue eyes. Brady was the golden boy. He had played varsity basketball as a freshman at a private high school in Chapel Hill and had been on a state traveling team for years before that. He was smart and active in student government, and *everyone* liked him. Growing up, Clay had preferred lacrosse and soccer but had never liked either as much as Brady liked basketball. His parents had told him he would find *his* thing when he got older, but he knew he wouldn't measure up to Brady, no matter what he did.

Brady shoved him away, and Clay tumbled forward, landing on his hands and knees in the sand. He glared up at his brother.

"Sorry," Brady said.

He offered his hand, but Clay pushed it away.

"I don't need your help!"

"I was just messing around, Clay. Don't take everything so seriously."

"Whatever," he grumbled.

Chris clapped him on the back when he stood.

Clay wasn't sure how Chris could stand being around Brady all the time. He was such an asshole. He liked everyone to walk in his shadow. As far as Clay could tell, Chris would have been a much better older brother.

Clay followed Brady and Chris up the stairs. His mother was lying on a lounger and only half-watching his six-year-old little sister, Savannah, splash in the pool with Chris's younger brother, Lucas, who was the same age as Savannah.

"Mom! Look what I can do!" She jumped up and down in the pool. "I beat Lucas in racing!" Savannah yelled. "Mom!"

"Yes, dear. That's lovely. Keep at it, and you'll be an Olympic swimmer someday."

Savannah beamed even though Clay was sure she had no idea what that meant, but it quelled her curiosity, and she went back to playing. His mother was talking to Chris's mother, Gina Atwood, who had a one-year-old Alice bouncing on her lap.

"Mom, what did you want?" Clay asked. "I was hanging out with my friends."

Marilyn looked up at him but turned her smile toward Brady. "There you are, boys. Your father is about to start grilling and wants your help."

"Got it," Brady said. "Is he in the study?"

"He wants *all* of us to grill?" Clay asked, exasperated.

"Your father is very busy, but he wants to spend time with you on our family vacation, Clay. Give him a chance, would you?" she asked. Her tone said there was to be no arguing, and she was irritated with him to boot.

"Don't listen to Clay. He's just in a bad mood because he had to leave his girlfriend behind," Brady teased.

"Another one?" Marilyn asked.

"She's not my girlfriend. She's just a friend."

"*Right*," Brady said under his breath.

"Well, if you want to invite your…friend over for dinner, there's plenty to go around."

"Girlfriend," Brady repeated.

"She's not my girlfriend!" he yelled, punching Brady in the shoulder. "Stop being such an asshole."

"Language, Clay!"

"He started it!" Clay yelled back.

"Enough. Both of you. Can't we just have one day of peace without you two bickering?" she asked. She turned to Chris's mother, apologetically saying, "I'm sorry, Gina. Boys, you know."

"You don't have to tell me twice. I get it."

She sighed and shook her head. "Now, go in and help your father. And I don't want to hear any more complaints from you, Clay Alexander!"

Clay cringed. He knew she meant business when she used his full name. "Fine."

He sulked past Brady and into the overly air-conditioned house. He found his father with Chris's father, Matthew, in the study. By the time Clay got up the nerve to walk through the door, his shoulders were straight, his chin was raised, and he held all the confidence his father, Jeff, expected of a Maxwell son, all the confidence that had been instilled in him from a very young age.

"Dad," Clay said, "Mom said you needed us."

Brady and Chris showed up a minute later. They were laughing boisterously at something Brady had probably said.

Show- off.

But the laughter cut off abruptly when they walked into the study.

Their father wasn't uncaring or unkind. He was a great dad actually. He'd just had a strict upbringing, and even when he tried to relax his standards toward his sons, he never seemed to manage it. The only one who got away with anything was little Savannah, and she got away with *everything.* His little angel could do no wrong.

"Come in and have a seat, boys. It'll just be a minute while I finish up this memo," Jeff said.

"Chris, why don't we go get the steaks out of the refrigerator?" Matthew said. He walked around the desk and moved over to Chris.

"Sure thing. You're going to let me grill yours this time, right?" he asked, elbowing his dad in the ribs.

"I don't want mine black and burned!"

"Aw, don't be so hard on me. That was my first time, and Pepper loved it," he said, referencing the Labrador they had at home.

"Well, Pepper isn't here, and I don't want her to have any more of my choice sirloins!"

Chris cracked up.

Clay could hear them joking back and forth all the way down the hallway. He wondered what that must be like as he turned back to his own father. He was handwriting the memo that he would mail off to his secretary in D.C. to type out and deliver for him.

It shouldn't matter that Clay couldn't joke around with his dad. He was important. A sitting senator in Washington. He drafted bills and created legislation, turning the tide of the country. It made his absences in their lives acceptable. And as Clay's mother continually reminded him, they were incredibly fortunate, and he should act like it.

Brady and Clay took the open seats in front of their father's desk. His leg bounced impatiently. *If we were going to have to sit there for another half hour, waiting for him to be done with his paperwork, why had he bothered to call us to help him grill?*

"Sorry," Jeff said. He pushed the paperwork away from him. "I didn't mean to keep you waiting. One day, you'll understand."

"I already understand," Brady said.

His father smiled a politician's smile. "I believe you do."

"I get it, too," Clay said immediately. He didn't. Not really. Sure, he understood the work his dad was doing, but he thought it was crappy that it came before his family.

Clay didn't want a family. Then, there would be no one in his life to disappoint.

"One day, Clay. One day at a time," his father said.

Clay's face fell.

"Now, tell me about your day while we go get the grill started."

Brady launched into a story about the day's events. He had a knack for telling stories in a way that made the listener feel like they were actually there. Even Clay could get engrossed in his brother's stories, but he saw the fabrications and exaggerations for what they were.

As such, Clay was mostly ignored the rest of the afternoon as they spent time around the grill and then throughout the rest of the afternoon while they ate the delicious food they'd made and lounged around the deck until the sun disappeared over the horizon.

"Jeff, that's your last one," Marilyn prodded her husband, trying to urge Savannah upstairs to go to sleep.

Gina was doing the same to Lucas while she held a passed out baby Alice in her arms.

His father laughed and held the beer out to his wife. "I've only had a couple, Marilyn."

"Don't get sloppy," she warned with a glint in her eye.

"Never. I'll come tuck in Savannah in a minute," he promised.

When she left, he conspiratorially leaned forward toward his sons. "Find a woman like that, boys. She'll make you happy forever."

Brady listened, enraptured by their father's attention. Clay just thought talking about his mom like that was disgusting.

"Let me tell you something, son," he said, placing his hand on Brady's shoulder.

Clay couldn't help feeling a pang of jealousy.

"Once you've found that woman, everything will fall into place. I just know it. Then, one day, you are going to be president of the United States."

Brady smiled triumphantly. "President?" he asked with longing in his voice.

"You're on the right path."

Brady as president? Clay almost snorted in disbelief. *Yeah, right.* Brady would make a terrible president. All he cared about was himself and how many people he could charm to be his admirers. Clay didn't wish his brother's form of coercion on anyone.

"And what am *I* going to be?" Jealous, he couldn't help but ask.

He hated that his father had just given his egotistical brother even more motivation to act like he was above everyone else, but still he hoped that his father would say the same for him. That Clay could be president. That Clay could achieve any dream he set before himself.

His father turned to him with a thoughtful smile. "Hmm…Clay, you're going to be the attorney general."

Clay raised his eyebrows. "What's an attorney general?"

"You're the number one lawyer in all the country. Top of your class at Yale, clerked for the Supreme Court, federal judge. Then, when the time is right and Brady has become president, he'll appoint you as attorney general." His father shrugged. "It worked for the Kennedys."

He and Matthew laughed at whatever joke he'd just made, but Clay didn't find it funny. He didn't find it funny *at all*.

Clay slouched back into his chair and turned away from the rest of the conversation. He didn't need to hear any more to know what his father thought about him. Apparently, his second son wasn't good enough.

A short while later, Brady and Chris got permission to ride their bikes to a friend's house as long as they would be home by midnight. Chris grumbled, but Brady agreed easily. He didn't break rules, and Clay was sure that he would be back at precisely midnight.

"Hey, can I go with you?" Clay asked hopefully.

Chris looked uncomfortable.

Brady frowned. "Sorry. It's a high school party. You wouldn't fit in." He sure didn't sound sorry.

He didn't want Clay to go with him. It was so obvious.

"Yeah. Sure. Of course. I'll just sit here by myself and die from boredom," Clay said dramatically. "Have a good time."

"It's not like that, Clay," Brady said. "It's just that no one your age will be there."

"Whatever. I'm going to the beach."

"Don't be gone long," his mother said, having come downstairs after laying Savannah down.

His father had disappeared right after her to tuck his youngest in.

"Yeah, yeah. I got it."

He trudged down the steps and through the sand. Fury was building in his gut. All he wanted to do was pummel something into oblivion. He'd gotten into a few fights in school because he couldn't control his ever-present temper. But he was getting better at it.

He ground his teeth together, balling his hands into fists at his sides and kicking at the sand. He was concentrating so hard on trying not to be angry that he didn't even see the figure sitting on the beach a few blocks away until he almost toppled over on top of her.

"Oh, hey," he said.

Andrea Billings scrubbed her face with her hands and then looked up at him. Her cheeks were splotchy, and her eyes were puffy, like she had been crying. "Hey, Clay. Sorry"—she hiccuped—"I'm a disaster."

He stood there uncomfortably for a minute. "Are you okay? Do you want to talk about it?"

She shrugged. "Just my parents arguing again. Doesn't matter. What about you? Why are you out here by yourself?"

He plopped down in the sand next to her. "Had to get away."

"Your brother bothering you again?"

"Yeah."

He had only known her a couple of days, and already, she just seemed to get it.

"My dad said something that just—ugh! It's so typical Brady, the perfect-son bullshit."

She laughed. "What's the fun in being perfect anyway?"

"Right?" he yelled.

"What did your dad say?"

"That he knew Brady was going to be the president one day. When I asked him what I would be, you know what he said?"

She shook her head.

"The attorney general. Like I want to be some stupid lawyer appointed by my brother. I'd rather be president myself."

"Well, *I* wouldn't want to be president! Can you imagine how much work it all is? My dad said the president never sleeps."

"Yeah, I guess you're right," he said, momentarily relieved.

"Though I guess there are perks," she said, giggling. "The president did get a blow job in his office."

Clay's eyes lit up. "That is a perk I could get on board with."

And then, without thinking about it, he leaned forward and kissed her. It was soft and unexpected. He didn't even know why he had done it. It just felt right. It felt like their moment.

When he pulled back, they both looked away, a little embarrassed at his brazenness. She stayed sitting there, staring out at the ocean, for a little while longer before saying anything else.

"Just so you know, I don't think you have to be the president or the attorney general or anything. I just think you have to be you, and that will be enough," Andrea said.

He smiled at her words. It was the first time anyone had said something like that to him. If only it were true.

He would die before remaining under Brady's shadow for the rest of his life. Maybe one day, *he* would outshine the golden boy.

Chapter 1

BOW TIES

"So, you really work for the Supreme Court?" the girl asked in disbelief.

Clay popped open the door to the cab they'd taken over to the building and tried to suppress a sigh of frustration. He fucking hated when people questioned him about his job. Yes, he knew he was one of the youngest clerks in history. He'd worked his ass off to get there, and he was damn proud of it. But still, it was better to have them question him than when they recognized his name.

Luckily, this girl hadn't. She stepped out of the cab and revealed the enormous rack he'd been staring at all night, and he remembered why he'd let her question him. It was going to be fun to have her look at him in disbelief when they actually walked inside, and then he'd fuck her against all those heavy law books on his bookshelf.

He figured fucking her in his office was a fitting going-away present since his term as a clerk was coming to a close.

"I really do," he told her.

She took his hand, and they walked up the steps and inside the building. It was the middle of the night a week before Christmas, and no one else was here. Even the annoying diligent douche who worked for the justice down the hall wasn't in the building.

"This is so cool," the girl said.

She seemed jittery with excitement. He doubted many people could actually boast that they'd had sex in an office at the Supreme Court. This was what dreams were made of.

He cracked a smile at his own thoughts.

They reached his office at the end of the hall, and he pulled his keys out of his pocket. Jiggling the key into the handle, he turned the knob and yanked the door open for her. She stepped inside to his personal hell for the last two years.

He'd spent half a year clerking for a federal court before he was called up to the Supreme Court. Some had said that he only got the position because of his name, the damn Maxwell name. But he didn't think top of his class at Yale Law had hurt anything.

"Wow," the girl said.

She walked right over to his bookcase, sending his brain into overdrive. He could just imagine pinning her body back against it. Definitely his plans for tonight. Easy enough.

"Clay, have you really read all of these?" she asked.

Fuck, he didn't even remember her name. Just that the skimpy green thing she considered a dress matched her eyes, and she had lips that looked like they belonged around his cock.

"You're asking too many questions," he said dismissively.

"That so?" She leaned back on the bookshelf facing him. "Is this better? This what you want?"

He arched an eyebrow as she ran her hand down her front in invitation. He didn't move. He liked the anticipation.

"Or would you rather have me here?" She stepped up to his desk and then laid her body across all the work he had to pick up before he cleared out his things this week.

"I think the bookshelf," he said, revealing a dimple for her.

"Mmm, me, too."

She crooked a finger at him, and he was about to oblige when his phone started ringing.

Fuck. Bad timing.

He raised a finger at Green Dress Chick and removed his phone from his pocket. A name flashed on the front of the screen that immediately brought a smile to his lips.

Andrea.

"Seriously?" the girl snapped from his desk.

"Have to take this," he said.

He turned away from the girl, ignoring her less than flattering comments. "Hello, love. This really isn't a good time."

"Is that so?"

"In the middle of something."

"What's her name?" Andrea asked. Her voice was high and musical, just like he had always found it throughout the past fifteen years they had known each other.

"Should I remember?" Because he didn't.

He didn't even know if he had bothered asking for her name. It hadn't mattered at the time.

"Your standards are slipping."

"I'm still with you. Can't be that low." Clay smirked.

"I'm out of your league, honey."

"Always have been," he agreed easily.

"Why do I put up with you anyway?" Andrea sounded bored, not irritated.

She was never irritated with him. Not really. She didn't give a shit about what he did. Just like he didn't care about what she did in her spare time.

Clay had met Andrea on the beach on Hilton Head when he was almost thirteen years old. Since then, they had spent every summer together on that beach, even after her parents had finally split up during her sophomore year of high school. She'd endured years of endless arguments between them. Then, after the divorce, there was limitless pampering from her mom to make up for the fights that had jaded Andrea's soft heart.

By the time they had gotten together at Yale during their freshman year of college, they were both very different people than they had been that one summer when he was embarrassed from kissing her on the beach.

Romance was wasted on them, so they had entered into the arrangement of a lifetime. They could do whatever they wanted, but at the end of the day, they would be together. Guard their hearts. No feelings would get hurt. They wouldn't turn out like her parents, and he wouldn't have anyone in his life to disappoint because of his behavior. It was perfect.

"You don't put up with me. You enjoy it. It's all my charm."

"Oh, right," she drawled. "That Maxwell charm. It does have a certain appeal."

"Every appeal," he said confidently. "So, I assume you called for a reason."

"I have a game for you," she said huskily.

"Right now?" he asked.

He glanced back over at the girl who had, seconds ago, been eager for him to fuck her against the bookshelves. Now, she just looked irritated.

"Don't tell me you're backing down from a challenge, Maxwell."

"You know I never do." He made a decision on the spot.

Andrea was an easy choice. He always chose her over everyone else. Ten years of the perfect arrangement and perfect sex had taught him that coming home to Andrea was better than any one-night stand.

"I'll call you back in ten."

"Make it five, or forfeit," she said before hanging up on him.

"All right. Let's go," he said briskly to the girl in his office.

The girl sat up on her elbows and stared up at him in disbelief. "Go where?"

"We're leaving. I'm sending you home."

"What?" she nearly shrieked.

"I'm not sleeping with you. Time for us to leave."

Her hysterics didn't seem to be working, so she changed tactics and gave him a seductive look. "What about your place?" Her eyes glittered with excitement.

"I don't think so," Clay said, bored.

It had been fun when it was a challenge. He liked challenges, but this was too easy. He could pick up any girl at a bar if he wanted to. At least put some fucking effort into it. And if he didn't get her out of this damn office, he was going to miss his opportunity to put in all his effort.

"Time to leave."

He yanked the door open without preamble. She pouted but had enough dignity not to say anything else. She begrudgingly followed him out the office, back down the hall, and outside. He had texted a cab service after hanging up with Andrea, and a cab was waiting for them when they made it into the fresh air.

"I can't fucking believe you're doing this," she said.

"Believe it."

"Was that even your office?"

He smirked. "Obviously."

"I don't know who the fuck called that would make you want to spirit me away so quickly." She looked down at the ground and then back into his eyes. "We could have had a really good time."

"We could have," he agreed. "But it was my girlfriend."

Her mouth dropped open. "You're an ass!"

She rushed into the cab and glared at him as the cab pulled away.

Well, that had been easier than he'd thought. That was the normal reaction he would get from people when he told them that he had a girlfriend. No one really understood their relationship, nor did they care to figure it out. It was easier to just let people believe he was a philandering asshole than to explain that they had been in a successful open relationship for the last ten years.

Easier to let people believe he was the bad boy of the Maxwell political dynasty than to clue them in on his long-term plan—top of his class at Yale, clerk at the Supreme Court, federal judge, attorney general. Thinking of it both excited him and made him feel sick. He wanted to live up to the man his father expected him to be, but following the mold made him crazy. It was a double-edged sword, a line he constantly skirted.

That girl would have been a treat for completing his clerkship and moving one step closer to the end goal on his path. Another thing completed on a checklist. Finishing didn't seem fulfilling in the same way it had when he was accepted to clerk. But, tomorrow, he would have to clear out his desk and get serious about deciding on which private practice offer he would accept.

He had been staring at three offers for over a week now, and since each position began in January, they were expecting an answer by Christmas…maybe New Year's at the latest.

But he didn't need to worry about that tonight. He could have Andrea as a treat instead.

Clay fished his cell phone out of his pocket again and smiled. *Four minutes. Perfect.*

He dialed Andrea's number and waited for her to answer while he waited outside of the building. It clicked over to voice mail.

He scowled down at the phone. "What the fuck?"

Then, it almost immediately lit up again.

"Can I help you?" she asked curtly.

Clay cracked a smile.

"So, where are you? I'll grab a cab now and meet you."

Andrea made a tinkling giggle. "Do you think you're the only one who can have fun, Clay Maxwell?"

A smile spread across his face. "You're bad, and it turns me on."

"Well, you'll have to do something about it by yourself. I have…other plans," she said breathily— for his benefit, he was sure.

His body itched from the challenge she was posing. Andrea always seemed to do this. He could fuck so many other girls, and then one little giggle from her would make him want to claim her all over again.

She was a continual challenge. She was beautiful with long blonde hair, bright blue eyes, and a tall, lean frame that he knew intimately. But every time he thought he had her figured out, every time he was sure she was going to do one thing, she would do something else. She liked to play games, and he liked her games.

Because, at the end of the day, he knew exactly where her head was in all of this. It wasn't seeking out a Harry Winston engagement ring. It wasn't demanding an *I love you* before bed. It wasn't a scowl for his philandering or the way he treated his brother or innumerable other reasons. It was just an arrangement for two people who cared about each other…in their own way.

"Pray tell, love. Who is the lucky bastard?" Clay asked.

He was already sliding into the cab that had appeared for him and adjusting the purple-striped bow tie at his neck.

Andrea came from old Southern plantation money. Her mother was a Southern pageant queen, and they had both been raised in the South Carolina Junior League. Her father owned half of Charleston and regularly purchased, stripped, and resold the other half. The Maxwells could stretch their lineage back to Thomas Jefferson himself. They had been in real estate in The Triangle area of North Carolina for just as long. Clay was a Southern boy through and through, and if there was one thing Andrea couldn't resist, it was when he acted like it.

"He's no one you know," she told him.

"I know everyone."

"Not this one."

"Stop teasing me."

She giggled. "Oh, but you don't really want me to do that, Clay. You probably want me to describe him on the phone. Should I start with his suit or how big I think he is?"

"Always good to know your competition," he said.

"Well, I don't have time. I have to get back to my game. I don't want him to think I have a doting boyfriend waiting for me at home."

Clay snorted. "Doting. Sounds just like me."

Andrea was silent for a moment, and if he couldn't hear the bar noise in the background, he might have thought she had hung up on him.

"Sometimes, it's not that far off," she said quietly.

"Right," he said with a laugh. "Doting, Andrea?"

"You're an ass."

"Yeah, you've always known that. Now, I'll show you doting. Where are you?"

"Don't ruin my game, Clay," she said without conviction.

She had called *him* after all.

They had rules, and they were simple. When they were together, it was just the two of them. When they were apart, anything was fair game. But when one of them called, ruining the other person's game was *exactly* the rule of thumb. He was coming to claim her, and she knew it. They had both known it as soon as he answered.

He could hear the telltale signs of excitement in her voice. He was sure she was pouting to look like she was upset.

"I would never," he lied.

"I don't ruin yours."

"You do if you can help it. Now, tell me," he demanded.

"Fine," she said. "But you'd better bring your A game. He's a keeper."

"Don't I always?"

She told him the name of the bar where she was. It wasn't far from his townhouse or his work, which made him wonder if she had picked it, hoping for this outcome. She was conniving, and he wouldn't put it past her.

Clay felt emboldened as he left to chase down his girl.

Chapter 2
GAMES

Clay stepped into the dimly lit bar. It was one of those upscale artsy places that Andrea frequented and he loathed. The actual artists wouldn't be caught dead in here, but art *enthusiasts* congregated in the space. And if Andrea liked anything, she liked throwing her fortune away at art shows.

He spotted her sitting at the horseshoe-style bar in the middle of the room, talking to her prey. She was in a demure black dress that hugged her lithe curves and two-thousand-dollar shoes that she had a closetful of at home. She was facing the entrance, which was likely strategic on her part. Her head had tipped up when he entered the bar, but aside from a passing glance, she didn't even acknowledge him. But she certainly knew he was here.

That was enough for now.

Bypassing her, he took a seat on a barstool with her in his line of vision. He didn't often drink by himself out in the city, so sitting alone was a change of pace. He believed it was better to have a wingman or two at his side when picking up women since they tended to travel in packs. It was lucky for him when his friends Cash and Ethan had ended up in D.C. after graduating from Yale Law. He'd had tons of friends growing up and in college, but these were the only two, other than Andrea, whom he could actually still stand.

They would probably laugh at him if they knew what he was up to. While they'd claimed to understand the thing he had with Andrea, they'd encourage his crazy lifestyle. Not that he needed encouragement.

Clay ordered a double Crown and Coke from a passing waitress and leaned back in his seat to observe his competition. The guy looked uppity in a black suit and tie. It fit but wasn't tailored to his build. He could use a haircut and a shave.

How had this idiot even caught Andrea's eye?

At least Andrea had made it easy on him.

He would bide his time for the perfect opportunity to make his move.

He went through three drinks in the hour. The bar was clearly an after-hours place because, in the short time it'd moved toward one in the morning, people flooded in. He could barely see Andrea now and knew it was about time. She had flirted her way through much of her conversation with this guy, and

Clay decided the poor sap was just a front. Andrea hardly seemed interested even though the guy was mooning over her. Andrea was not the kind of girl for that.

"Anyone sitting here?" a girl asked, coming up beside him.

Clay turned to face the girl. She was hot. Like smoking hot. He'd say she wasn't his type, but hot was his type. Tall, brunette with freckled olive-toned skin that drew attention to her perfect pink lips. Unfortunately, he preferred blondes and dresses. This girl wore a pantsuit. He hated pantsuits. He understood them as a necessity for women who worked in the business sector, but the misogynistic pig in him loved to get a good look at legs in a pencil skirt.

She slid her charcoal jacket off her shoulders to reveal the silky burgundy sleeveless top underneath. Better but not great.

Clay finally shrugged. "Nope. Go ahead."

"Thanks. It's fucking packed in here."

"Yeah. Didn't realize the place would fill with hipsters. It's like we splashed water on them."

"Gremlins," the woman said with a laugh. "Nice."

"Yeah. If only they hadn't multiplied in the last couple of years, then these bars wouldn't be so in."

"Right. So true. I wouldn't be caught dead in here if my boyfriend didn't like the scene." She wrinkled her nose. "It's hard enough, getting over here from the Hill, with goddamn traffic."

Boyfriend. Why did that suddenly make her more attractive?

"And where is this boyfriend of yours?" he inquired, momentarily forgetting his game.

She shrugged. "It'd be just like the ass not to show up after making me drive all the way over here. As if I don't have more important shit to do."

Clay smirked. It sounded like something he'd probably do.

"Sounds like a stand-up guy."

"The worst."

Clay almost laughed. She was serious. He was about to ask why she'd stay with the guy if he was like that, but then he glanced over at Andrea. She was still flirting shamelessly with Bad Suit, and Clay was over here, talking to his second stranger for the night.

He and Andrea both put up with each other's shit. It worked for them. Had been for almost ten years.

The bartender finally responded to the woman waving cash over the bar, trying to get her attention.

"I'll take a double vodka on the rocks. Grey Goose. Just keep them coming."

He eyed her with appreciation, and she just smiled wryly. "It's been a long day."

Clay held his hands up. "Who am I to judge?"

The bartender pushed the vodka over to the woman and passed another Crown and Coke to Clay, who hadn't even asked for it. It was his fourth. He didn't even know how many other drinks he'd had tonight.

As he took an appreciative sip of the whiskey, his phone pinged.

> *Where are you? I thought you'd make this harder.*

"Girlfriend?" the brunette asked.

"Something like that."

"She stand you up, too?"

Clay saw Andrea arch an eyebrow over Bad Suit's shoulder. He raised his eyebrows. She tilted her head toward the restroom, and he smiled, letting her know he'd gotten the message. Loud and clear.

"Not exactly," he responded. "Excuse me for a minute."

"Should I save your seat?"

He wasn't sure if she sounded hopeful. Most girls would be falling all over themselves by now, but she didn't seem to be that kind of girl, which was interesting. She just continued to sip her vodka, straight up, unperturbed.

"Yeah. Unless that boyfriend of yours shows up." Clay winked.

"All right. I'm Gigi, by the way."

She dropped her suit jacket over his seat and put her hand out for him to shake. He startled slightly at the introduction, as if this were a business meeting and not two people meeting up at a bar. He didn't even remember the last girl's name. This was a lot less than flirting.

Wait, is she even flirting with me?

Huh. Maybe not.

He reached out and took her hand. She had a firm grip, which meant she worked in a profession where people looked down on her. She needed this for authority. He liked a firm grip…handshake and otherwise.

"Clay."

"Nice to meet you, Clay. I've got your seat until my lecherous boyfriend shows up."

He grinned. He couldn't help it.

He wedged his way through the crowd, receiving disgruntled shouts from the people he'd unceremoniously shoved out of his way. When he finally made it back to the restrooms, he found Andrea standing outside the door, as if waiting for the next chance to go inside, which he knew she never did. Queuing was not one of Andrea's specialties.

"Hello, gorgeous," he said, approaching her.

"You, sir, are in big trouble."

"Tell me all about it."

A girl left the restroom, and Clay pushed Andrea inside. The girl gave them a strange look, but there were other restrooms for people who needed it. He locked it from the inside and turned to face his girl. He grabbed her around the middle and hauled her against him. She was so small, always had been. She'd been obsessed with her weight in college and ended up in a lot of counseling to try to fix the issue, but she'd always be small.

He pressed her body back against the door, and she met his gaze with a determined one of her own.

"Clandestine," she murmured in a tone that made it seem as if she were unimpressed.

"You said I was in trouble," he prompted.

With her words, blood was already pumping to all the right places. Fuck, she turned him on. The chase, the rendezvous, the game.

His hands slipped down her black dress, slinky and sophisticated, and he knew it cost a fortune. Everything that Andrea liked did. Instead of going for her lips, he nuzzled her neck, making her arch against him, and then he trailed rough kisses over the territory he was claiming.

"Yes," she said, trying to seem unaffected, "you came to ruin my fun, and then you didn't even make a move. Clay Maxwell, whatever has gotten into you?"

"You're too hasty." He nipped at her neck, and she squeaked. Oh, how he loved that sound. "I was assessing the situation and determining when to go in for the kill."

He forcefully grabbed her leg and pulled it up around his waist. Her dress slid past her upper thigh, nearly revealing what was underneath. He slipped his hand under the material and realized with satisfaction that there was *nothing* underneath.

"Oh, dirty," he growled playfully. "You were ready for me."

"I was, but you're too slow. I'm planning to leave with him."

"Like hell you are!" Clay barked out.

"What? You can have your fun for the night, but I can't?" Her eyes issued a challenge.

"I haven't had any yet," he growled, "but I will now."

Clay's hand slipped back under her dress until he found her pussy, hot and aching for him. She enjoyed this as much as he did, and he'd remind her exactly how much. He wanted to just take her against the door, but he'd rather she beg him for it later.

Without a second thought, he slipped his finger between her lips and trailed it through her wetness before massaging her clit. He had perfect access from this angle, and the only way it would be better was if he could bury his face in between her legs and feel her come all over him. She'd definitely beg then.

"Mmm," she purred, grinding against his hand.

Abruptly, he removed his finger from her clit and pushed two fingers up inside her. She was dripping wet, and he coated his thumb before circling her clit and finger-fucking her hard. It'd be so much better when he got his cock up inside her, but for now, this would do. His dick was as hard as a rock, and it was practically painful as he watched her eyes roll back into her head while her pleasure mounted.

"You're not playing fair," she groaned.

"Only way I know how."

"Oh, please, make me come." She looked at him, her eyes hooded. "If you can."

Motherfucking challenge accepted.

She knew what he was capable of, but he reveled in showing her just how much pleasure she could get from just his fingers. He knew how to ply her body to his command. She writhed underneath him, barely holding on. He'd seen that look for ten years now. He shoved against her, reminding her exactly what she would get, if only she begged. Her fingers brushed against his erection through his suit pants, and all he wanted was for her to take it out.

Then, she let out one final moan and came all over his fingers, leaving him slippery wet and dying to get his cock into her pussy.

She huffed as she tried to regain her composure. He let her leg drop and used a nearby paper towel to mop up his hand.

She was still leaning back against the door, staring at him. "I like the bow tie."

"I know." He grinned, revealing his dimples.

"You always know just what I like."

"How about we go home, and I'll show you exactly what you like?" He leaned in close and growled low in her ear, "Fuck you at my leisure, make you come at my command. Or do you want to be spanked tonight, baby? Or more?"

Her breathing was heavy when he pulled back and looked into her dilated baby blues. "Oh, Clay…" She patted him twice on the cheek. "Maybe another time."

"What?" he demanded.

"You lost tonight. Game over."

She turned to go, and he slammed his hand back on the door. Someone banged on it from the outside and yelled at them to hurry the fuck up.

"What the fuck?"

Andrea softened but only slightly. "I don't want to be seconds tonight, *baby*."

Then, she strode out of the restroom, leaving him alone, wondering how the hell that had just happened.

Chapter 3

A LIFE OF BAD DECISIONS

This wasn't how their little game was supposed to end.

It *never* ended this way.

He hadn't waited that much longer than usual to approach her. After they'd talked, then they would go back and fuck the night away. He wasn't sure if either of them had ever refused before. It was against the rules.

Whenever she played, he always left the girl he had been talking to for a night with Andrea. There wasn't a girl alive that he'd trade the game for. Well, maybe one, but since she was about to marry his brother, it didn't count.

Andrea could be a bitch to everyone, but then again, he was a total ass. That was how they worked. This was where they made sense.

Under the fury that was simmering to the surface though was confusion. *Why would she choose Bad Suit over me?* He'd understand if she hadn't invited him to play, but this was different. She had made him leave his own game for hers and then turned him down.

Clay tried to clear his head, but anger just hit him stronger. He returned to his barstool with single-minded determination. When he made it back, Andrea and Bad Suit were already gone, which only pissed him off more. He hadn't even gotten to confront the douche. Jackass was going to get to enjoy all of Clay's hard work. Think he'd gotten Andrea soaking wet and caused the tremors between her legs.

Dick.

"You're back," Gigi said when he finally returned.

"Yeah. Got held up."

But a guy was sitting in his seat. He was average height with moppy dark hair and a beard. He was pasty pale in his purple V-neck shirt and skinny jeans, which frankly proved that the guy had a small dick.

"Who's this, Gi?" the guy asked possessively.

"Clay. We just met."

"That's fast," he said, eyeing Clay. "Even for you."

"We just met!" she nearly shrieking. She smacked him on the arm.

"Yeah, buddy. Don't worry. I was only warming your seat." Clay was in such a piss-poor mood after Andrea that he added a wink for effect.

The guy glowered at him. He clearly didn't miss what Clay was saying. Truth was, he was in such a mood he'd probably fuck Gigi if he could get her away from Small Dick. But, really, he was itching for a fight right now to burn off the adrenaline. For a little while, it might even be better than a lay with a stranger.

Anyway, he knew he could take this guy.

But, instead of reacting to Clay, he blew up on Gigi. "Great, Gi! Just fucking great!" Small Dick slammed a twenty on the bar and reached for his jacket. "I'm not dealing with this shit again. Who knew that if I'd shown up a little earlier, I'd have found you fucking someone you'd just met? What else is new?"

Gigi's brown eyes nearly popped out of her face at the words. "Christ, Marcus! What the fuck is your deal? I legit just met him because this was the only fucking seat, and *you* were late."

"So, if I'd been on time, you wouldn't have done this shit?" he demanded. "I bet."

"Man, you have some issues," Clay muttered. "I'm not into your girl. I have enough trouble on my own." And she just walked out the door.

"Seriously, nothing happened!" Gigi said.

"Nothing better have fucking happened." Marcus turned to face Clay menacingly. He narrowed his eyes. "Have we met before?"

"Doubtful." Clay didn't associate with people like Marcus.

"Wait, no. I've seen you on TV, I think."

Clay shrugged his shoulders. He didn't like where this was going. He never liked when people recognized him—his face or his name. Because that meant only one thing…

"Your brother is Brady Maxwell, right?"

That.

It meant that.

Fucking Brady.

Clay glowered. Douche had to touch on the one other subject that'd set him off.

Marcus's smile grew as he realized he'd struck gold. "Yeah. That's right. That's where I know you. Brady's the one fucking underage college students and reporters and still managing to get his slimy ass reelected to Congress."

Clay openly glared at him. His anger had hit an inferno. All of the alcohol simmered in his veins, throwing his logic to the wind. A lot had changed between Clay and Brady since he and Liz had gotten together. Clay still thought Brady was a pompous, self-important dick, and at another time, he would have let other people call his brother on it.

But not now.

Not about Liz.

She was single-handedly the best thing that had ever happened to the Maxwells. Crazy to think about after all the shit they'd gone through to get where they were at the moment.

Clay didn't even respond to Marcus's comment. He just let his fist fly. It connected with the douche's cheek with a satisfying crack. It hurt like a bitch and split Clay's knuckles open, but damn, did it look good when Marcus rocked backward from the force of the hit. Clay followed it up with a punch to the gut. Marcus doubled over, gasping for breath, when Clay brought his knee up to connect with Marcus's nose, which broke on contact.

"Fuck!" Gigi swore.

Clay righted the guy and grabbed him by the front of his coat. He slammed Marcus backward against the bar. "Don't ever fucking talk about my family, you piece of shit."

Blood was pouring from Marcus's nose, and Clay was drawing attention to them.

"Let him go!" Gigi cried, yanking on Clay's arms. "That's enough. Let him go, Clay."

"What the fuck?" Marcus wheezed. He was clutching his nose.

"Go fuck yourself," Clay spat.

"I could press fucking assault charges, you asswipe!"

Clay laughed. "I'd just love to see that."

"My girlfriend is a fucking attorney."

Clay smiled, glancing at Gigi, whose olive skin had paled considerably. She looked frightened.

"Another thing we have in common, and I'm one of the best in the goddamn city. So, again, go fuck yourself."

"Just leave," Gigi told him. "He's not going to press charges. Just get out of here. For your brother's sake, if not your own."

Clay laughed humorlessly. "Whatever."

He stumbled out of the bar and into the cold bitter air. It immediately sobered him up some, and he shook out his hand. The fog had started to lift, and pain returned slightly with the shift.

What the fuck is wrong with me?

He shouldn't have let Andrea upset him. Not enough to purposely pick a bar fight with a stranger.

He had definitely assaulted that guy, unprovoked. He'd be fucked if Marcus did actually press charges. Didn't matter if Clay was one of the best lawyers in the city. People were always out for blood when it came to the perfect Maxwells.

And he'd drawn first blood.

He wiped his hands down his face. He needed to just go the fuck home and sleep off this shit. Deal with it in the morning with a clear head.

He stumbled down the street, away from the bar, removing his phone from his jacket pocket. He typed out a text to Andrea as he walked in the general direction of his apartment.

> *Thinnkk o me as he fcks u n kno I cld b makin you cum.*

He was about to send it when he got an incoming text.

> *Savi's coming into town for NYE.*
> *Liz wants you to bring Andrea if you're both free.*

Clay stared at the crisp text message from his perfect older brother. He hadn't seen their younger sister, Savannah, since the election. She was a junior at the University of North Carolina at Chapel Hill, majoring in journalism, and was always fucking busy. It'd be good to see her even if she and Brady would gang up on him.

Clay responded eloquently.

> *Fuck you.*

A response came almost immediately.

Always a pleasure, Clay.

Clay nearly threw the phone, and then he remembered the text to Andrea. He pressed Send, his anger heating back up. *Fuck everyone tonight.*

"Stop right there."

The cold barrel of a gun was pressed against his temple.

Clay froze in place. *Shit! Fuck! Shit! Fuck, fuck, fuck! Oh, fucking fuck, fuck! What the fuck?*

All traces of alcohol immediately dissipated from his system, and he was on red alert. Fear hit him fresh, and his bravado was gone. For the first time in his life, he didn't have a single smart-ass remark to come back with. At least…not one that wouldn't get him killed.

"Give me everything you have on you. Right now!" he cried, his hand shaking slightly as he held the gun aloft. "And no sudden movements, pretty boy."

"Just throw your shit over here," yelled another voice off to Clay's right, past the guy holding the gun. "And make it fucking quick."

He couldn't see either of the assholes who were holding him at gunpoint and robbing him blind. He couldn't even turn to look and get the incriminating information he'd need in court…if he survived this.

Fuck! No!

He would survive this. He'd comply. They'd get what they wanted and be gone. Most armed robberies didn't end in death. They were thieves, not murderers. He knew the statistics. He needed to get this under control. But he was still shaking violently as he reached into his back pocket.

"Now, you piece of shit!" the guy next to him yelled. He pressed the gun harder against Clay's temple, and sweat collected on his brow. "Keep going! What? You think your life is worth shit? It's not. You're fucking nothing. It'd be a motherfucking mercy to pull this trigger and put this bullet where it belonged. Now, move."

Clay tossed the wallet in the direction he'd heard the other guy move. He heard the guy pick it up and start rifling through it.

"Nice. You must think you're untouchable if you're walking around the streets with fifteen hundred dollars in cash on you. He was just asking for it. We should put him out of his misery."

Clay clamped his mouth shut. He wanted to think that he'd be a badass vigilante in this situation and get the drop on these fuckers. But, with the barrel of the gun pressed to his temple, he was keenly aware of his own mortality.

"What else you got, pretty boy?"

The second guy patted him down and stripped him of the Rolex on his wrist, his iPhone, the keys in his pocket, and even the cuff links on his shirt. They were worth a fortune even if these idiots didn't know it.

"Okay. I've done everything you said. Now, let me go."

The first guy laughed. "Let you go? So, you can go run to the police?"

He didn't even see the sucker-punch coming. It hit him square in the jaw, then the kidney, the stomach, and his chest. He doubled over, fighting for breath, as pain exploded in his vision. One guy pushed him over, and Clay dropped to his knees as the other one joined in. They both cursed his very existence as they proceeded to beat the ever-living shit out of him.

Clay curled into a ball on the ground as they kicked his stomach and ribs and back over and over. He felt something break and couldn't keep from crying out. He couldn't get enough air in.

Karma had never struck so true.

For a split second, he thought they'd leave him there like that. He couldn't get up to go to the police. They'd done what they came for. They needed to just slink back into the dark depths from where they'd come from.

Then, the gun pressed into the back of his head. Clay groaned and looked up into the eyes of his attacker.

He memorized every feature in that split second—dark hair, dark eyes, pale skin, a scar on his left cheek, tattoo on his neck, a bird, jagged edge to his eyebrow—as the guy screamed in his face, "This is what you deserve, you piece of shit!"

Clay was sure this was the end. After everything, this was how he was going to go, mugged and beaten to within inches of his life, lying in a dirty alley.

Fuck.

Then, the gun landed heavily on his temple. His skull crunched against the gravel, and he fell into darkness.

Chapter 4
WAKE ME UP

B*eep. Beep. Beep.*

"Ugh," Clay groaned. He had a splitting headache, and everything felt fuzzy.

"Clay!" a girl cried. "You're awake!"

He cringed at the volume before slowly cracking his eyes open. A gorgeous blonde was leaning over him.

"Hey, sexy," he croaked.

The woman shot him an exasperated look. "Is that any way to talk to your future sister-in-law?"

"Sorry, Liz," he ground out. "Wanna fuck?"

Liz laughed and shook her head, as if she'd expected nothing less. "Well, at least we know there's no more damage done than what was already wrong with your head."

Everything else slowly came into focus. The bright lights of the hospital room, the itchy blanket lying across his torso, the gentle thrum of the equipment surrounding him.

"What the fuck happened?"

Liz frowned. Her blonde hair swished over one shoulder, drawing his eyes lower, lower, lower, and then they quickly shot back up to meet her baby blues.

She was chewing on her bottom lip. "What exactly do you remember?"

He strained to remember how he had gotten here, but he was drawing a blank. "Andrea left with Bad Suit."

"Right. She mentioned she'd left the bar you were at."

Though Liz's eyes said that Andrea hadn't said she'd left with someone else. The extent of their game wasn't common knowledge. He wasn't surprised she'd left that part out.

"I should probably go get her. She's really been beating herself up about all of this."

"Wait," he said, grabbing her hand. "Tell me what happened."

"You were robbed," she said plainly. The corners of her mouth turned down. "Someone found you unconscious in the gutter without your ID or anything. You didn't even have your coat or shoes, and you were so messed up."

"Bastards took my shoes!" he growled as everything slowly came back to him. He grimaced as he remembered the brutal beating he'd taken in the alley.

"You were brought to the hospital, and they IDed you here. Brady's trying to keep it all quiet and out of the news."

"Oh, of course he is," Clay drawled. He leaned back and closed his eyes.

Liz reached down and squeezed his hand. "He cares about you, Clay. This isn't about him."

"It's always about him."

Liz sighed, and then she leaned forward and kissed his forehead. "Some things never change, do they?"

Clay shrugged.

"Well, the police will want to hear your story. Plus, everyone else is out in the lobby, waiting for you to wake up. I'll go get them, but..."

"Why you?"

"What?"

"Why were you waiting in here for me to wake up?" he asked.

Liz smiled. "Because I could handle it."

He furrowed his brow. "What the hell does that mean?"

"Honestly, Clay, everyone else was too distraught. You looked really bad when you first got here. Andrea burst into tears and fled...literally fled. I said I'd stay and look after you."

"Oh," he said, surprised by this revelation. "Thanks."

"Anytime. You'd do the same for me."

"Would I?" he asked with a grin.

Liz shook her head. "I'm going to get everyone now. Is there anything you need?"

"Aim the next kiss a little lower?"

She stood and rolled her eyes. "Oh, Clay…"

Liz left the room, and he caught sight of her long, lean legs. It was a nice sight even if he had to see it after waking up in a goddamn hospital.

He still couldn't believe those fuckers had jumped him. He'd made himself an easy target—drunk, stumbling, on his phone, not aware of his surroundings. He might as well have asked them to put that gun to his head and strip him clean. Didn't make it any fucking better though. At least he knew what one guy looked like. That was his only shred of hope in all of this. He'd gotten one solid look at his attacker before he'd blacked out.

When the door opened, a doctor entered the room, followed by an older nurse, and started checking on him. "Good to see you're awake. You were in pretty bad shape when you were brought in last night."

"I still feel like I'm in shit shape," Clay said.

"You sustained two cracked ribs, significant bruising, and a concussion. I didn't think you would be in great shape."

"Ugh," he groaned. "How long is all that going to take to fucking heal?"

"I would say at least six weeks for those ribs."

Clay laughed and wheezed at the pain. "I don't have six weeks."

"The first two weeks will be the most important for you to manage the pain at home and try not to do anything that would damage it further. Unfortunately, there isn't much more we can do on that front, except help make it manageable."

"Fuck."

"You should feel very lucky that you didn't sustain worse injuries. I hope the cops find the person responsible."

The doctor left after they'd run a few tests that hurt like a motherfucker. Who knew breathing tests could hurt so fucking much?

The door opened again, and in came Clay's parents. His father was tall and proud with salt-and-pepper hair and wrinkles on his forehead from the strenuous task of running the country into the ground—otherwise known as being a US senator. His mother was as beautiful and serene as ever with her short blonde hair and soft smile.

Clay was surprised they were even here.

"You gave us quite a scare," Marilyn said, taking his hand.

His father stood on the other side of the bed. His hands were at his sides, and he looked uncomfortable.

"We're both just glad you're all right," Marilyn said. "Aren't we, Jeff?"

A look passed between them. It was a signal Clay had seen a lot growing up. *Show some emotion to your child!*

"Of course we're happy you're all right," Jeff said with a rare smile. "You had us all worried."

"I'd hate to do that," Clay managed. His ribs were hurting worse than ever, and this conversation wasn't helping.

"How are you feeling?" Marilyn asked.

"Like shit."

"I'll see if I can find the nurse and have her come in and up the pain medication." She turned and left the room, leaving him all alone with his father.

He was a daunting man. Always had been to Clay. Brady had always gotten along better with him. Clay had always been teased for being a mama's boy. Just lying here made him want to stand up because that was what was proper in their house. But he couldn't move.

Jeff cleared his throat. "Did you decide which law firm you're going to work with now that you're not clerking any longer?"

Straight to business. "No," he said flatly.

"Well, you'll have to decide. Not much time left."

"Yeah, I'll get right on that," he said dryly.

"They'll want to know by New Year's," he continued, as if he hadn't heard the sarcasm in Clay's voice. "I think you should probably take the Cooper and Nielson offer. Their reputation is solid, and you can quickly move up the chain."

"Just what I want."

"Good, good. Well," he said with a fucking politician's smile, "I'll just check on your mother."

"Great. You do that," Clay said.

Jeff turned and started walking toward the door. Clay wanted to make some snide remark about him leaving without even really asking if his own son was okay, but it wasn't worth it. Years of this wall between them wasn't going to come crumbling down from one particularly gruesome mugging. Clay expected no more, no less.

Andrea peeked her head in the door. Finally, the moment he had been waiting for.

"Hey," she whispered.

She looked like a total wreck. Her eyes were red and puffy. Her hair was in a messy ponytail. She wore expensive yoga pants and a tank top with a running jacket and all black Nikes. She didn't have a scrap of makeup on, and she was chewing on her manicured nails as she entered.

And, despite all that, she still looked gorgeous. He was so used to her being all dolled up under several layers of makeup with perfect supermodel platinum-blonde curls, wearing Jimmy Choos and an endless assortment of those tacky Lilly Pulitzer dresses. But her walking into his hospital room, distraught as hell, was the sexiest he'd ever seen her.

"Clay," she croaked, walking uneasily to his side, "I'm sure you don't want to see me."

In fact, it was exactly the opposite. He distinctly remembered her leaving and wanted to know if she'd been with the douche while he had been beaten to within an inch of his life. Not that he blamed her for this shit, but still. It was a matter of pride.

"Why?" he asked finally.

"Why? Because this is all my fault."

"You hired two guys to beat me up and rob me?"

She groaned. "No!" she grumbled. Her spine straightened, and she seemed to come back to herself a bit with his joke. "But I should have left with you, and then this wouldn't have happened."

"Obviously, you should have left with me," Clay said flippantly.

Andrea sniffled. "I know. I should have."

"So…did you fuck him?"

"Clay, it doesn't matter." Andrea reached out and took his hand in hers. "I feel awful enough without recounting the rest of the night."

"You've never felt bad about the game before."

"It never resulted with you being in the hospital either."

"Some assholes robbed me, Andrea. That's not your fault. That's not my fault. That's not the game's fault."

She swallowed. "It feels like it."

He crooked his finger at her. "Come here."

Andrea leaned forward and softly pressed her lips to Clay's. He wanted to breathe her in and take what belonged to him. He didn't want to consider why she wouldn't answer the question about fucking Bad Suit. It sent an unpleasant twist through his chest.

"Maybe we should stop," Andrea whispered against his lips.

"No, I think we should definitely keep going."

She laughed humorlessly. "Your ribs are cracked, so we definitely have to stop this, but I meant…the game."

Clay's eyes widened. "How hard did that gun hit me?"

"I'm serious, Clay."

"We've had an open relationship like this since college, Andrea. It doesn't make sense to stop just because of one bad incident. This works for us," he earnestly told her. It always had. *What would we do without our games? Without our open honesty about what we wanted from the other?*

She looked down, as if considering his words. "You've never been…jealous?" she whispered the last word, glancing back at him.

Clay recalled the fiery anger that had built inside him last night when Andrea left the bar without him. But he just shook his head. "No."

"Oh. Okay." She looked uncertain as to how to proceed. "How about we just be us for New Year's? As long as you're okay to move around."

"Don't worry about me, baby. I'll be on my feet today. Something like this can't hold me down."

He smiled confidently, but she didn't look half as confident as he felt. It was unsettling, coming from her.

"Well, if you think you'll be ready, then I'll tell Liz that we'll be with her and Brady and Savannah then. Okay?"

He gingerly brought her hand up to his lips and kissed her. "Okay."

She cracked a halfhearted smile. Damn, she was taking this hard. Even harder than him. This wasn't like Andrea at all. He'd never seen her shaken before. She was as quick with a snide remark and sexual gesture as he was. She'd been as into their agreement as he was…maybe more so. She had fucking initiated it after all.

Just when Clay was about to open up and ask her more about it, Brady stepped into the room. "Hope I'm not interrupting," he said with a smile for Andrea's sake.

Clay nodded his head at his older brother, the bright light that always overshadowed him. "Look who showed."

"Sorry I wasn't here earlier. I was on the phone with Heather, trying to handle some damage control. I didn't think you'd want this getting out everywhere."

Clay felt like this incident was another part of the political machine he was locked in.

He knew he should be appreciative that Brady had phoned his press secretary, Heather Ferrington. She was a hot fucking blonde, and Clay couldn't figure out why Brady had never banged her.

"I'm sure," Clay retorted.

With Brady in the room, Andrea sat up straight. None of the vulnerability she had just revealed to Clay showed through when she addressed his brother, "I'm going to go see how your mother is doing. Good seeing you, Brady."

He nodded at her as she passed him to exit the room. Clay hated her absence but appreciated the fact that she knew he had to face Brady alone.

"Quite the predicament you've found yourself in," Brady said. He walked to the end of the bed and drummed his fingers on the plastic footboard. "How are you feeling?"

"Like I need another dose of morphine."

"Mom is looking into that," he said dismissively. "Want to tell me how you ended up in that alley?"

"What are you? The fucking PI?"

"I'm simply interested in what happened, Clay. The doctor said your blood alcohol level was through the roof. It had to have been for you to wander the streets, away from the bar Andrea said you'd been in."

"Fuck you," Clay growled.

Brady frowned. "I'm not interrogating you. The police want to speak with you after this. They'll do the interrogating I'm sure. I'm just trying to understand. Why didn't you just call a cab?"

"Why don't you go to hell?"

Brady's politician mask fell away, and for a split second, Clay saw how shaken Brady really was. He just looked like his older brother again. Clay sighed, and just that easily, he dropped his own anger.

"I'm glad you're okay," Brady said.

"Me, too," Clay said.

"Seriously, if you want to talk to me about it, I'm here. I know we've had our differences over the years, but I'm always here for you."

Clay clenched his hands into fists, grasping the covers and not meeting his brother's eyes. "They said I was worthless and a piece of shit. Said that I deserved to die. They screamed it in my face while one held the barrel of a gun to my temple."

"Fuck," Brady said gruffly.

"I can't describe what it was like."

"Do you think it was premeditated? Did they target you?"

Clay grimaced. "No. Do you think it would be better if it were?"

Brady's eyes traveled over Clay's bruised body, wrapped ribs, and broken knuckles, and he shook his head. "No."

"Me neither."

"We'll find them, Clay. We'll have justice."

Clay nodded and wished he had as much faith in the legal system as Brady did. But he knew too much, and sometimes, the bad guys just got away. Sometimes, the bad guys won.

Chapter 5

BAD SUIT

C lay scrubbed his face with his hand and tried to wipe away the frustration of these damn broken ribs. It had been nearly two weeks, and it still hurt like a bitch. He chased the two pain pills with a swallow of scotch. That would drown out the pain for a few hours while he dealt with this goddamn New Year's party.

"Well, I'm sure *that* mixes well," Andrea's slow drawl carried down the stairs of their second-story house in the suburbs of northern Virginia, just outside of D.C. They both had their own apartments in the city, but when they wanted to leave that behind, they came here to their place.

Clay finished off the scotch and set it back down on the bar. "It does."

"Are you already drunk?"

"Course not. Do you know how much liquor that takes?"

"Yes."

Clay's eyes traveled the length of her shimmery champagne floor-length dress that hugged every tiny curve on her body. He wished the pain meds would kick in right about now, so he could rip that dress off without wheezing through the activity.

"Don't drink that much tonight," Andrea told him. She walked forward and brushed her fingers over the bow tie of his fitted Armani tuxedo. "There. Perfect."

"Thanks, babe." He grinned.

It was good to see Andrea all done up again. Even if it was annoying that she'd spent the last several hours upstairs with a personal stylist doing her hair and makeup, he couldn't argue with results. It was night and day from the Lululemon and Nikes she'd been wearing around the house as she insisted on taking care of him.

Smothering him was more like it. Sure, he had been beaten up and had a few broken ribs, but he could still handle his life like a man. Frankly, he was glad to be getting out of the house even if it was for this stupid party.

At least most of the worst swelling had gone down, and he was okay on his feet again. The doctor had said he would have another month to recover before he should be doing any physical activity, but he was too stir-crazy to listen.

Andrea must have seen something change in his expression because she frowned. "Are you feeling okay? We don't have to go."

"When you look like that, you might be right."

She looked like she wanted to fight him on that, but instead, she just trailed her hand up into his hair. "You're thinking about fucking me, aren't you?"

"It's been two weeks," he groaned. He pulled her body up against his and tried not to wince at the contact.

Andrea simpered exaggeratedly. "And you miss me?"

"You keep looking at me like that, and I'll show you how much."

"Another night, lover. Need to make sure you're...up for it." She raised her eyebrows.

"I'm sure you'll take care of that."

"I'm sure I will."

Clay leaned forward and planted a kiss on her lips. This felt good and right. Andrea hadn't been this flirtatious since the night she'd left without, opting to go home with Bad Suit. He still hadn't fucking figured out what had happened with that douche, but he knew better than to bring it up when she was finally in a better mood.

They took the waiting limo into the city. Andrea popped open champagne in the backseat and was sipping from a crystal flute as she absentmindedly browsed on her phone. Clay stared out the tinted window. He liked to act like the attack hadn't been bothering him at all, but now that he was faced with his first public appearance, he couldn't stop thinking about it. He swallowed hard and tried to drown it out, but his aching ribs were a constant reminder.

"Are you excited to see your sister?" Andrea asked. She glanced up at him and frowned. "You look a little pale, Clay."

"I'm fine."

"Are you sure it's okay to take those pills with alcohol?"

"We both know it's not, Andrea. Just drop it."

She returned to her phone. "Fine."

"And, sure…I guess I'm excited to see Savannah." Clay shrugged.

"Do you know if she's bringing her boyfriend? What's his name again?"

"Easton, I think."

"I'm surprised she hasn't finally started dating Lucas."

"What?" Clay sputtered. *Savannah and Lucas? Chris's younger brother?*

Andrea looked up from her phone with an amused turn to her lips. "Surely, you know they've been hooking up on and off for years. It's rather obvious."

"I'll murder him."

Andrea giggled. "I like when you turn all alpha, but I don't think any murdering is going to happen, especially if she brings the boyfriend. Try not to do anything stupid tonight, okay?" Her words seemed to carry more weight than just in reference to his little sister's love life.

"Do I ever?"

She quirked an eyebrow in response.

The rest of the car ride was a natural silence as they traversed the hellish D.C. traffic. The pain meds kicked in about halfway to their destination, and already, he could feel the slight buzz helping to numb the pain.

They pulled up in front of a swank hotel on the water that was bustling with people. A red carpet was rolled out in front of the location, and Clay half-expected paparazzi to be hounding the elite guests entering. But it seemed to be just the standard fare for the evening.

Clay removed the gold monogrammed tickets from his suit jacket to hand to the man at the front door.

"Clay and Andrea Maxwell," the man said, checking off his list. "Right this way."

Clay opened his mouth to tell him that they weren't married, but Andrea gently nudged him, and he closed his mouth. She smiled up at him a little dreamily, and he was afraid to know what that look meant. She wrapped her arm around his elbow, and they walked inside.

The ballroom was dimly lit with posh gold and silver decorations. Clay beelined for the bar and ordered a whiskey and another glass of champagne for Andrea. He swore, she was worse than he was. She'd had three glasses in the limo.

He sipped the contents and searched for Brady in the crowd. It was easy to find him. He just had to look for the gaggle of people who wanted to kiss his ass.

Andrea followed Clay over to the group of supporters that somehow always seemed to find Brady, even at exclusive events such as this.

Brady's fame had only risen after the public declaration of his relationship, followed by engagement, with Liz. They'd been in the middle of a heated reelection campaign for his House of Representatives seat in North Carolina when it came out that Brady had slept with a college reporter. Shit had hit the fan, miring him in months of bad press right before the election. But Brady and Liz had ridden out the wave, despite the nasty things thrown their way—some in an attempt to unseat the Maxwell political dynasty and others just jealous that Liz had snagged the most eligible bachelor in both D.C and North Carolina. It just proved that any press, even bad press, could work in his brother's favor.

"You made it!" Brady said with a genuine smile when Clay pushed through the throng of people.

He firmly shook his brother's hand. "Yep. Just like you'd requested, Congressman."

Brady looked like he wanted to roll his eyes, but he just kept that smile on. "Well, I'm glad you're here. You, too, Andrea."

He pulled her into a hug, but she quickly stepped away.

"So, was it you who put our tickets under the same name?" Clay asked Brady.

"What are you talking about?"

"Clay and Andrea Maxwell," Clay said pointedly. "You're the only one around here getting married."

Brady's eyes found Andrea's, and she smiled and then hurried over to Liz, who was wearing a knockout dress.

"I didn't secure the tickets. Andrea did," Brady told him.

"What?" Clay asked.

Why would Andrea have put our names down together like that? She had never done that before, and she was the last person he knew who would even want that.

Brady shrugged. "Maybe she's finally starting to like you," he joked. "How are you feeling anyway?"

"Perfectly fit as ever."

"Look who finally showed up," Savannah said, when she wandered over with her boyfriend, Easton.

"Just your favorite brother."

Savannah wrinkled her nose. "That's debatable."

"Are you drinking?" Clay asked, staring down into her clear glass.

"I've been drinking since I was fifteen. You were the one who used to sneak it out for me," she said, as if remembering a fond memory. "At least now I'm legal."

"God, you're twenty-one? You're so old now, Savi. What are you going to do with your life?"

"If I'm old, what does that make you two?" Savannah raised her eyebrows at her two brothers. "Seven and ten years older than me…you both must be ancient!"

Brady and Clay laughed. And, for once, it felt like family bonding. Clay didn't know the last time that had happened.

"Congressman, do you mind if I spare a minute of your time?" a woman said, coming up to his side and interrupting the moment.

Oh right. That's why.

Clay didn't bother excusing himself. He just slumped away from the obnoxious intruder and wandered toward Andrea. He wanted to know why she had put their names together like that. It shouldn't have bothered him that much, except she'd never done it before. Coupling that with the smothering after his accident, and he really didn't know what was up with her.

But, when he got near her, she just took his hand and led him out onto the dance floor. When she pressed her body against his, he decided to let it drop for now. It wasn't that important. They would figure it out.

After a couple of dances, he hated to admit that he was winded and aching. His ribs were throbbing, and a headache was burning in the back of his head. He found an empty seat at a table and watched his friends mingle. Liz came to check on him at some point, but he waved her away and held up his drink. His best friend. His one true solace.

The night wore on with the practiced ease of the D.C. elite. The pain in his side kept him on the outskirts of a crowd he normally reveled in, but tonight, he watched them differently. Maybe it was the obscene amount of alcohol he had been consuming, but something in the scene had lost its luster.

"Darling," Andrea crooned into his ear. She snaked her hand around his neck. "You have to come out and enjoy the party. It's almost midnight."

"I'll enjoy the party later when I have you back in my bed."

"If you can't even party," she said, coming around to sink into his lap, "then how will you fuck me properly?"

"My dick is fully functional."

Andrea ran her nails down his face and planted a soft kiss on his lips. "You are mine, aren't you?"

"What do you mean?"

"You are mine, Clay Maxwell, and no one else's."

"I like to think I belong to myself," he said cautiously.

"We're not playing games tonight. How do you really feel about me?"

"I don't know where all these questions are coming from," he said.

He stood and easily deposited her to her feet. She was a good head or more shorter than him, but something in her eyes made him feel small.

"I just want to know what I am to you. It shouldn't be so difficult to discuss," she said crisply.

"Yeah, well, I thought we already knew the answer to that. You're my girl."

A triumphant smile played on her lips.

"But we're still the same as we always were."

Then, it drained from her face.

"What? Do you want to change the way things are?"

"No," Andrea said immediately. "Why would I want that?"

Clay didn't feel like delving any deeper into that conversation. He grabbed Andrea's hand and pulled her back out onto the dance floor. He just wanted to get to midnight, get home and pop some more pain meds, and then ring in the New Year properly.

They found Brady and Liz in the crowd. Liz was standing next to a small woman with a black bob and blunt bangs, who was gesturing animatedly. She looked oddly familiar.

"Oh my God!" Andrea cried when she saw whom Liz was talking to. "Jamie!" She flung herself at the girl.

"Andrea!" Jamie said, returning the hug.

"Clay, you remember Jamie Lane from the art exhibit?" Andrea said by way of introduction.

Of course, Andrea only ever got this excited about art. He was pretty sure this was actually the sister to Liz's ex-boyfriend, Hayden. Small fucking world.

"Yes. You bought all of her paintings at her last exhibit. Cost a fucking fortune," he drawled.

Jamie colored slightly and looked between Liz and Andrea. "It's so good to see y'all."

"I can't believe you're here," Liz said. "I didn't even know you ran in this circle."

"My artwork has been getting around to some big names, and those people like to dole out favors."

"Congratulations! I'm so happy for you!" Liz said.

"Thank you so much!" Jamie cried. "I'm just, you know, so happy to see you happy, too. Oh, and, Andrea," she said, as if remembering something, "did you get ahold of that art gallery owner I introduced you to when you were looking for new pieces?"

Andrea's lips thinned. "Um…which one?"

"It was, like, a month ago, I guess. Maybe six weeks? You know, the one from that last exhibit I saw you at. Asher McWalter."

Andrea hadn't mentioned that to him. *Strange.*

"Oh, right," she said, glancing away, as if she wanted to be anywhere but in this conversation. "Yes. We, uh…we spoke. Briefly."

Fuck. He knew what that meant. *But why the hell is she nervous? If she's fucked the guy, then why is she purposefully avoiding my gaze?* That meant something was wrong. Something that he wasn't supposed to know about.

"Who is Asher McWalter?" Clay asked, forcing her to look at him.

She frowned. "Nobody."

"He runs this amazing art exhibit downtown," Jamie said.

Sensing the building tension between Clay and Andrea, Liz put her hand on Jamie's shoulder. "How about I buy you a drink?"

"Oh. Sure," Jamie said with a frown.

Then, they disappeared.

"Well?" Clay prompted.

Andrea met his gaze. Christ, she was so strong. Even though she didn't want to say whatever was about to come out of her mouth, she still looked him in the eyes and crushed him.

"He's an art gallery owner who I met about a month before your attack. He's the guy you saw me with the night of your…robbery."

Clay's mouth went dry as the crowd started counting down to midnight. *Bad Suit.* "You mean to tell me that you've been fucking that douche bag for over a month?"

She nodded minutely.

"You told me to come fight for you in that bar, knowing you were going home with him. He wasn't some stranger you'd picked up. That was planned," he growled. "You let me show up and you let me finger-fuck you in the restroom," he spat.

"Clay…"

"You broke the rules, Andrea. No wonder you want to end the game. Why the fuck did you leave with that douche?"

"Fuck, isn't it obvious? I wanted to make you jealous," she cried.

Clay's eyebrows rose. "You left me alone, pissed off and horny, only for me to get jumped and have the shit beaten out of me…because you wanted me to be *jealous*?"

She gritted her teeth. "I didn't know that would happen. I didn't *want* it to happen."

"Five, four, three, two, one!" the crowd cheered all around them as they watched the ball hit the ground in Times Square, the festivities being shown on a giant projection screen on the wall.

But Clay and Andrea just stared at each other, as if in a duel.

"Well, are you going to kiss me?" she demanded as everyone made out around them.

He was so pissed. Unbelievably, horribly pissed. He couldn't think straight; he was so angry. A rage filled him to his core to know what Andrea had done.

Their game was simple. It had worked for ten years until Asher McWalter had walked into her life.

Clay let his anger feed him as he grabbed her roughly by the back of her neck and kissed her like it would be their last breath.

Chapter 6
LIMOS

In the back of the limo, Clay shredded Andrea's expensive dress between his hands. Whatever had passed between them during that midnight kiss hadn't dissipated in the time it took them to get out of the ballroom and into their waiting limo. In fact, it had only heightened their emotions. All Clay wanted was to rip Andrea's clothes off and claim her body.

Fuck his ribs. He was getting laid. Right here. Right now.

"This dress cost a fucking fortune," she murmured.

Not that she gave a fuck. He could see it in her eyes. She'd rather have the material in pieces on the floor of this limo than around her body.

"Tell someone who gives a fuck, baby."

"Well, you'll have to buy me another one."

He bore down on her, sliding his hands up her bare calves. He grabbed the slit he'd torn into the dress between his hands, deviously grinned up at her, and wrenched it into two until it hit her upper thigh.

Andrea exhaled loudly and squirmed. He knew she was trying to seem unaffected, but he wouldn't have any of that fucking shit.

"I'll do as I please, and you'll like it," he told her.

She raised her eyebrows. "Aren't you all domineering?"

"Shh," he said. "You broke the rules, baby. It's my turn."

Her eyes widened, and then he saw it—the fire that he so craved from her. She was crazy if she thought she was getting off scot-fucking-free for her part in what had happened to him. Yeah, he wasn't an idiot. She wasn't responsible for him getting jumped, but what she'd done pained him more. It went against the foundation of their relationship. And he was fucking pissed.

"You think I'm just going to lie here and let you do whatever you want?" she demanded, sitting up onto one elbow. "You said yourself, nothing has fucking changed between us."

"That was before I knew you were fucking with me, Andrea," he growled, his voice rising an octave.

She plopped back down onto the leather interior. "I wasn't fucking, fucking with you."

"Then, what the hell were you doing?"

Andrea opened her mouth to explain, but he'd had enough talk from her. There was no way she could explain her actions. She'd toyed with him.

Wanted him to be jealous about her being with Bad Suit—douche bag Asher McWalter—as if the guy could ever live up to Clay…as if he could give Clay a reason to be jealous.

"If you would just let me…"

He dug his fingers into her thighs until she stopped talking. He crawled his hands up her perfect milky-white skin, hoping he'd leave fingerprint bruises all up her inner thighs to remind her just whose girl she was.

She groaned, grasping the seat and lifting her ass, urging him on.

He tore the remaining piece of her dress, stripping away her last vestige of modesty, revealing once again that she wasn't wearing anything at all underneath it.

"Making a habit of this?" he asked.

"You like it."

"I wear bow ties, and you go commando. I think I got the better end of the deal."

Her eyes fluttered closed again when his fingers finally made it all the way up her legs. Clay pressed them open wide and teasingly circled his finger, so he was close to touching her where she was clearly demanding but not quite. He could sense her frustration and desperation, see it in her brow. When he saw her eyes start to flicker back open to demand he touch her, he slipped his fingers between her lips and slicked them with her wetness.

And, fuck, was she wet.

He plunged two fingers deep inside her and then drew them up against her walls in just the way he knew she liked. She whimpered softly, and the sound was music to his ears. Leaning forward, he roughly swirled his tongue around her clit until she was bucking beneath him.

The back of the limo had never held so much appeal to him. He forgot all about his aching ribs and the echoes of their argument. Instead, he just focused on this one task—making her come. And she would, goddamn it. He could fucking guarantee that. He was good at many things, but sex was his specialty.

Andrea pushed her pussy up against his face, begging for the release he was holding just out of range. If she wanted to toy with him, he could toy with her. Oh, sure, she would come—when he let her.

"Clay…" she moaned.

"Say it again."

"Clay fucking Maxwell."

"That's right," he said with a grin.

Then, he circled his tongue around her clit, and she came all over his face.

He didn't waste any time. She lay there, panting. The second fucking orgasm he'd given her, unreciprocated, in two weeks. He was damn sure he was getting his own tonight—more than once, if he could ignore his damn ribs long enough.

Clay unceremoniously yanked down the zipper of his tuxedo pants, pulled his dick out, and maneuvered to enter her. She shuddered as he thrust up inside her. Her walls were still contracting from the pleasure he'd just provided, and he could feel the heady remnants of her orgasm.

He wasn't easy on her body either. Leaning his elbow on the cushion by her head, he drove deep and long into her, claiming her body. She moaned, tightening all around him. Her hands cupped his face.

All remnants of their fight had fled her face. She looked up at him with dreamy hooded eyes, and all he saw was how beautiful she was. Even though he was taking her punishment out on her body, he still found her gorgeous beneath him.

"I love when you take me like this," she said, digging her nails into his hair.

"Hard?"

"And rough," she agreed.

He pounded into her harder at the words. Fuck, it'd been two fucking weeks. He was pretty sure that was a record.

And then she was shuddering underneath him again. She came out of nowhere, and in response, his body jerked and bucked as she squeezed him, tilted her head back, and cried out his name. He couldn't help it. There was no stopping it. With that kind of reaction, his dick had its own fucking mind. He leaned forward and exploded inside her, lost in the throes of release.

When he returned to himself, he slipped out of her and crashed back onto the limo seat next to her. She eased into the tiny space next to him, lying on her side, her chest heaving.

"Goddamn it, Clay," she whispered.

"Mmm," he murmured. He was feeling really drowsy. Since his ribs were now on fire—maybe physical activity had been a bad idea—he thought sleeping sounded pretty awesome.

"How can I stay mad at you now?" she said.

"Why the fuck are you mad at me?" he bit out. "You're the one who broke the rules."

"Rules are meant to be broken."

"I'm a lawyer, honey. Try again."

"That means you know *exactly* how to bend and break the rules to *your* liking," she said. "I've learned a thing or two from you over the years. Don't forget; I was there for the three *miserable* years of law school."

"Oh, fuck, not this again." He closed his eyes against the same conversation they'd had on multiple occasions. "Just because we made it through law school together doesn't entitle you to anything."

"Every other couple we knew has broken up or gotten divorced!" she reminded him. "Every one!"

"That's because one person would get pissed that the other one was fucking other people. You and I didn't give a shit about that. We had an arrangement with rules. Remember? That's why we survived my three years in law school."

"You're so thick sometimes."

He smirked. "I definitely am. You just felt how thick I am."

Andrea snorted and sat up. Without a second thought, she grabbed the ends of her destroyed dress, tied them into a knot on the side of her leg, and somehow managed to regain all her dignity. "Not everything is about your dick."

"Just most things."

Andrea was silent the rest of the way back to their house. He let her brood. He was pissed enough for the both of them.

At some point, he must have dozed off because Andrea shook him awake when the limo had stopped. Clearly, he was more exhausted than he'd known. And the pain meds were wearing off.

They entered their house together, and Clay went straight for the pill bottle. He took another one to douse the flames in his sides. When he rounded back toward the foyer, Andrea was standing with her hands on her hips, staring at him.

"We should talk," she said.

"Do I look like I'm in the mood to talk?"

"I don't care."

He ran his hand back through his hair and started up the stairs.

She stomped after him. "Are you really just going to ignore me?"

"Talk if you must talk, woman."

"I don't feel like I should have to apologize about Asher."

Clay ground his teeth. "The fact that you're using that douche's name in my house—"

"*Our* house," she spat back. "Any other night, you wouldn't have given two shits that I'd been seeing him. How many other girls have you seen through our games?"

Clay shrugged. "More than one."

"Right. So, don't come back all high and fucking mighty."

"Have you seen him since that night?" Clay asked.

He glanced at her as they both walked into their massive master bedroom with the giant four-poster king-size bed in the center.

"What? No, of course not," she said, something flashing in her eyes. She almost looked hurt that he had even asked.

Or guilty. Huh.

"Good."

"And why do you even care?" she demanded. "You claim you aren't jealous, but you are. You claim you don't want a real relationship, yet you want me to be there for everything for you. You claim that this makes you happy, but it doesn't."

"You agreed to all of this, Andrea!" he bellowed. "You're not the girlfriend type. You're not the marrying type. You don't want your heart broken. You don't want to be left alone, like your parents left each other. You make the same fucking claims that I do."

Her eyes spit fire at him. "And what if I've changed?"

"You haven't."

"How can you possibly know that?"

Clay laughed and shook his head. He couldn't believe he was hearing this. "Because you like the games. You thrive on the games. You said it yourself…we survived three years of law school when no one else did." He swept his hand through her long blonde hair, pushing it off her shoulders and exposing her collarbones. "You know I care about you. You know you're my girl. At the end of the day, I come home to you. We *work* this way."

He could tell that she wanted to say something else, but instead, she just turned away from him and walked into her walk-in closet. Clay dropped his hand with a sigh. Everything hurt too much for this conversation.

Andrea reappeared a couple of minutes later in a silk negligee that barely graced the tops of her thighs.

"I'm going to sleep," she said. Then, she strode right past him, crawled into the enormous bed, and turned on her side with her back facing the middle of the bed.

Christ.

He stripped out of his tuxedo and pulled back the covers to lie next to her. The bed was big enough that, if they wanted to, they never had to touch each other. Some nights, it was a blessing. Tonight, it felt like a giant chasm had ripped the bed in two.

Ignoring her obvious dismissal, Clay bridged the distance between them, wrapped a protective arm around her waist, and dragged her body against his. She was stiff as a board beneath his touch.

"Andrea," he whispered, "come on."

"I hate this," she admitted.

"Me, too."

She shook her head, and he wasn't sure what she was thinking. Surely, she meant that she hated they were fighting over something ridiculous. *Why change when things are good?*

Eventually, her body relaxed into him, and much of her weight pressed back into his chest. It was a reassuring soft embrace, something they'd done for years. And even though he was still upset about Bad Suit, he couldn't help but feel content as he fell asleep with his girl in his arms.

Chapter 7

YOU

Their relationship was tense the next week before Clay started his new law job. He wouldn't give up an inch on the Bad Suit fiasco. Andrea seemed even more stolid than ever and refused to talk to him further on any of the topics that had come up on New Year's. The only good thing that had come of that week was that his ribs were finally healing and had stopped causing him excessive amounts of pain.

Just in time for him to start putting in long hours at the new office.

He'd decided on Cooper & Nielson. His father was right, as much as Clay begrudged him that.

Cooper & Nielson was the best firm in the city, and it was the perfect stepping-stone to getting him the experience he needed to become a judge. That would be another check mark on his to-do list to becoming attorney general.

He frowned as he thought about it while tying the knot of his pink-checkered tie. One more thing to make good old dad finally proud of him.

"Where are you off to this early?" Andrea asked. She appeared out of the walk-in closet in a knee-length blue dress. Her hair was pulled back off her face, and she looked so hot.

They'd never argued for this long before. Normally, whatever was bothering them, they would just get over—or, more accurately…fuck out. But, so far, no such luck. In fact, there'd been no fucking since the limo. Something he definitely needed to change.

"Work, baby." He walked over and kissed her cheek. "Someone has to pay the bills."

Her lips upturned. "We both have trust funds. No one needs to pay the bills."

"Well, you're the only one living off of yours."

Andrea scoffed at him and ran her hands up the front of his suit. "For one, I earn a decent living, selling art. Something you've still yet to grasp. And second," she cut in before he could laugh at her for considering her hobby a job, "this is a two-thousand-dollar suit."

"Which is not a big deal since I just made my Supreme Court flirting bonus," he said with a wink.

Every year, the top law firms across the country would "flirt" with Supreme Court clerks. Each justice had four, and the retired clerks even had one each to do their bidding…all of the real behind-the-scenes work. It was grueling, backbreaking work that Clay had put in during the last two years. But the average bonuses for clerks who entered into a top firm started at $250,000 on top of the salary at the firm, coming in as a third-year associate. His was getting more than that because he'd made them wait…and beg. It wasn't a bad gig.

"Whatever you want to believe," she said.

"Are you going to be here when I get back?"

She raised her eyebrows. "What do you take me for? A kept woman? I have business in town."

Clay's face darkened. "With whom?"

She patted his cheek. "An art dealer. Don't wait up."

"Are you meeting…Asher again?" he asked as she walked toward the door.

She sighed. "No, Clay. You know I haven't had contact with him."

And then she left.

He hated to admit that the tension had left his chest with her answer. He wasn't…jealous. He was still just…just really irritated about the whole thing, and he didn't want her seeing the douche again.

Clay took his Porsche into the city, grumbling all the while about the traffic. He never could understand why drivers were so horrible here. Back home in Chapel Hill, there wasn't nearly this much traffic or congestion. He missed being there sometimes. He missed his cabin on the north side of town and his parents' mansion outside of Durham. He missed Southern hospitality and fashion and cooking. He'd been out of the South for too long, but it would always be home.

He pulled into the parking garage for Cooper & Nielson, sliding the pass that they had given him over the sensor. The bar jerked up, and he entered the subterranean enclosure. For once, he felt like he was with his people. Every car he passed was exceedingly luxurious, polished to perfection, and practically dripping with wealth. It was clear; status and money spoke volumes. His Porsche glided into a vacant spot right between a Mercedes and a Lexus. It was like sinking his dick into expensive pussy.

He took the elevator up to the top floor where he was supposed to meet his new boss Ted Cooper, cofounder of Cooper & Nielson.

"You must be Mr. Maxwell," Cooper's secretary said when he walked into the office. She was a redheaded woman in her late forties with a stiff smile. She looked like she didn't leave the desk often.

"That's right."

She typed something on the computer keyboard and then wrote something down in small illegible hand on a giant desk calendar. "Good. Mr. Cooper will be finished in just a moment."

"Excellent."

She glanced back up at him. "You wouldn't happen to know Congressman Maxwell?"

Clay sighed. Of course…Brady. "Yes, Brady is my brother," he said immediately.

She furrowed her brow. "Oh, I meant Senator Maxwell. I met him when he was still in the House of Representatives. Can't get a handle on him being a senator."

His father had been a senator for nearly two decades. At least this wasn't about Brady. "Yes, that's my father."

"Great man," she said with a genuine smile.

"Clay Maxwell," a voice called from the doorway of an office.

"Mr. Cooper." Clay walked forward and shook hands with the wizened old white dude who was a legend in D.C. law.

"Excellent to have you on board, son."

"I'm honored to be here, sir."

Clay was thankful that he'd gone through all of his introductory materials for the job earlier in the week. He had already been prepped, and he was ready to go. All he needed was to get set up in his own office and be handed cases. He knew what to do from there.

"I just wanted to say, welcome aboard, and introduce you to your colleagues who will be around to answer any questions. You'll, of course, have your own team in place, but there's always a learning curve." Ted patted Clay's back. "I'm sure it'll be less with someone from your background."

Clay smiled graciously. He hadn't put those two years into clerking for nothing.

Ted directed him back to the elevator, and they took it down two floors. He walked with Clay down the hallway, making polite conversation. Clay was surprised that he was having this chat with the top dog at a mega firm. That signing bonus must have really meant something. And, to think, all of this was just one big stepping-stone to the real prize.

"Here we are," Ted said.

It was a nice open room with offices on the perimeter and space for secretaries, paralegals, and the rest of the staff in the center.

"Let's go find Miss De Rosa. She will be your key point of contact."

They stopped in front of an office space with a heavy curtain covering the window that looked into the office. Seeing Mr. Cooper, the secretary buzzed for the attorney inside.

A few seconds later, the door popped open and a girl stepped out.

"You!" the girl cried.

Clay's eyebrows rose. *Well, fuck.*

"Hey, Gigi," he said casually, as if they were old friends rather than mild acquaintances before he'd broken her boyfriend's nose in a bar fight.

"What are *you* doing here?"

"Didn't you hear? I'm the new attorney."

"Wait…*you're* the Supreme Court clerk?" she asked, her big brown eyes wide.

It was like she had forgotten that he'd said he was the best lawyer in the city.

He just smirked in response.

"Well, I'm glad that you two seem to know each other," Ted butted in. "Miss De Rosa, please help Mr. Maxwell with whatever he needs."

She gritted her teeth and nodded. "Of course, sir."

He wondered exactly what "whatever he needs" meant. She still had some pretty killer lips on her that he wouldn't mind exploring. But, damn, she still had on a fucking pantsuit. At least it all fit together now. She wasn't just an attorney; she was a big attorney at Cooper & Neilson. The handshake, large quantities of vodka, and unfortunately, the pantsuit all made sense.

"Great. Well then, I'll leave you in her capable hands." Ted nodded and then left them alone.

At that comment, Clay couldn't help but arch an eyebrow at her.

She groaned and pointed at the door. "My office. Now."

He swaggered inside without complaint, and she slammed the door behind him. The office was large with towering bookshelves across one wall, packed to bursting with legal books, most of which he recognized. She had a formidable desk facing a pair of leather chairs. A large window opened up to the street beyond their building. It wasn't a great view or anything, but it had its own industrial appeal.

"Sit," she snapped.

He folded into a seat in front of her desk, placed one foot over his knee, and bridged his fingers in front of his chest. "So, Miss De Rosa," he said flirtatiously.

"Don't speak," she snapped.

"You like them silent. That's fine with me."

She glared at him, openly glared, like she thought he was a maggot.

"Look, that playboy charm might work on other women of lesser caliber than me," she said confidently, "but it will *not* work on me. This is a strictly professional working relationship. Clear?"

"Sure," he agreed easily.

"Good." She was still fiery and looked pissed that he was here. "I hate that I even have to do this, but I was told that you were supposed to shadow me for the next couple of weeks."

There it was.

"What?" he demanded. "Shadow you?"

She shrugged. "If you're the best attorney in the city, you probably don't need that, do you?" she asked, spitting his words back at him.

"Of course I don't need that," he growled low.

"Fabulous. I'll let Mr. Cooper know that you're set to take on your own cases without my help." She jotted something down on a piece of paper and then looked back up at him. "Unfortunately, I do have to work with you for the rest of the day. I'd just prefer if we pretended like this was our first interaction."

"Sure thing," he said easily.

"And interact as infrequently as possible after today," she added.

"So, you'll forget that you flirted with me, and I'll forget that I punched Small Dick in the face."

Gigi sputtered. "What did you just say?"

"The lecherous boyfriend," he reminded her.

She snapped her eyes closed and pressed her hand to her forehead. He thought she'd smiled for a second, but it was gone when she looked at him again.

"It'd be in your best interest not to mention that nickname for my boyfriend or my boyfriend's name at all. Now, can we get to work?"

She was definitely way hotter when she was ordering him around. He liked that. Even though she acted like she hated him, at least this was an easy flirtation. He didn't have to think about the consequences of his actions and worry about anything like he did with Andrea at home. Like why her silence frustrated him, why the thought of her with Bad Suit infuriated him, and why he couldn't seem to stop thinking about her—

"Well?" Gigi said.

He pulled himself out of his thoughts and came back to the present. "Let's get to work."

A few hours later, Clay was tired and hungry. He'd had a nice break from his clerking duties. They were extremely taxing, mentally and physically, and it turned out that, even with the fat paycheck, this wasn't going to be any different. In fact, he was going to have to work just as hard to prove that he was worth the paycheck they were giving him.

He was hunched over Gigi's desk, working through a long legal document, when the door opened behind him. Gigi's head popped up from where she was buried under a pile of books.

"Hey, Gi."

"Marcus," she said. Her voice had a hint of panic. *Ah. Small Dick.*

She glanced down at the large-faced watch on her wrist. "Is it…is it lunch already?"

"Yeah. I was thinking we could try that Indian place again," Marcus said.

Clay could feel him coming nearer to the desk. He looked up at Gigi, and she shook her head ever so slightly. So, the boyfriend didn't know that he was here. That wouldn't be a good thing for him to find out now, as it would end up blowing up in the middle of her office. *Awesome.*

"Is this your new intern, Gi?" Marcus asked.

"He's, uh…"

"Not an intern," Clay said.

He straightened from where he'd been hunched over and turned to face Marcus. He registered Clay's face immediately, and he went from shock to anger in a split second.

"What the fuck are you doing here?" he cried. "Gigi, how the fuck did you think it would be okay to see him again?"

"He's a new lawyer here, Marcus. I had no choice. Cooper left him with me," she said in a rush.

"Likely fucking story. Had you been seeing each other before he broke my fucking nose?" Marcus demanded.

"No! We'd never met before that night. This is just a coincidence." She came around the desk with her palms out, as if to calm him down.

"I don't believe in coincidences." His eyes shot between Gigi and Clay. "That's it. I've had enough. I can't do this anymore."

"What?" she cried.

"I'm breaking up with you. I should have done it two years ago when you slept with that stranger, but I didn't."

"Marcus, that was forever ago, and we weren't even *officially* dating yet. Plus, *you've* slept with someone else since then!" she snapped.

Suddenly, it was like Clay was intruding on two years of pent-up anger. He leaned back against the desk, crossed his arms, and wished he had popcorn for the show.

"Don't bring that shit up like you know what you're talking about, Gi," Marcus said.

"I know *exactly* what I'm talking about, and I'm tired of it. You can't come in here and yell at me for having someone in my office when I had no control over the situation, and then go around, accusing me of doing something you have been doing for most of our relationship!"

"Fine, I'm done." Marcus turned on his heel and strode out of the room.

Gigi glared at Clay. "Look what you fucking did."

Then, she ran out of the room after the guy, leaving Clay all alone in her office, still starving.

He grumbled and then sank back into a chair. He figured it'd be better to wait for her. And it was.

She came back about ten minutes later. No tears marred her cheeks. She just looked sad and frustrated.

"So…that didn't go so well?"

She didn't even glance at him. "No."

"Long time coming?"

She shrugged. "I don't want to talk about it."

"Cool. How about a double shot of Grey Goose at lunch?"

Her eyes finally found him. "You're an ass."

"Not the first time I've heard that."

Gigi reached down and picked up a black purse off the ground. She hoisted it onto her shoulder and said, "You're buying."

"It's a date."

"Don't hold your breath."

Chapter 8
SMALL DICK

Lunch was uneventful.

Clay wasn't much of a comforter to begin with, and Gigi looked like the last thing she wanted was for someone to comfort her. In fact, she seemed more like the type of girl to drown herself in alcohol instead of talking about her problems. And that was exactly what she did. The double shot of vodka had multiplied to the point where he actually had to cut her off. He wasn't sure if he'd ever done that for someone before. But, Christ, they still had work to do that afternoon.

"I don't want to go back," Gigi said. She had her hand on her forehead. "I can't stand another grueling day in that building."

"You don't like it?" he asked. He had just paid the check and was trying to urge her out of her seat.

"Oh, I fucking love it. Why else would I have gotten a hundred thousand dollars in debt to slave away at a crazy mega firm? I mean…you have to be insane to want this."

"Pretty much."

"I'm shocked you're doing it. Can't you just ride the connection train to get whatever you want?" she slurred slightly.

Clay's brow furrowed as they exited the pub.

"You're a Maxwell after all."

"Yeah, I guess I could," he said stiffly.

She didn't need to know that he was doing this for a specific reason. She was kind of drunk, and he was supposed to be shadowing her for the next couple of weeks. He didn't normally mix business with pleasure. He'd made exceptions, but none of them had ended well. Made it easier when he didn't have to remember their names.

"Oh, ho!" she slurred. "Want to make a name for yourself without Daddy's help then? I saw how you reacted when Marcus"—she hiccuped over his name—"mentioned your brother."

"Let's not talk about him."

She nodded. "Marcus is a dick."

"Small Dick."

She laughed and nodded. "Not entirely inaccurate."

"No dude can wear skinny jeans like that if he's packing."

Clay managed to get her into the passenger seat of his Porsche. He was glad that he'd driven. It wasn't often when he was the responsible one. This was a weird change, as if he'd somehow stepped into a parallel universe of his life.

Gigi babbled on the entire way back to the office. It wasn't far, but he hadn't wanted to walk outside in the fucking frigid temperature. D.C. always turned bitter cold right before the inauguration, and he wasn't looking forward to standing outside through that shit again.

Clay parked his car and killed the engine when he realized Gigi must have said something to him. "What?"

She trailed her finger down his face. "You're handsome."

He smirked. "I know."

"Jerk," she said halfheartedly. "You're a mistake, aren't you?"

"Yes," he said because he recognized that, in this instance, it was true.

Gigi was hot. But she wasn't some casual acquaintance. He'd have to see her every day. He'd have to work with her on cases.

Plus…Andrea.

A smile crooked onto his face at the thought of her. Even if they were on rocky terms, that didn't mean he wanted to make the same mistake she'd made with Bad Suit. He didn't want a relationship. He'd already seen what one looked like, thanks to Gigi and Small Dick. He already had one that was perfect just the way it was.

So, he acted like the dick she expected. "I don't like pantsuits."

She jolted slightly. "Well, you can take it off."

Damn. "I'm not interested," he said tersely.

"Yes, you are."

Yes, I am. Damn, how did I turn a hot chick down?

"Just because your boyfriend broke up with you doesn't mean that you need to spread your legs for the first guy who is nice to you," he said cruelly.

Her eyes hardened, and she straightened immediately. She jerked the car door open and was already halfway across the parking garage when he got out of the car. The elevator took long enough that he caught up with her.

All the humor was gone from her face. She stepped into the elevator and turned to stare straight into Clay's face. "You work on your cases; I'll work on my cases. Otherwise, you can go to hell."

The door slid closed, and he sighed. *Jesus Christ!* This was going to be a fucking shitty situation. He'd known he shouldn't have listened to his dad about the law firm.

~

The next week was miserable. Gigi acted as if he didn't exist. Not that he gave a fuck, but it made it difficult to do anything when he was supposed to be working with her. This was why he didn't get involved with people at work. They made shit complicated. It didn't have to be complicated.

By the time Friday rolled around, Clay was fucking ready to get out of the place. The office closed around four o'clock, but he knew enough people would be working well into the night and some even during the long weekend. But not him. Not yet at least.

Clay sent a text to his friends, Ethan and Cash, and headed out the door.

Drinks tonight?

Gigi walked into the elevator next to him. She crossed her arms and avoided looking at him. He didn't know what her deal was. So, he'd turned her down. She'd been pretty demanding about wanting to fuck him. As far as he was concerned, he'd done her a favor. She didn't need to be a bitch about it.

"You're taking over your own cases on Monday. I just spoke with Mr. Cooper," she snapped.

"So, she does speak," he drawled.

She glared at him. "And you shouldn't."

Clay shrugged. Lately, everyone had been blowing things way out of proportion.

"You know, I thought you were a nice guy when I met you at the bar that first day, but I should have known better after you punched Marcus. Not sure why it took me so long to realize it when you showed back up."

"You were drunk. I don't fault you for not being coherent."

Gigi rolled her eyes and crossed her arms. She seemed determined not to say anything again.

He climbed into his Porsche and drove the twenty minutes to his bachelor townhouse downtown. Then, he called a cab to take him to the bar. As much as he enjoyed showing up places with his Porsche, drinking and driving wasn't high on his list. If he never had to go to the hospital again, that would be fine by him.

Soon, he was at a local bar, The Hill. It was aptly named for its location but nothing else. The place was dingy, and he knew of the dirty things that happened after-hours when congressmen and their interns would leave for the evening. He'd seen it all on Capitol Hill.

It was a place that Andrea would never frequent. It was one of the reasons Ethan and Cash liked it—though the easy female patrons were probably the biggest one.

"Clay!" Ethan said. He grabbed Clay's hand and shook it forcefully. His dark hair brushed over his forehead, and he flicked his head to get it out of his eyes. "It's been fucking forever, man."

"Just a couple of weeks."

Cash approached from the other side. "How's the old ball and chain?" he asked, jokingly elbowing Clay in the side.

Clay tried not to wince. *Douche.* "Andrea is the same as ever."

"She still trying to get you to stop fucking around?" Cash asked.

"Andrea has never cared about who I've slept with," he said with a grin. "Why would she start caring now?"

"Fuck if I know," Cash said. He wrapped his hand around a beer and shoved it into Clay's hand.

Even though these guys had gone through law school with him, it wasn't as if they were his confidants. He couldn't tell them that Andrea actually had been acting weird, like she cared about who he fucked. He didn't get it. But Ethan was more intuitive and slightly less of a douche bag, so he seemed to understand that Clay was bluffing about the statement. That was probably because he was one of the guys who'd gotten divorced during law school.

Andrea hadn't really even been around this week. Normally, Clay wouldn't have even noticed. He'd usually just stay in the city, and they'd live their own lives. But ever since New Year's, he'd been heading back to their house, surprised to find it empty or, to his chagrin, Andrea there but distant.

He wasn't a total idiot. He knew something was up with her. He just didn't want to try to fix what wasn't broken. And he had a feeling that was what she wanted.

"We don't need to worry about that hot piece of ass you have waiting for you at home," Cash announced. "Let's find some for you here."

Ethan laughed. "Shouldn't be hard. Clay isn't picky."

"Neither are you two dipshits," Clay growled.

He really wasn't picky. He liked them hot and leggy. Blonde and skinny. But he'd take just hot. Hot worked for him.

"I need it after this chick I've been working with at Cooper and Nielson. Her boyfriend broke up with her, so she thought I'd fuck a pantsuit. She's been frigid ever since."

"Frigid is not worth the effort," Cash drawled. He leaned his bulky build back against the bar and downed half of his Bud Light without blinking. He was a huge guy from southern Georgia with dark hair that he frequently let grow out too long for D.C. standards.

"Not worth your effort at least," Ethan interjected.

"Yeah, well, we don't want to end up like Ethan fucking his boss."

"You still doing that?" Clay asked.

Ethan shrugged but smiled nonchalantly. "Every now and then."

"Only when her husband is out of town," Cash said.

Clay laughed along with his friends. He never would have guessed Ethan would be the one fucking the boss. Seemed much more like Cash to him, but Ethan must like it to be going back for more.

Over the next hour, Clay let the long week of work fall off his shoulders. His life had been stressful ever since the attack, and it was nice to just let the grind go and hang out with his friends.

A group of girls turned up in the bar at one point, and Cash dived right in. He had none of the sly, sexy game that Clay exuded. He was an act-first-think-later type, but girls tended to like that. Unlike Ethan. Clay had always said that his game was that he had no game. Ethan would pick up chicks most nights without even realizing that was what he was doing.

Cash seemed to have automatically zeroed in on the brunette ringleader, but Clay's eyes were drawn to the cute redhead to the girl's left. A cute redhead wasn't his normal MO, but he liked the way she kept shooting furtive looks his way. He could work with that.

Plus, he knew that if he didn't approach her now, he'd lose out to Ethan, who had a major thing for gingers. They were his kryptonite. Just as Ethan was about to walk over to Cash, Clay strolled over to the redhead. As he approached, she smiled up at him under hooded blue eyes with long thick lashes.

"Hey," she breathed.

"Hey yourself." Clay leaned his side into the bar and smiled his dimpled smile that always brought girls to their knees.

"I'm Bethany."

"Nice to meet you, Bethany," Clay purred. He liked the way she breathed in deeply when he'd said her name.

Bethany giggled and averted her gaze. "You don't remember me, do you?" she asked after a minute of silence.

Shit!

His eyes shot to Cash, who was talking up the brunette and not paying attention. *Did the dipshit know these girls?* This was the biggest fucking issue with frequenting the same bar over and over.

"Don't worry," she said, brushing it aside. "It's not a big deal."

"Really?"

"I'd just dumped my boyfriend and needed a quickie. You were hot and obliged," she admitted with a soft pink blush on her cheeks.

"Were?" he asked with a smirk.

She giggled again. "Are. You're definitely still hot."

"Well, we could make this time more memorable…"

"I got back together with the boyfriend."

"How unfortunate for him that I'm here tonight then."

She bit her lip and glanced down at his mouth, as if contemplating his suggestion. When she took a step toward him and not back toward her friends, he knew he had her. *God, this is so easy.* He swore, sometimes, he didn't even have to put in any effort at all. With or without this boyfriend she'd spoken of, he still managed to get her eating out of the palm of his hand.

She leaned forward toward him. "Well, I don't know. Maybe we could…"

Clay sighed and took his phone out of his pocket, ignoring whatever else she was going to say. He pretended to be engrossed in an urgent text message and held his hand up.

There was no challenge here. He had already fucked this girl and couldn't even remember her. *Why settle for cute when I have fucking hot at home?*

With satisfaction, he sent a text out to Andrea.

Hey, baby, I have a game for you.

Redhead was looking at him with a sneer on her face. Guess it wasn't much of a game if he didn't put in effort to keep her interested. Fuck, he didn't feel like caring tonight.

Andrea called a second later, and instead of making an excuse to Redhead, he just walked away to answer.

"Hey, babe."

"Hello, Mr. Maxwell," she said crisply. "You have a game for me? I thought we'd decided on no more games."

"You're right. No game tonight. Just you."

"Is that so?"

"Just you, Andrea."

"Well, I'm at an art gallery at the moment. If you come over, you might get some pussy later."

"Might?" he asked. A smile broadened his face. He loved when his girl talked dirty to him.

"Don't you want to come here and find out?"

Chapter 9

CAVEMAN

The goddamn art gallery was on the other side of town.

If Clay hadn't felt like Andrea's words were a challenge, he would have said fuck it as soon as he saw the address. She couldn't have known where he was at the moment, but it was at least forty-five minutes from his office. *Thank fuck for Uber drivers!*

When he finally exited the Escalade that had driven him across town, he was glad that he hadn't changed out of his suit from work. Everyone else in the place was dressed to the nines, as if this were a black-tie event. He might actually be underdressed for the occasion, which never happened. He carefully straightened his tie, all the while wondering where Andrea had sent him.

A woman at the door handed him a program. Without looking at it, he promptly discarded it as he passed a table. He wasn't here for the event. He was here for Andrea.

His eyes traveled the crowded rooms bursting with expensive artwork and snooty artsy types. The walls were perfectly stark white with white columns interspersed in the room. Everything was tasteful and chic. Very modern. Very rich. Money was dripping from the clientele, and he was surprised to find he recognized a few people. This must be very exclusive and prestigious to draw such a crowd. No wonder Andrea was here.

"Clay!" someone called from behind him.

He turned to face the voice and saw that Jamie girl he'd met on New Year's. She smiled and waved, trotting over to him with a guy behind her.

"Hey! I thought you'd have been here ages ago!" Jamie said.

Clay furrowed his brows. *Why?*

"Oh, this is my husband, James."

"Nice to meet you," he said, shaking James's hand. "Have you seen Andrea?"

"I think she's in the next room, talking to a collector. She's sold a ton of work here tonight."

"Oh, yeah?" he asked slowly, not sure what she meant by that.

"Yeah. All of my pieces are gone. She's brilliant, that one. You're lucky to have a girlfriend like her. She has quite an eye for artwork and has proven to be a savvy entrepreneur in our art community," Jamie gushed.

"Indeed," Clay said.

His head was spinning. From what Jamie had said, it sounded like Andrea wasn't here to purchase artwork, like normal…but she was running the show? He was really confused by that. He knew that she had said she was involved in selling artwork, but she'd never mentioned that it had gotten to this level.

How did I miss this? Did she just not tell me, or have I been oblivious to her success?

He didn't even remember her inviting him to this event, let alone telling him that she was hosting it as her own art business.

"Excuse me. I'm going to go look for my girlfriend," he said with a curt nod.

Jamie and her husband disappeared into the crowd as Clay went in search of Andrea. He found her exactly where Jamie had said she would be, talking to an older woman who was apparently a collector. Andrea had her back to Clay and was gesturing to some piece of art with a few brushstrokes on the canvas. He would hardly consider it art, but he knew Andrea had paid a small fortune for it.

Clay assessed Andrea from afar, glad that she couldn't see him, as he got his thoughts together. She looked gorgeous from head to toe. Her platinum-blonde hair was slicked back into a French twist, and she had demure pearls dangling from her ears that went perfectly with her tight black dress. Well, it wasn't too tight. He just had an active imagination. It was perfectly fitting for what she was here for. And the shoes, some four-inch designer heels with red lacquered soles, made her calves and ass look sexy as hell. He wasn't sure a day would pass when he didn't find her as beautiful as that first day they'd met on the beach.

Andrea seemed to finish up whatever business she'd been working on and turned, as if sensing his eyes on her. She smiled at the sight of him, and he approached her.

"Well, hello there," he said.

"Clay," she said softly, "you made it."

"No wonder you couldn't play tonight, if you were busy organizing all of this." He spread his arms wide and gave her an easy smile. It wasn't about the game. This was about her. Them.

"I'm really glad you came. I didn't know if you would," she admitted. "I honestly thought you'd forgotten the whole thing until I got your text."

Well, fuck! He was supposed to have known about this already. He couldn't remember her telling him about it, but he'd been so out of it since the attack that it must have totally slipped his mind. They were both usually really good about being there for each other.

So, he just smiled and said, "This is important to you. Of course I'm here."

Andrea's baby blues went lazy and satisfied at his comment. They spoke volumes about what his words meant to her. She slid her hand up his jacket. "Well, I'm glad. Even if you are underdressed."

He shrugged. "I still look hot."

"And smell like an ashtray," she added. Andrea rolled her eyes. "Were you out with Cash and Ethan before this?"

Clay shrugged and threw an arm around her narrow waist. "I'm here with you now."

"Well, let me introduce you to some people then." Andrea immediately shifted back into professional mode.

This was what it was like when they were at events together. That same old familiar feeling. The ease with which they settled into the facade of being a real normal couple. His hand on her waist, her eyes finding his, sharing private thoughts in a glance. They had been like this for so long; it was as easy as breathing.

Except, this time, it was different. Just a slight difference but a difference nonetheless. Andrea had been standing at his back for his career, his dreams, for so long, he had never realized the shift it would be for him to be standing at her back for once.

All the people here were for Andrea. Some of the people she introduced him to were her colleagues and patrons. What he'd always thought was a brainless fascination with spending an insane amount of money on art seemed to have turned into a real career.

This whole time, he must have been fucking blind not to notice.

But he noticed now. And he felt something stirring in his chest for her. Pride. Even if he didn't understand this world, he was glad that she was happy in it.

Andrea kissed the cheeks of a woman in a flowing long gown and said something in French he just barely caught. His French was rusty, but he was pretty sure they were talking about him.

"Yes. This is my boyfriend, Clay," Andrea said, gesturing to him.

"Pleasure to finally meet you. Your Andrea is quite a treat," the woman said in a thick accent. "I've not seen anyone with such an eye since my belated husband."

"She is striking, isn't she?" Clay said.

He put his arm around Andrea, and she beamed.

"That woman owns half of Paris, I swear," Andrea told him once they were out of earshot. "Her husband was an art collector, and apparently, she's grown to like American art even though she thinks that Americans are a bit crass."

"We are," Clay agreed. "What did she say about me?"

"Oh, you heard," Andrea said, pulling him farther away. "She said you were too handsome not to have at my side at all times."

Clay bent down and kissed her temple. "She's right."

"I'm so glad you're here," she said again. "I have to do some more business, but let me show you this one project."

Clay obliged her and followed her into another room where a large portrait was showcased. It was of a woman he'd never seen before. She was stripped naked and staring out a large glass-paned window plastered with rain. Tears leaked from her eyes, and she looked distraught. It was romanticized in some way. Her breasts were covered. Her legs crossed. She didn't look obscene. Just missing something…and it wasn't her clothes.

"I wasn't going to get rid of it," Andrea told him. "But I knew it would fetch a fortune."

"It speaks to you," he admitted. He wasn't big into art, but even he could tell that the work was special.

"It does. She does."

"How much is it going for?" he asked curiously. *Why would she ever get rid of something she loves so much?*

"Half a million."

Clay choked and sputtered, "Jesus, Andrea…"

She nodded. "I know. The artist recently passed. I'd purchased this the last time we were in the French Riviera, and now, it's worth a hundred times what I paid for it. Seemed too good to pass up."

Clay didn't argue with her. It was too good to pass up. They didn't need the money by any means, but that kind of increase in value was incredible. And, like the stock market, who knew how long that value would last? Everyone was probably scooping up all the paintings from the artist while they were available. Then, the bubble would likely burst, and Andrea would be left with a painting worth the five grand she'd paid for it.

"And it'll sell tonight?"

She nodded. "I've already had five prospective buyers. It might go into auction if they all decide to bid."

"All the better for you."

Sadness crept into her eyes at the loss of the painting, but she quickly hid it. He knew how much it pained her to get rid of this. She was first and foremost a lover of art. Even if she was making a career out of it, it wouldn't still the sting of losing one of her pieces.

"Andrea, there you are. I've been looking all over for you." A man approached from behind them and pulled Andrea into a hug before Clay even realized whom it was.

As soon as he did, his jaw clenched, his hands balled into fists, and his entire body stiffened.

Bad Suit. Asher McWalter. *What the fuck is he doing here?*

He stared daggers at the douche bag's back. He stepped forward to pry Bad Suit's slimy fingers off of what belonged to Clay when Andrea hastily sidestepped his advance.

"Oh, Asher," she said crisply. It was her business voice. "I didn't realize you were even here."

"Just arrived. Had to close the gallery," he said evenly. "You know how it is."

Clay loudly cleared his throat, stood up as straight as possible, and stared down at the guy with pure fury in his eyes. He wasn't at a bar. He couldn't throw a punch. But he didn't need to. He didn't need to be physical with this guy. It was pretty obvious that anything he threw the douche bag's way would crush him.

But this guy had gotten Andrea to leave that bar with him. He'd taken Andrea home and fucked Clay's girl on the night when she was supposed to have left with him. He knew he probably shouldn't lay his entire attack on this guy's doorstep, but that didn't stop him from doing it.

Andrea took one look at Clay's face and stepped easily into his arms. She put her hand on his suit, like she wanted to hold him back. Her smile was cautious. "Asher, this is Clay. Clay…Asher."

Asher glanced uncertainly between them. He probably didn't know that Andrea had a boyfriend. None of Clay's conquests knew about her. Except, well, Liz, but that was an accident when he had run into her at Hilton Head. Not that he'd gone through with it with Liz.

When neither of them moved, Andrea kept talking, "Asher owns a gallery uptown. I've found some great pieces there. Jamie was featured there once."

Clay didn't take his eyes off of Asher. Andrea was filling him on information he already knew. The girl never mumbled, so she must be nervous as shit to have them standing in the same room, breathing the same air.

Andrea glanced up at him with a pleading look on her face. It was brief. She would never show her emotions for that long. He just knew that she wanted him to fucking say something.

"That right? Art galleries seem to be all the rage right now," Clay drawled.

"And Clay is…he's an attorney," Andrea said, clearly not thinking his comment was sufficient. "He just finished up as a clerk at the Supreme Court and is now at the top firm in D.C."

"Attorney," Asher said, staring him down. "Heard they're a dime a dozen."

Clay grinned. "That's not the only thing I've heard is a dime a dozen."

Clay was in full-on standoff mode. He'd never encountered someone who would do this. Not that Andrea wasn't sought after by any means, but the former conquests were usually fleeting. They certainly didn't show up when he was around, and they didn't have the balls to tell him he was a dime a dozen. He'd been with Andrea for ten years officially—fifteen, if all the summers at Hilton Head were included. Asher was infringing on his territory, and he could go straight to hell for all Clay cared.

"But it's all right," Clay said.

Clay tugged Andrea closer to him and teasingly brought his lips down on hers. She squirmed for a minute, clearly uncertain about doing this at her event under the close scrutiny of the last guy she had been fucking. But she eventually gave in and kissed him back.

"Andrea," Asher said with a pointed cough.

"You did know she had a boyfriend, right?" Clay asked, not letting Andrea say a word.

He could hear a slight groan next to him, but he ignored her. He was too focused on the look of confusion on Asher's face.

"You're her…boyfriend?"

"Obviously."

"Since when? Two or three weeks, Andrea?"

Clay laughed derisively. "Weeks? Try years. But it's interesting how you think you can talk to her when she's been mine since we were thirteen."

"Clay," Andrea whispered, "just let it go."

Asher was looking at Andrea now, and Clay could see the guy was hurt by his words. *Good. The poor sap. Thought she'd actually cared about him and wasn't just another game.*

"No, he needs to know, baby," Clay told her. "She's mine. So, whatever you're thinking, I'd turn around and walk away because it's never fucking happening."

Asher took one more look at Andrea, gritted his teeth, and then disappeared.

Good riddance.

Andrea smacked Clay on the arm, bringing him back to reality. "Why did you have to do that?"

"What do you mean, why did I have to do that?" Clay asked. "He can't have you, Andrea."

"He already *knows* that I don't want to date him, Clay. He knows. I told him after the attack. I had no interest in him anymore. You didn't have to rub salt in the wound."

He dipped his head real close to her again. His nose brushed against hers, and he ran a hand down her back. "You're wrong about that. That was exactly what I needed to do because, now, he knows *why* you ditched his ass. And that you're with me, Andrea. With me."

He kissed her again, full on the mouth. Something had possessed him when he saw Asher and the way he looked at Andrea. Something had crawled straight out of Clay's chest and breathed fire.

But the look on her face now brought it all back into perspective. He wasn't sure he'd ever seen her look at him like that. Like putty in his hands. Complete and total adoration. Guess she didn't mind that he'd put his foot down, which was good because he wouldn't have been able to stop even if he'd wanted to.

~

That night, they didn't even make it back to their house in the suburbs. Andrea's place was closer, and he didn't even care at this point. He just wanted to be with her. They stumbled through the door, and Clay hoisted her into his arms and went straight to her bedroom.

She sank into the down comforter with a sigh. "What you said back there," she murmured.

He stripped out of his suit. "What did I say?"

"That I'm with you."

"Of course you're with me," he insisted.

He reached for her black dress and slid it off her body, finding her without underwear and only in a skimpy black bra. She flicked it off and tossed it across the bedroom.

"Come here." She crooked her fingers at him, and he obliged.

He had been fantasizing about sliding his dick inside her body ever since he'd seen her in that fucking dress at the gallery. Plus, he was just so fucking proud of her. He didn't know how much money she had made tonight, but it didn't even matter with that smile on her face.

He started at her knee, leaving a trail of kisses up her inner thigh. He blew hot on her most sensitive area before moving up her stomach and to her tits. Fuck, he loved her tits. He flicked his tongue over one as he took the other between his fingers.

She moaned, wrapping her legs around him and drawing him closer. "Oh, Clay, I've been thinking about you all day."

"Fuck, me, too."

"I just want you inside me," she purred.

"Plenty of time for that."

She shivered as he switched to the other nipple, his hands roaming her body and taking in every curve.

"Say that you're mine," she whispered.

"You're mine," he repeated against her skin.

She laughed softly. "No. Say that I'm yours."

"I'm yours."

"Oh, yes, I love the sound of that."

"If you keep crying out like that, I'm not going to be able to control myself."

"Then, don't," she said.

She positioned herself against his cock and rubbed up and down on him. It was fucking hot and showed him how wet she already was.

"Fuck," Clay groaned.

He aligned their bodies and then thrust into her. She moaned loudly, only making him push harder into her. God, she felt amazing. Her nails dug into his back. Their bodies smacked together.

It wasn't like this with anyone else. Andrea seemed to know his body as well as he knew hers.

He slammed into her over and over again. She tilted her head up to stare into his eyes. Something was stirring in those eyes. Her face was awash with passion and desire, but still, there was something else.

"Oh, Clay," she groaned. "Finish me off, baby."

And he did. He thrust into her a few more times, and then they both lay back on the bed, spent.

"That was amazing," she whispered, curling into his shoulder.

He shifted to go clean up, but she reached out and grabbed his arm. "Will you stay the night?"

"Where did you think I was going?" he asked with a laugh.

"I don't know."

"Just the bathroom. I'll be back."

When he returned, she cleaned herself up and then wrapped herself around him.

He felt like he was about to pass out from the exhausting round of sex when she whispered so softly that he barely heard it, "I like being yours…and I'm glad you're mine."

He didn't say anything. He didn't know what to say. They had been each other's for so long…so nothing really needed to be said.

He just kissed the top of her head, listened to her sigh contentedly, and fell asleep with her in his arms.

Chapter 10

INAUGURAL BLISS

The day had finally arrived—the presidential inauguration. D.C. bulged to bursting with visitors hoping to catch just a short glimpse of the new president as she took her oath into office. Last election had brought in a record two million additional people into the already busy city, and this year was predicted to be even larger. Everyone wanted to remember how they'd stood on the sidelines in the freezing weather to watch history being made.

Clay had watched the sidelines of history his entire life. Since congressmen were required to be in attendance, his family had been at so many different inaugurations that he had lost count. This one was just like all the others—crisp and cold with the early morning haze burning off from the sun's rays peeking through the clouds. Thankfully, it wasn't raining. He'd sat through rain before, and everyone had gotten terribly sick afterward. No, he hoped the rain would hold off until tomorrow at least.

Instead, he'd have to make do with shivering in the many layers he'd packed under his peacoat while he labored through speech after speech. He was pretty tired of the sidelines, to be honest, but at least he had a *seat*, unlike the droves of people stretching into the distance.

His mother was seated next to him, chatting away with the Atwoods—Gina and Matthew. Their children—Chris, Lucas, and Alice—were in the row behind him with Savannah and her boyfriend, Easton.

Andrea was currently bundled up in the seat next to him. She had one hand tucked into the pocket of his jacket. He laced their fingers together, which brought a huge smile to her face—one she had been wearing every day since the art gallery.

"Oh my God," Liz cried, rushing over toward them through the crowd and interrupting the moment between him and Andrea.

But Andrea just smiled. She'd been in such a great mood. The sex had been mind-blowing with her being so happy like this. And he'd thought it'd been killer before.

"What's going on?" Andrea asked.

Liz plopped into the chair next to Andrea. "It is a madhouse! Be glad that Clay is already with you," she said, brushing her long blonde hair out of her face. "Brady got all caveman on me when I said I had to find my *own* seat! He didn't want me to leave his side, but it's not like I can sit with all the congressmen!"

"He just likes having you with him," Andrea said sensibly.

Liz brightened at the words. "Yeah. He's a little protective."

"A little?"

"A lot," she admitted. "But he had to be during all the election chaos we had to deal with."

Andrea tapped Liz on the hand. "Honey, that runs in the Maxwell blood."

Clay snorted.

"I've noticed," Liz said, looking pointedly at Clay.

"You're lucky though," Andrea said. "Brady is a great guy. A respectable man. It was nice to see him settle down and with someone who could keep up with him."

That sounded strangely like a compliment. Clay had never really been sure what Andrea thought of Liz. Their first meeting, in which Andrea had called Liz boring and promptly told him not to fuck her, had been pretty memorable. Since then, the two hadn't exactly gotten off on the right foot, but it seemed that they both were becoming more accommodating to the other. He didn't even know when that had happened. He seemed to be missing a lot lately.

Liz shot Andrea a surprised look, and then her gaze moved down to her engagement ring. "I'm glad to see him settle down, especially with everything we've been through."

"This is good for you two."

"Thanks, Andrea," Liz said with a warm smile.

Clay pretended not to be paying attention when Liz leaned over and whispered to Andrea, "And what about you and your Maxwell brother? Can you get the black-sheep bad boy to settle down? Can you tame his ways?"

Andrea laughed. "I don't want to tame him. I like him the way he is—wild and mine."

Clay sighed in relief at her words. That was exactly what he'd wanted to hear. Nothing had changed. She liked things just the way they were.

"To each their own," Liz muttered under her breath.

At that time, all conversation ceased as the inauguration began. It was an hour full of ceremony heaped upon more ceremony. The president's official term would begin at noon on the twentieth of January. They all listened to a famous pop artist sing the national anthem. The president was sworn into office and gave a lengthy speech. Then, the ceremony ended with a benediction. An hour later, the new president would move into the White House, and the United States would shift ever so slightly.

"That'll be Brady one day," Liz murmured. She looked emotional about the inauguration. Must have been her first.

Clay humphed at her words. "We'll see."

She looked at him with her penetrating deep stare. "Yes, we will."

At the end of the official inauguration, Clay knew that there would be endless events that he'd be forced to participate in. It was the woes of being in a political dynasty. He and Savannah, though neither had any interest in politics, would forever be swept up in the machine.

Though brisk, windy, and chilly, the day went by quickly. Andrea stood at his side for the long day of events. The perfect socialite, she knew everyone, seamlessly fitting into every conversation and navigating the D.C. elite even better than he could, which was a feat in and of itself.

More people than he could have ever realized asked her about her art business. She would animatedly go on and on about the endeavor and offer them a private viewing or to keep a lookout for a piece they'd been searching for. Her networking skills seemed to be the highlight of her career. She knew everyone, so everyone wanted to work with her. And since she was part of the elite, they trusted her and thus flocked to her.

"You're going to run out of artwork at this rate," Clay joked.

Andrea squeezed his arm where she was holding on to it. She had just been speaking with a couple about finding a few new paintings for their house. The woman had even asked her to come to their suburban mansion to look at the space and get her point of view on what she thought would be the best. Everything would obviously be generously paid for.

"I could never run out of artwork, but it does seem like we're going to need to travel more," she admitted.

"I wish I could."

"The new job is holding you back," she joked, leaning into him and smiling at another couple they had seen at the last luncheon.

"Holding me back or propelling me toward my real future as the attorney general?"

Andrea wrinkled her nose. "Why do you even want that job, Clay?"

"You know why."

"Because your dad mentioned it once when he told Brady he should be president?"

"And look where Brady is now," Clay pointed out.

"You don't have to stand in his shadow," she murmured. "You're your own man, Clay."

"This is what I want," he said fiercely.

"Okay," she agreed easily. "There's that fiery passion. I missed it."

"I'll show you fiery passion."

He bent down and nipped her ear. Her eyes drifted around the room, as if to find a place they could sneak off to, but there was no such place. Not here with everyone they knew in attendance and thousands of people they didn't know crowding the space. There wasn't a place in D.C. where they could be alone right now.

"I have an idea," Clay murmured.

"I'm listening."

"You come back to my place."

Andrea groaned. "You want me to come to your bachelor pad? You should have gotten a hotel in the city."

"Come on, Andrea. Just you and me. Alone."

"Can I burn the sheets?"

"Whatever turns you on, baby."

"No," she said with a sad sigh. "We should stay and be here for your parents and Brady. Liz is new at all of this. She's navigating it well, but she's not used to this kind of stuff. I kind of like helping her with it when I can."

Clay's eyes widened. "Who are you, and what have you done with my girlfriend?"

"Oh, don't think I've turned into a sap on you. She's just…nice."

"She is."

"And," she said quickly, "you didn't fuck her."

He laughed. "No, I didn't."

"So, I can actually welcome her into the family. I want her and Brady to do well, you know?" Andrea's eyes swept over to where Brady had his arm locked protectively around Liz's waist.

They were deep in conversation with some other couple. Liz looked radiant and undeniably happy.

"I know just what you mean."

"Clay Maxwell!" Andrea said. "Are *you* becoming a sap on me?"

"No."

"But you want your *brother* to be happy? With a girl *you* pursued?"

Clay shrugged. "When you put it like that…"

Andrea stood on her tiptoes and kissed his cheek. "Don't worry. I won't tell your brother that you actually love him."

"You're insane, woman."

"I just know you too well, Mr. Maxwell."

"Well, if you aren't going to get to know me better in a more…biblical sense, then you'd better go over there and help my future sister-in-law."

Andrea giggled and walked over to Liz. She linked arms with Liz and drew her away from Brady. Brady's eyes locked with Clay's across the distance, and he nodded curtly, as if entrusting him with his most precious cargo. Clay nodded back and watched as

Andrea worked her magic with Liz in the room for the next hour.

By the time they could finally extricate themselves from the day's events to get ready for the inaugural ball later that evening, they were both wiped out, and Andrea was late for her hairstylist appointment at her apartment. Just because of the crowds, it was hell, getting back to her place. But Clay knew he'd have a while to wait as Andrea got ready for the events of the night.

Andrea kissed him deeply on the lips before scampering upstairs. He changed into his tux and waited for her…for what felt like forever. And, when she reappeared, he missed everything she was wearing and simply stared at the beautiful woman. All he saw were long and lean legs, sexy, curvy hips, soft breasts spilling out of the top, and that perfect face smiling back at him.

"Fuck."

"That good?"

"Hell yeah. Better than good." He stepped up to her and ran his hands over every square inch of material he could touch. "More like, I'm going to tear this dress off, like I did the last one, to get to exactly what I want underneath it."

Andrea smirked at him and planted a light kiss on his lips. "As much as I'd adore that, I thought we could maybe…talk for a minute?"

"You'd rather talk than spend the next ten minutes fucking before the limo arrives?"

She just walked across the room and took a seat on the sofa. He followed her, leaning back into the corner and draping his arm across the back.

"It's not that I want to skip having sex with you. The sex has been…amazing. Even better than normal, and it's always really great," she said. Andrea didn't fidget or squirm like he thought most girls would when she had something serious she wanted to say to him. She just looked him square in the eyes and delivered her carefully constructed speech. "But I want more than great sex, Clay."

"You do?" he asked cautiously.

"When you were attacked, something…changed. It shifted the paradigm of our relationship. It made me realize how much you mean to me, and I think it showed you how much I mean to you. I know I did something incredibly stupid by trying to make you jealous, and you got hurt. I can never tell you how sorry I am."

"I don't blame you for what happened, Andrea."

"I know. And I appreciate that."

She took a deep breath, and he saw a flicker of fear cross her features.

What could be so important that it would rattle Andrea?

"I just want us to be on the same page. When we were at the art gallery and you stood up to Asher for me…" Her hand went to her stomach. "I have never been happier than in that moment. You claimed me as your own. You were completely serious when you were protective of me. For a moment, I knew that must be what Liz felt like when she was with Brady."

"What?" Clay choked out.

Fire alarms were going off in his head.

This was not the conversation he'd thought they were going to be having. *She thinks that we're like Liz and Brady? She thinks that the paradigm of our relationship has shifted because I scared off that douche bag?*

"Ever since that happened, I've really felt like you and I are in tune, in sync. And I've realized that I like the direction we've taken."

"You…do?"

She nodded. "This is what I never knew I wanted. For so long, I thought that it would be easier to close myself off to escape the abandonment I'd always felt from my parents. But it's been fifteen years, Clay. Ten years of dating. I don't think we're going anywhere. And I just want this to stay that way, not to go back to being closed off and uncaring."

"Okay," he said slowly.

"Do you get what I'm saying?" she asked. Her blue eyes were wide and hopeful.

"Yeah," he answered carefully. "You want us to stay the same."

She slowly breathed out through her nose. "No, I want us to grow. I think we're growing. I want to be with you, Clay. This works for us."

He nodded, his head buzzing with her words. She seemed satisfied that he was nodding along, but internally, he was freaking the fuck out.

What exactly did growing together mean? Did that mean she wanted to change how things had been? Did she want us to stop sleeping around?

Until this moment, he hadn't realized how serious Andrea had been about ending all the games.

"So…where do we go from here?" he asked.

"Why don't we just go to the ball as a couple and see where the night takes us?"

Chapter 11

SAME PAGE, DIFFERENT BOOK

F*uck.*

Oh, fuck.

He had fucked up.

He had definitely fucked up.

Andrea thought they were on the same page. She thought that what had happened with Bad Suit and the way Clay had acted that night had changed things. She thought the attack had changed things.

As far as Clay was concerned, the only things that had changed were that he had wheezed for a few weeks, and he was fifteen hundred dollars poorer.

This shit with Andrea felt the same as it had every day before it. Did he care about her? Of course. He always had. He always would. She was that person to him. The one he'd never walk away from, who always totally got him, no explanation necessary.

But that didn't mean they were on the same page. Because Andrea was talking about mushy feelings that he, as a grown-ass man, was not interested in thinking about. Shit had been fucking fine for too long to *shift the paradigm* of their relationship.

He hadn't thought that claiming her in front of Bad Suit would have this kind of reaction. *Has she already been thinking like this, and the night at the art gallery has just solidified it?*

What he did know…was that he was freaking out.

He was trying to control it. They still had to get through the ball tonight. But the idea of a relationship, a real goddamn relationship, made him want to turn tail and run in the other fucking direction.

Andrea kept shooting him curious glances in the short limo ride to the inaugural ball. He probably should have said something to ease her anxiety. It wasn't like he was leaving, but they needed to have another conversation about this *new* direction. He just figured that having that conversation right before they were about to go out in public wasn't the best idea.

They arrived at the inaugural ball in style. Their limo dropped them off at the front entrance, and Clay helped Andrea out of the car before they walked into the room. It was a giant space, big enough for the enormous crowd that was supposed to arrive tonight. Cash bars were sporadically placed around the room, and there were light hors d'oeuvres on tables. Clay knew the after-party was where the real action would happen, but this event allowed lobbyists to schmooze with politicians in a fluid manner since dinner wouldn't actually be served. He couldn't wait to get shit-faced at the after-party. It was like the *Vanity Fair* Oscars after-party for politicians.

Andrea wrapped her hand around his elbow and smiled. "Shall we?"

He nodded, and they meandered through the room. They found Brady in a more secluded area with Liz on his arm. As Clay and Andrea approached, Brady was chatting with some of his fellow politicians.

Liz extended her left hand to the group. "Yes. This June. We're both very excited," she said.

"A wedding for the ages," one woman said, leaning forward and examining the ring.

Clay knew that he should be able to recognize most of the people here, but his thoughts were back in Andrea's apartment.

"It's going to be beautiful," Andrea said.

"It's going to be sweltering," Clay corrected. "Asheville in June. Even with the mountains, it's going to be hot and humid."

"You wear a suit every day. It'll be fine," Andrea said.

"Oh, don't complain, Clay," Liz teased. "It'll be you next anyway."

"Excuse me?"

"Clay," Andrea warned.

Brady laughed and clapped his brother on the back. "Don't take everything so seriously, Clay. She just meant that you and Andrea have been together forever. You're clearly a match. It's not crazy to think that you'd be next getting married. God forbid, it's Savannah!"

The rest of the group burst into laughter, as if what Brady had said was the most hilarious thing they'd ever heard. Of course, Clay knew that Savannah wouldn't be getting married anytime soon. She was seven years younger than him. There was no way. Over his dead body.

So, that technically made him next on the list. But that didn't mean right now. And it certainly didn't mean anytime soon with Andrea talking about changing their relationship. Marriage and babies weren't high on his list. Actually, they'd never even touched the list.

"I need a drink," he said before turning and walking away.

No one followed him. He was better off. He needed to get his shit together and figure out what he was going to say to Andrea later.

A few minutes later, he returned with a whiskey in hand and a glass of champagne for Andrea. He hoped, after a glass or two of this, he would be able to relax a little. He certainly needed it.

Andrea intercepted him and took the champagne from him. "How thoughtful."

"Mmm," he said, taking another sip of his whiskey. He'd asked the bartender to pour him a shot before he got this one, but apparently, that was in poor taste. So, he'd had to down one of these before collecting her champagne.

"Are you okay?" she asked.

"Let's talk about it later."

"Clay…"

"Later, Andrea."

"You can't admit something is wrong and then not tell me what it is," she insisted. "I do have emotions, you know?"

"You made that quite clear."

"What does that mean?" she snapped. Her eyebrows rose sharply.

"It means that, because you have developed those emotions out of nowhere, you should not ask me to talk through them with you in public," he said plainly.

She narrowed her eyes and then tossed back the champagne like it was a fucking shot. *Damn! That's impressive.* He'd practically cringed, watching her do it.

"You think, because I've decided to tell you how I feel, I'll just let you walk all over me? I'm not, nor will I ever be, one of those girls you can treat like shit and ignore, Clay Maxwell," she said evenly. "I've known you for fifteen years. I've been in your bed for nearly as long. I know you inside and out. I'm not an idiot. I know that what Brady said back there freaked you the fuck out."

"And?" he snapped.

"And what?"

"And what do you think? Do you think this is leading us to that shit? Is that what you meant when you said we were like Brady and Liz?"

"God! Why do you have to jump to conclusions?" she demanded. She grabbed his arm and pulled him farther away from the crowd. "Did I say I wanted us to get married and have kids?"

"No, but…"

"No. I didn't say that. I said I wanted us to be a couple. So, why can't we act like that?"

"Because this isn't *us*, Andrea!"

"What isn't us?" she asked. "*This* is exactly us. This is what we do. We go to functions together. We play boyfriend and girlfriend. We pretend to be just like everyone else. How is this any different?"

"Because we're not pretending. You actually want us to be like that," he told her. "And I don't know if I want that."

Andrea took a small step back. "You seemed like you wanted that when we talked at my place. You seemed on board. Why won't you just try with me, Clay? Just try? I mean, you claimed me as your girlfriend to Asher. You pushed him away, fucking ran him off, so that he'd never even look at me again, but you don't want me?"

"I want you," he said. He dropped a hand onto her hip and pulled her closer. "I really, really want you."

"Ugh!" she snapped. She pushed him away from her. "Not like that. That's not what I meant at all, and you know it!"

"What? So, now, you don't want to have sex with me?"

"This isn't about sex. This is about you being terrified of having a relationship. I mean, I would understand if it were someone you had just met. If you were so afraid of doing this because you didn't really know the person and had no clue how they would treat you. But this is me," she said. Her voice dipped down, and she sounded so vulnerable. Tears formed in the corners of her eyes, and she closed them to try to keep them at bay. "This is me, Clay."

"I know it is."

"I know everything about you. I like that you're a scoundrel and a sarcastic ass. I like that you value your family as much as you get frustrated with the entire process. I know you. If you can't let me past your guard, like I've let you past my guard, then you'll never let anyone in."

Clay couldn't hear any of this. Of course Andrea knew him. She always had. That was why their arrangement had worked. That didn't mean they needed to change it.

"But why would you want to change something that works? What we have works," he told her. "It was always has."

Andrea feebly shook her head. "It doesn't work for me anymore. I want more. I *deserve* more. I've grown up, and I need something more than this." Her blue eyes were sad. "Honestly, Asher was willing to give me more."

"You're really going to bring up that douche like that?"

"Yes! Don't you see what I'm saying? I could have more. I could have a real relationship, but I want it with *you*." She reached out and laced their fingers together. "I want to make this work with you."

"I don't need this." He pulled away from her.

"What? You don't need what?" Andrea reached for him.

"This," he said calmly.

How could I keep having this conversation without her understanding? He didn't need this argument. She was asking for more than he was willing to give. He wasn't ready for that. He just wanted to keep things the way they were.

"This," she repeated. She gestured between them.

"Yeah."

Andrea glanced off, away from him. She seemed to be trying to collect her thoughts. Her face hardened. Something in her shifted. He had no idea what she was thinking. *Couldn't she tell that she was ruining everything?*

"Have you fucked anyone else since the night of your attack?" she asked. Her voice was hard, lacking all the emotion that had been there moments ago.

"What?"

"You know exactly what I mean. Have you fucked anyone?"

"I've fucked you."

"Anyone *else*?"

Clay stared into her eyes as he realized…no, he hadn't been with anyone else. He'd had the opportunity. Gigi had thrown herself at him. The girl at the bar had offered herself up. There'd been several other occasions where he could have easily taken someone home with him, but he hadn't.

"Well?" she asked.

"No. Just you," he said through gritted teeth.

"I see. So, we live in the same house. We go to all the same functions. You call me your girlfriend. We haven't played any games since the attack, and you're only fucking me. Please explain to me how we're not already in the relationship that you so desperately claim not to want to be in?"

Well, when she put it that way.

He took a step back, balking at the thought. "Just because I haven't slept with anyone doesn't mean I never want to sleep with anyone else ever again."

Andrea swallowed at his words, but otherwise, she gave no sign that what he'd said had hurt her.

"So, you want me to be yours, but you don't really want me?"

"What? Of course I want you."

"Right. Because, of course," she spat, rolling her eyes, "you want me. You want to run other guys off. You're jealous at the thought of me being with someone else. But you won't admit that we're really dating and really together. You want the opportunity to fuck someone else even if you never do. You want to keep our relationship stagnant for selfish reasons. You want your cake and to eat it, too."

"I'm not jealous—"

"I'm not cake, Clay!" she snapped. "If you really don't want this, then go and fuck someone else tonight!"

He stared at her as if she had lost her mind. "You want me to fuck someone else?"

"If that's what you *really* want, then go ahead. Go find someone here. Just break all the stupid rules. Show me how much I mean to you."

Clay shook his head. She had gone insane. *But isn't she telling the truth?* He wanted to continue screwing around and doing whatever he wanted. He wanted to keep things just the way they were because it worked for him. And, now, she was getting pissy because he'd told her the truth.

"Fine!" he shouted, anger bubbling up to the surface.

"Fine!"

"Enjoy your evening."

"I hope she's worth it," Andrea barked.

Clay shook his head at her bold statement and slammed her back with one of his own, "Oh, she will be."

Andrea recoiled at the words, and without a look backward, he turned with his drink in hand and went in search of the hottest fucking girl in the room.

Chapter 12

YOU DID THIS TO YOURSELF

Clay woke up the next morning to a wall of pain. He cradled his head in his hands as he rolled over in bed and tried to escape the light filtering in through the window. He flung the covers up to shelter his body, but it did no good. He couldn't go back to sleep. Not with this massive hangover.

What the hell did I drink last night to warrant this?

He couldn't remember.

He opened his bleary eyes and glanced around the room. It was empty, save for him. The bed was mussed, but it didn't look like anyone else had been in it. At least, he didn't think he'd had anyone else here.

Everything was a little fuzzy around the edges. The last thing he remembered was yelling at Andrea and making a fucking fool of himself at the inaugural ball. Apparently, he'd then drunk enough to black out. Whatever other shit had gone down last night, someone else would have to fill him in. He was too hungover to figure it out.

He stepped out of bed.

Naked.

Buck naked.

His tuxedo was a string of clothes leading out of the bedroom of his second-story townhouse and down the stairs, as if he had taken each piece off while making his way to the bedroom. But, normally, when that happened, he'd see a dress, followed by a red lace bra and finally the matching thong. A pair of high heels would be strewed across the floor. None of that was here this morning.

Just him, completely nude. All alone.

What a night!

Clay rolled his eyes and headed to the bathroom to dig out some Tylenol. He chased it down with a glass of water and then hopped into a long, luxurious shower to chase away the aftereffects of what felt like an entire bottle of whiskey pounding against his skull.

An hour later, he'd changed into a pair of dark wash jeans and a Carolina blue polo. He was starving but wanted to head over to the house. He probably needed to talk to Andrea about that shitty conversation they'd had. That wasn't how he'd wanted to have that talk. It was definitely not supposed to go down like that. He'd just pop over to the house, and they could go out to brunch.

He'd kill to be back in Chapel Hill right now and get some real Southern-style brunch. Maybe they could go back home for a weekend here soon. It'd be good to check on his house down there and just get out of the city for a while.

He pulled out his phone, surprised that he didn't have any other messages or calls from the night before, and then shot Andrea a text.

> *Hey, can we talk? I'm stopping by the house. Brunch?*

Clay revved his Porsche and took off for the suburbs without an answer. He hoped she was there or else it would be a futile drive, but she usually got out of the city when it was this busy.

He double-checked his phone when he was driving through their neighborhood. "Huh. Still no response."

He was surprised. She typically responded quickly. Maybe she was still asleep. She could be a late sleeper, especially after a long night.

Ignoring the feeling of unease that crept over him, he parked in the two-car garage. Andrea's Mercedes was missing, but it hadn't been there last night either. She'd left it at her apartment in town when they took the limo. The limo had probably brought her back here anyway.

He opened the door of the garage into the immaculate kitchen. Andrea had had it custom-designed. Not that either of them cooked. She would bake every now and again, but they'd both been too busy lately to play house.

"Andrea!" he called.

He stepped over the threshold and into the foyer. Then, he stopped dead in his tracks. His eyes roamed the walls. The foyer, the living room, the hallway down to the dining room and den.

Every single wall was *empty*.

His stomach flopped. *Shit.*

Normally, the walls were covered in priceless artwork that Andrea had collected over the years. The living room had had a landscape motif. The foyer, a welcoming branch of modern art that he'd never understood. The walkway had had portraits. She'd always said it was like greeting friends. The steps up to the second floor had been covered in floral paintings that complemented and mirrored each other.

Now, they were blank.

Stark.

White.

Empty.

His heart thudded in his chest. A terror like he had never known before seized him. His hands shook, and he fisted them at his sides, as if he could will them to listen to him.

But they betrayed him. His entire body betrayed him. How could something so simple… make everything feel so lost?

The house felt too big.

Too inhospitable.

Too unwelcoming.

Until that moment, he'd never once realized how much the artwork had breathed life into their place. How her hobby, obsession, career had brightened not just the house, but also their life together. How it had made a house, a home.

He rushed up the stairs, taking them two at a time, with only one thought in his mind. He needed to talk to Andrea.

"Andrea!" he yelled. "Andrea!"

No response. And he still didn't have a response on his phone.

Fuck.

"Fuck!"

He slammed the door open to the master suite. No artwork. Not a single goddamn piece. He turned and pressed the closet door open. He leaned heavy against the doorframe, unable to believe what he was seeing.

The closet was bare.

Not one single pair of Jimmy Choos. Not one designer dress. Not one ten-thousand-dollar handbag.

It was as if Andrea had never been here.

As if he had dreamed her existence into this place.

He shuddered at the emptiness of the home that they had built.

Clay choked on words. Andrea was gone. It was plain and simple. Clear as day before him. She had left. Not just the house, but clearly him as well. She had taken everything here that belonged to her and disappeared.

Never had he ever imagined a life Andrea didn't exist in. Ten years ago, they'd formed their pact. And he'd somehow destroyed it all in one night of drunken debauchery.

"No," he muttered. "She can't do this."

He wrenched out his phone and dialed her number, determined to convince her that she had made a horrible mistake. She couldn't leave him. Andrea was the one with abandonment issues. There was no way that she would just leave without a word. Without one goddamn word.

The call went to voice mail, and he heard her sweet voice on the other line.

"Hi, this is Andrea Billings. Sorry I've missed your call, but…"

Clay ended it before she could finish. He couldn't leave a message. What he needed to say had to be done in person.

He stormed back down the stairs and out to his Porsche. He ignored traffic and floored it over to her apartment. He was lucky that no cops were looking to pick up an asshole in a Porsche going ninety in a forty-five. He slammed on the brakes, leaving skid marks on her street, before parking illegally in front of her building. He hopped out of the car, took the elevator up to her place, pulled out his key, and slid it into the hole.

It wouldn't turn.

He stared, dumbstruck, down at the door. He'd been here last night. He'd used this very key *last night* to get into Andrea's apartment where they had gotten ready together for the ball. He jiggled the lock a dozen times before realization dawned on him.

She'd changed the locks.

His jaw dropped, and he stared uselessly at the handle. His hands were shaking again. His body ached from the extremes she'd gone to.

It couldn't end like this. It made no sense. Last night was no different than any other night. *What the fuck did she think had happened?*

He'd hurt her with his words. He knew that. But he hadn't actually slept with anyone. He hadn't even been fucking coherent enough to get it up, and he'd woken up alone. He hadn't gone through with his threat. There was a difference between hurting Andrea with words when they argued and actually going through with something that would destroy her. She had to know that.

But she clearly didn't.

Clay banged on the door until his fist was bruised. He yelled against the door. "Andrea! Come out here right now! I know you're inside! Just talk to me!"

He yelled until the next-door neighbor came out and asked if everything was okay. He was making a scene.

Fuck, I'm making a scene.

Clay dialed her number again and listened all the way through the voice mail this time. "Andrea, what the fuck is going on? Your stuff is all gone at the house, and my key doesn't work at your apartment. Where the hell are you? We need to talk. I don't know what happened last night that made you want to do all of this, but it's not what you think. I swear. Just talk to me."

He hung up before he could say anything else stupid, and he took the stairs back down to the ground level to burn off steam.

Seated in his car once more, he didn't feel any better at all. He needed to talk to her. He needed to talk to someone who could explain this to him. Definitely not Ethan or Cash. They'd probably just laugh at him and say he'd had it coming or he was better off. He didn't feel better off.

He stared at his phone and realized there was no one else. Andrea was always the person he would run to when things got tough. She was the one he talked to and joked with and fucked when he needed someone. She was his person.

Instead, he dialed Liz's number. He didn't know what had made him do it, but he couldn't just sit here alone. And even though he and Liz had had their differences, he knew he could rely on her.

He dialed the number, and after only one ring, it went straight to voice mail.

"What the fuck?"

He tried again. Same result.

So, Liz knew and wouldn't talk to him. That meant only one thing.

Brady actually answered the phone. "I had a feeling you'd call."

"What the fuck is going on?" Clay asked.

"I really hoped you would have the answer to that."

"Andrea is gone. She won't answer my calls or texts. She's moved out all of her stuff from our house in the suburbs and changed the locks at her apartment."

"I see. I had gathered that from the furious shouts Liz had been ranting about all morning," Brady said. "Do you want to meet up and talk about it? In this case, I don't think it's too early to go get a beer."

"Fuck, I need one."

Clay couldn't believe the kind of day he was having. First, his girlfriend of ten years had left him. And, now, he was having a beer at noon on Saturday with his older brother, who he'd spent longer than the last ten years feeling torn between disgust and envy.

Brady sank down into a seat at the quiet brunch location they'd decided on. It was halfway between Brady and Liz's place and Clay's townhouse. He'd gotten a back booth, away from prying eyes and ears, and he was happy to see it had a functioning bar. He probably shouldn't be drinking after what alcohol had done to him last night, but he couldn't face this day completely sober.

"Damn, you got yourself in a mess," Brady said as soon as the beers were in front of them.

Clay shook his head. He still couldn't fathom how he'd gotten here. "Yeah, I just don't fucking get it."

"Well, all the women are pissed as hell. I don't even want to be in my own place with all the uproar. What exactly did you do?" Brady asked.

"I said some stupid shit to Andrea last night," he admitted. He didn't know why he was being this honest with Brady when he'd normally crack a dumb joke, but there literally wasn't anyone else to tell. It felt kind of nice to confide in Brady.

"What kind of stupid shit?"

Clay sighed. "She kept going on about how she wanted to change our relationship so that we were a couple and not…whatever we'd been the last decade."

"And that is?" Brady prodded.

"You know how we were. We had an open relationship. We didn't care what the other person did, except when we were together."

Brady's jaw clenched. "I did know that was what you and Andrea had been this whole time, but just the thought of doing that with Liz makes me want to go ballistic."

"Yeah, well, y'all are different."

"Doesn't sound like Andrea is that different. What did you say to her wanting to change your relationship?"

"I told her I didn't want to," Clay said, as if this were the most obvious thing in the world. "She told me, if I didn't really want a relationship, then I should go sleep with someone else. So, I told her I would."

Brady put his head in his hands. "When a woman tells you to do something that stupid, you should never listen. It's like saying *fine* to end an argument."

Clay blanched.

"She said *fine* at the end of the argument? Oh, you're fucked," Brady said. He held up his pint glass. "Here's to living in the doghouse."

"I just need to talk to her. If I can talk to her, I can tell her that I didn't actually sleep with anyone else. It didn't really happen."

"Even if she believed you, Clay—and with your track record"—Brady frowned—"I don't think she'd care. It's not so much whether or not you slept with someone; it's that you ignored how she was feeling and said you were going to do it just to hurt her."

"That's some fucked up mind game right there."

Brady sighed and took another swig of his beer. Clay had already finished his.

"It might feel like a mind game, but to be honest, for a long time, I've been waiting for Andrea to realize she wants a real relationship. Savi and I always teased you about getting married for a reason. I honestly thought that was the trajectory you were on. I'm pretty sure Andrea thought that as well. So, if you weren't there with her, then she was probably feeling led on and used, little brother."

"That's bullshit! We talked about this," Clay said in frustration. "We decided how our relationship was going to be. She knew!"

Brady held his hands up. "I don't doubt that, but she still left for a reason."

"Well, fuck, what do I do? I have to talk to her. We need to work this out," Clay said.

"I'd just give her some space. Trust me. I fucked up with Liz a lot. *A lot.* I think I took *fucked up* to a whole new level," he admitted. His eyes were dark and distant, as if remembering that time still haunted him. "I should have fought harder. I shouldn't have ignored how she was feeling, even when I knew she was hurting. There's a lot that I wish I could turn back and correct. But I don't regret letting her figure out her thoughts on her own. She needed that time. I needed that time. Maybe I should have come back into her life earlier, and then she wouldn't have had to deal with shit from that douche bag she dated, but it made us stronger. When Andrea's ready, she'll talk to you again."

Clay nodded. Brady's advice was sound, but in that moment, all Clay wanted to do was tear D.C. apart to find Andrea and convince her that leaving was a horrible, terrible mistake. But, to his chagrin, she wanted nothing to do with him.

So, he was stuck here at a bar, taking his brother's advice, and giving his girlfriend, his constant companion, the space she needed and deserved. And he fucking hated it.

Chapter 13
SUFFERING

Giving Andrea the space she needed and not busting down the door to her apartment was an exercise in restraint. He hadn't even known that he had that much control in one finger, let alone in his whole body. He also hadn't known that her walking out would hurt this much.

And it hurt like a fucking bitch.

Fifteen years was a long-ass time to be with someone.

He didn't even *remember* what a time in his life before Andrea was like. He'd been a kid. She was his entire adult life. She was the girl at every event. She was the girl he would come home to. *Without her, what the hell am I supposed to do?*

He'd found that answer at the bottom of a bottle all weekend.

Sure, I'm wallowing in self-pity, but who could blame me? His girlfriend had just left him, and he didn't know how to pick up the pieces of their life together. He had always been so confident and cocky in the fact that he had his *own* life. It was completely separate from her. The part of him that never needed anyone. Now, he knew that was a lie.

There was no separate part of his life. Even his bachelor-pad townhouse made him think of her, and she rarely, if ever, came over here. She always complained it smelled like a rock star's tour bus even though he paid for a cleaning service.

It was easier to be so drunk that he couldn't think or see straight all weekend than to be sober and sitting around, thinking about her all the damn time.

She had proven her point. Loud and clear. He got it.

She was pissed. She'd wanted things to change, and he'd been a dick. Maybe if he had responded less like…*himself*, then things would look different today. But, instead, he'd told her he was going to go fuck someone else and break all the goddamn rules. After he'd just been so pissed at her for doing the same.

At least he hadn't actually slept with anyone. Brady had filled him in on the fact that he'd flirted with half of the women at the inaugural ball before everyone at the party had lost track of him that night, but Clay knew he hadn't slept with anyone. He wasn't sure it would have even been humanly possible to sleep with someone with that much alcohol in his system.

～

Monday morning dawned bright and early. He felt and looked like shit from the long weekend. Dark circles rimmed his eyes, and despite the shower, he still smelled like he was oozing alcohol from his pores. He found it hard to give a damn.

He entered his office without a word to anyone else there. He closed the door and laid his head down on the cold hard desk. Shit, he felt horrible.

The door to his office burst open.

"What the fuck are you doing, just sitting there?" Gigi asked.

She wasn't in a pantsuit today. Instead, she had on a pencil skirt with a button-up tucked into it. She wore black-rimmed glasses that looked hot as fuck, too.

"Just a few more minutes," he said, closing his eyes again.

"Are you out of your mind? Do you know what time it is? Do you know what *day* it is?"

"Monday?" he croaked.

"Yes! Monday! Monday morning, when we have a meeting with a partner to hand over your freaking cases."

His eyes popped open. *Well, shit.* With the kind of weekend he'd had, he hadn't even thought about his meeting with the boss this morning. He needed to prove he was worth their extra three hundred grand.

Clay stood and tried to brush out the wrinkles in his suit coat.

Gigi groaned and hastily shut the door. "Christ, you're trying to get us both fired, aren't you?" she asked.

"No."

She stormed over to him and started straightening his jacket and shirt. Then, she barreled straight forward and ran her fingers through his hair. Normally, this would have been pretty sexual, but she was very matter-of-fact about the entire thing.

She shook her head as she fixed him. "You smell like a bar," she said. "What the fuck did you do all weekend?"

Clay shrugged. "My girlfriend broke up with me."

She stilled with her fingers still in his hair. Her dark brown eyes rose to meet his, and she had a sad frown on her lips. "Oh." Then, realization seemed to trigger in her. She shoved him away from her. "If you had a girlfriend this whole time, then why didn't you just say that? You acted like a total jackass to me when I was drunk, and all you had to do was say you were with someone."

Clay didn't answer her right away. He could have said that, but that was never his answer to problems. Andrea wasn't his scapegoat. He was just an ass.

"Well?"

"It didn't matter. We'd been in an open relationship for a long time."

"Yeah. Well, that sounds like it worked out great for you."

Clay internally winced at that comment. On the outside, he remained as stoic as ever. "Literally every woman I know hates me right now. Let's just not."

Gigi sighed. "You're right. That's not fair of me. I don't know the details or what happened."

"Yeah. I'm not exactly an open book either."

"You do look like you're thoroughly suffering though." She bit her bottom lip and observed him.

"Thoroughly suffering is one way to put it," he said dryly.

"You still look like a hot mess."

"At least I'm still hot."

"And arrogant."

"But hot?"

"And an asshole. So, your breakup didn't rid you of any of your less redeeming traits."

Clay laughed softly. It felt good. "Thanks."

"Well, if you're ready, I think that's all I can do for you. Cooper is normally drunk by noon most days anyway. He might not even be able to smell the alcohol."

"I suppose alcoholism runs in the business," Clay joked.

"It's a tough job. Not everyone is cut out for it."

"That's the truth."

"Anyway, let's get moving, Maxwell. We have a meeting to get to."

Clay groaned but nodded, following Gigi out of the office. She glanced over at him once they reached the elevators.

"What?"

"Were you at the inauguration?"

He shrugged. "Yeah. Every year."

"Damn. I couldn't make it. I was stuck at work."

"You worked all weekend?" he asked.

"Don't have anything better to do." She pressed the button for the fourth floor. "Plus, this case is killing me. Literally."

"You should loosen up some, De Rosa."

She gave him the side eye. "As if loosening up has helped *you* any. Perhaps you should dig in and get a little more serious here. I can tell you think this place is a stepping-stone for you."

"Oh, yeah?" he asked curiously.

"It's written all over you. I can't *believe* they paid you a signing bonus, knowing that you're on your way to being a district attorney or a judge. It's written all over your résumé, all over your family," she told him intuitively.

"So what if it is a stepping-stone?" He was very intrigued now. Of course his résumé looked like he was on an upward trajectory. He *was*.

Gigi pursed her lips. "You'll move up, no matter where you go and what you do. You're a Maxwell. Name recognition is important for a reason, but if you didn't just slide by here and you actually worked with me instead, we could do some good things on the way up."

"Like what?"

She sighed, as if she hated admitting this out loud. "Help people, Clay. We could help people."

"That sounds like pro bono work."

"I'm just saying that we have a lot of power, and instead of stepping on the little people, we could maybe help them. I've been there. I know what they suffer." She eyed him up and down. "I don't know if you've ever really suffered before, but I'm kind of putting myself out there on a limb. Mind helping me off the ledge and agreeing to help?"

"So…what? You want me to spend a few more extra hours at the office to work on cases? Other cases?" he guessed.

She shrugged. "If you still have a job after this, then yeah. Why not?"

Why not? That was the question.

Honestly, when had I ever done anything for anyone but myself?

Helping people wasn't the reason he'd become a lawyer. He wasn't a social worker. But maybe helping people would be just the thing he needed. And, for a second, it dulled the ache in his chest and gave him something to think about for a future that had looked so bleak only moments before.

~

Their meeting ran over with the boss man, and by the end of it, Clay was second-guessing agreeing to help Gigi with more work. It'd been bad at the Supreme Court, and this workload was nearly on that level. He had a ton of cases of his own. Not that he'd ever been put off by having a lot of work to do. He usually just barreled through it with a single-minded madness for it, but he didn't know when he'd have time to work in anything else.

The best thing about the heavy workload was that he had next to no time to think about Andrea.

He spent the next week in a blind stupor. He and Gigi would be the first ones at the office and the last ones to leave every day. Their relationship was, to his utter surprise, completely platonic.

Ever since they'd reconciled, they'd formed a shaky friendship. It was something strange and new for him—to sit with a woman for hours on end and just talk about work. Of course, he still noticed her clothes…and the fact that she wore less pantsuits. But he wasn't trying to get under her skirts, and she made no moves toward him.

It was nice.

It was like having a friend.

The second week of silence from Andrea, he started working on other projects Gigi had handed to him now that she kind of trusted him. Cases he rarely would have looked at before—disability cases, domestic violence, housing disputes. But the majority of them were dealing with the orphanage that Cooper & Nielson sponsored ever year at their annual gala event. In some way, these matters took his mind off of his own issues far more easily than big corporate law cases.

But at night was when it got tricky.

The breakup was hitting him much harder than he could have ever imagined. Even harder than that because he'd never once even *imagined* a breakup. Away from work, the only way he could forget the insanity that was now his life was when alcohol would numb the pain.

"Hey," Gigi said, sticking her head into his office, "I'm about to head out. You want to get a drink or something?"

"Yes." He grabbed his coat as he stood. "I most definitely need a drink."

"Why am I not surprised?" She led the way to the elevator.

"Hey, you invited me. You can't then insult my drinking habits."

Gigi raised her eyebrows as the elevator deposited them into the parking garage. "Oh, I definitely can."

"Whatever. You drink like a fish, too." He clicked the fob for his Porsche, unlocking the car.

"I never said that I didn't have a problem," she said, dumping her purse on the floor of his Porsche and sinking into the passenger seat. "I just said you have a bigger problem."

He smirked his classic dimple grin at her. It had been harder and harder to find it since Andrea had left. Fuck, it had already been two weeks. He tried to block the thought from his head, but it just reared up without warning.

Gigi and he decided on a place a short distance from the office. Nowhere he used to frequent with the guys. Nowhere that Andrea would show up. Just a regular bar that would be happy to serve him whiskey while Gigi downed vodka like a champ.

"So, tell me what really happened with you and your girlfriend," she prodded after they were a few drinks in. "You never really said what happened."

Clay tossed back his whiskey and shot her an exasperated glance. "I was hoping you'd never ask."

"Well, I'm asking now. So, lay it on me."

"I don't know. After we ended up at Yale together, we were in a relationship for ten years. We'd been talking for the five years before that. She has abandonment issues because of her parents' divorce and I..." He paused, not sure how much he was ready to divulge.

"You?"

"I have a lot to live up to," he admitted.

"No shit. Your dad and brother are in Congress. No wonder you work so hard."

He shrugged. "Whatever. Andrea and I decided we'd have an open relationship. No one would get hurt, but that night when I first met you, I got attacked. I was robbed and beaten to within an inch of my life. I was lucky someone had found me and brought me to the hospital."

"Fuck," she groaned. "That's awful."

"Yeah. I guess Andrea thought that changed shit."

"That would definitely change shit."

"But then she wanted it to mean things I just wasn't ready for."

"Like what?"

Clay shrugged. *Everything.* He hadn't been ready for anything she was sending his way. She had wanted more than the arrangement they'd had, and he hadn't been ready to hear that. He knew that now. He'd been spooked. The thought of changing the way things were terrified him. She had gone and changed things anyway.

He knew that he hadn't been fully with it since leaving the Supreme Court. Too locked in his own head about moving forward with Daddy's plan for his life that he'd neglected her and himself.

He was damn sure that, if he got that second chance, then he wasn't going to make the same mistake twice.

"A real relationship. We argued about it, and she thinks I slept with someone else."

"Did you?" Gigi asked with raised eyebrows.

"No. But I told her I was going to."

"Why would you do that?" she demanded. "Guys are such idiots."

"I don't know. I was drunk, and we were arguing. I just wanted to make her as mad as I was. Now, she won't even talk to me."

"Well, I wouldn't talk to your dumb ass either," Gigi said. "After ten years, and you're bugging because the girl wants a relationship? That's madness. I thought Marcus and I were fucked up."

Clay laughed. "You and Small Dick were fucked up."

Gigi finished off her double shot of Grey Goose and leaned forward toward him. She poked him in the chest twice. Hard. "You know you love her, right?"

"I…what?"

"You love her. That's why you're totally insane right now."

"Yeah," he said softly. Then, he called for another round of drinks. "Course I love her. Doesn't mean a damn thing to her right now."

Chapter 14

SNOWBALLS & AVALANCHES

There was always a moment.

That one moment that changed everything.

Clay's moment was named Candace.

It had been a month of radio silence. Andrea hadn't called or texted. She hadn't been on any social media accounts. Her life associated with him had essentially been blocked since the inauguration.

Silence was deafening.

It was needy and greedy.

It ate him up from the inside out.

It cracked him around the edges, broke down his walls, and left room for the Candaces of the world to crawl in and wreak havoc.

He had promised himself that he wasn't going to give in. All he'd been thinking about for a fucking month straight was Andrea. He swore, he was going to wait to hear from her. He was going to convince her to come back and make all those promises she wanted to hear…that he feared he would break.

Other women weren't the answer.

Rationally.

Logically.

It made perfect sense to him. Fucking a dumb brunette over the sink of the bar restroom wasn't going to make him suddenly feel better. But there was always the difference between knowing and *knowing*.

One head didn't exactly talk to the other.

And he'd fucking tried to stay away. He knew what he wanted. But what he wanted didn't even want to talk to him, let alone fuck him. She wanted to leave him in that long deafening silence without even a sliver of hope. Not even a note on the goddamn table. Not even a single fucking text message proclaiming him a douche bag.

He'd wanted a chance to explain himself, to fix the shit he'd said. But she wouldn't give it to him. She didn't want an explanation. She wanted to get the fuck out of his life and leave him high and dry. That was her right—to be a strong woman and tell him, for all intents and purposes, to go fuck himself. He still hated it—the silence, the absence, the pain.

So, he'd given in.

He'd held off all night. All fucking night.

Ethan and Cash had found it hysterical. Having never really liked Andrea or gotten to know the new incredible woman she'd grown into—another thing that Clay knew was his fault. The guys were stoked that he and Andrea had broken up. Both egged Clay on not to just continue the life he'd been living, but to also embrace the new freedom to fuck whomever he wanted, whenever he wanted, however he wanted.

But he hadn't.

Until Candace. Until she weaseled her way onto his fucking lap, teased him with filthy fucking words, dragged him hand over fist to the restroom, and begged him to take her like the dirty slut she was.

Her words.

It was like an avalanche. It all started with one tiny snowball. Then, as it picked up speed, it cascaded down the mountain, clearing out everything in its path.

Candace was his snowball. Just one tipped him straight over the edge, like a reformed junkie doing his first line of coke after rehab.

Like an idiot, he was back at the bar every night, running through women as fast as he could go through them, trying to find an ounce of what he was looking for in any of them. He never found it. It wasn't there anymore. It was pure unadulterated sex. No feelings, no emotions. Just lust and desire and fucking.

It was fine for a while since it kept him occupied. Blew off steam from the long workdays. Kept his friends from needling him. Kept him from thinking. Period.

There was already a girl for tonight. He'd picked her out when he walked into the place. Ethan and

Cash hit on her friends, but she'd been eyeing him all night. He hated putting in effort now. It used to be fun—the chase, the game. There was no game now. That, Andrea had completely abolished.

"Are you going to go talk to her?" Cash asked, nudging him in the direction of the girl.

"No."

Ethan gave him a sympathetic look. Clay was sure he hadn't been as sympathetic when Ethan's wife, Terri, had left him in law school. Or maybe he was mistaking the look.

Fuck, this wasn't even what he wanted.

He glanced over at the chick. She caught his gaze and nodded her head to the side. She raised her eyebrows and then started walking toward the side entrance. Subtle.

"I have to make a phone call," Clay said, standing.

"Are you kidding me?" Cash asked. "That girl just invited you to go fuck her."

Clay shrugged. "I've had better. Why don't you go get her off?"

He dropped two twenties on the bar and then walked in the opposite direction of the girl. Silence was getting to him tonight. He'd told Brady that he wouldn't call. She wanted space. He'd give her space. But, tonight…he just didn't care about that promise. He wanted to talk to her.

He dialed Andrea's number before he lost the nerve.

He didn't think she'd answer. He thought she might have even changed her phone number. The locks had changed. *What other damage could she inflict?*

But, to his surprise, the line clicked over.

She didn't say anything at first, as if she were debating with herself as to why she had picked up the phone. He didn't have the answer to that, but he'd sure like to.

"Andrea?" he said.

Then, after a slow deep breath for courage, she said softly, "Hey."

"Hey."

"Why are you calling me?"

He heard in her voice how she was clinging to that hardened exterior she'd built up for years. The snotty bitch who didn't let anything touch her. He'd broken through to her before. He could do it again.

"I just wanted to talk."

Andrea paused and sighed. "It sounds like you're at a bar."

"What else do I have to do?"

She didn't respond.

"What do you want, Clay?"

"I want answers, Andrea."

She scoffed. "You *have* answers."

"We haven't spoken in weeks."

"And we shouldn't be talking right now."

"You busy? Are you somewhere important?" Clay pressed his phone harder against his ear and moved deeper into the hallway, away from the noise.

She was so quiet. She clearly did not want to be having this conversation.

"As a matter of fact, I am."

Clay knew just what that meant. "What's his name?" he drawled lazily.

"Clay, don't."

"You have a game for me tonight? Is that why you answered?"

"Clay…"

"Any real competition?" he asked. He could practically see her squirming on the other end of the phone.

"That's not why I answered, and it'd better not be why you called."

No, it wasn't. He'd called because he missed her. Because fucking everything that walked did nothing for him. "I want you back, Andrea."

"No, you don't," she said firmly. "You keep saying *I*. I want this. I want that. Well, I don't care what *you* want. What about what *I* want?"

"Fuck, Andrea, what do you want?" he asked, running a hand back through his disheveled hair.

"It doesn't matter because you can't give it to me."

Clay cringed, glad that she couldn't see him. He hadn't had enough alcohol for this. "How do you know I can't give it to you if you don't tell me what it is?"

Andrea laughed. "I told you already, Clay, and you made your choice perfectly clear. So, I'm going to go now."

"Andrea," he said, keeping her from hanging up on him in anger.

"What?"

"Why'd you really pick up?"

"I guess I'm just a masochist," she murmured into the phone.

"You've always been one of those, but that's not it." He could sense there was something else.

"Fine. It's late, and I still worry about you." She sighed, as if the admission hurt her. "So, don't call me again unless you're really in trouble."

The line went dead in his hands, and he felt like chucking his phone across the room.

Well, that hadn't gone as he'd planned. He was pissed and frustrated and didn't know what the fuck to do. Sleeping around hadn't helped. Drowning in booze hadn't helped. Talking to her definitely hadn't helped.

Maybe it was time to just let the bullshit go.

~

"Are you sure you want to do this?" Gigi asked him.

She held a crisp white envelope in her hand. The Cooper & Nielson logo was embossed on the front. A gold foil sticker had been placed over the flap with a raised C&N. The party invitation was sleek and powerful and the absolute only way to get into the exclusive annual event.

"I'm sure."

"I thought that, when you called me to pick you up the night you talked to Andrea on the phone, you were a real idiot, but this…" She plucked the other invitation from his hand and held the pair aloft. "This is mental."

"It's my chance."

"You broke up two months ago, Clay," Gigi said softly. "I hate to say it, but the likelihood of her, one, being excited that you're randomly showing up to see her, and two, accepting your invitation to a gala event are pretty slim."

Clay shrugged unperturbed. "Big gestures run in the family."

"Oh, so, *now*, you want to be associated with your family?"

"What do you want me to do, Gigi? Do you think I should just let her go? Wash fifteen years down the drain?" he asked.

"I didn't say that, idiot. I just want to make sure you know what you're walking into."

"Well, thanks for your kindness, De Rosa, but I have a feeling that I'm just going to have to be an idiot either way with her."

"Not sure you know how to be anything else."

"Now that, that's settled," he said with a grin.

He should have been wallowing after that conversation with Andrea. It should have turned him on his head and made him dive headfirst into a drunken pit. That was how he had always reacted to bad situations in the past. He was practically an alcoholic with his drinking tendencies. He never went anywhere without a drink in hand.

But something had clicked when he talked to Andrea.

She'd admitted that she worried about him.

And, if she worried about him, that meant she thought about him.

And, if she thought about him, that meant there was hope.

And, if there was hope, then the shit he'd been pulling the last couple of weeks needed to stop.

When he'd asked Gigi for her help, she'd looked at him in wide-eyed wonder. He was pretty sure she legitimately thought he was insane. *But who else could I ask?*

She was the closest thing he'd come to know as a friend in a really long time. Liz was on Andrea's side at this point. Brady was too busy with work, not that

Clay really wanted to ask for his help. And the guys were against him ever seriously dating again.

So, Clay had decided to take matters into his own hands.

He'd cut back his drinking habits. Stopped fucking around. No more revolving door of women.

And it'd been easy. Well, easy enough at least.

"Do you want me to go with you?" she asked. She looked nervous for him. "I could drive you."

"I appreciate it, but no. I need to do this alone."

She shook her head and straightened the bow tie of his suit. "Well, at least you look hot."

"That's a constant."

Gigi smacked his sleeve. "Just go get your girl."

Clay retrieved the gala invites from Gigi, and she shot him one last anxious look.

"Let me know how it goes."

He shot her a dimpled grin. "Will do."

Then, he left the office, took his Porsche uptown, and parked in front of a small modern-looking building. He knew he was in the right place by the other cars he followed into the lot. High-end clients were here to purchase expensive artwork. The pulse of the most privileged and influential in D.C. were in one building. But he wasn't here for them.

He was here for her.

He stepped out of his car, straightened his bow tie one more time, and then walked toward the building with newfound hope to correct his errors.

Chapter 15

HIS MOMENT

Clay's feet carried him into the building. It looked much the same as the last event he'd been to. Crowded with people, the walls lined with artwork, the bar line being the longest thing in sight.

As he entered, a waiter approached him to offer him a glass of champagne on the house.

Clay smiled at the man and shook his head. "No, thank you."

He'd declined a drink. Champagne, sure. Something he rarely, if ever, drank to begin with. But, hey, it was a start. He really wanted to be sober for this.

On the walls, there were so many pieces of art that he'd never seen before. Either Andrea had been hoarding art more than he knew, or she'd been traveling a ton to procure pieces for this exhibit. She had a collector's eye for it. That was for sure.

As he scanned the opening line of pieces, he read the tags that said where the painter was from, and they hadn't been to a number of these places in years. Marseilles, Barcelona, Vienna, Venice, Amsterdam. *Had she taken a European tour in the time that we'd been apart?*

As he scanned the paintings, he kept one eye open for Andrea. He didn't want to run into her without some forewarning on his part. He wasn't here to embarrass her or make her uncomfortable. He didn't want to put her off her step when she finally saw him. It'd be better to talk to her in a more secluded area. But he wanted to be here for her even if she didn't know the extent of it.

He had his eye on the nearest exit when he felt hard eyes on the back of his head. He whirled around and saw a head of blonde hair walking furiously toward him in a tight blue dress.

"What do you think you're doing?" Liz asked, Brady hot on her heels.

She grabbed Clay's arm and started wrenching him out of the gallery. He easily followed her with a humorous glint in his eyes.

"You should leave." She pointed toward the exit when they were far enough away from the main group of Andrea's clients.

Brady had his huge mass mostly blocking them from view.

"I can't leave," Clay told her.

"Yes, you can, and you will."

"Liz," Brady said warningly.

She looked up at Brady with her big blue eyes, and for a second, her expression softened. "You know he can't be here."

"Andrea can't keep running forever," Brady said firmly. "This isn't fair to him either."

"I'm still standing right here," Clay said.

"What are you doing here?" Liz asked. The edge was gone from her voice. She looked sad and resigned. Like she wanted to help him but thought the effort would be futile.

"I just came by to see how things were going for her."

"Does she know you're here?" Liz asked.

"No," he admitted.

"No, of course not. She would have told me."

"Look, I'm not here to cause her any trouble," Clay insisted. He just needed to see Andrea and ask her a question. Then, he'd go.

"You can't control whether or not it causes her trouble," Brady told him.

Clay ran a hand back through his hair. "Yeah, but how much longer do I have to wait for her to come to me? She's as stubborn as I am, and we both know that's never going to happen. So, you're telling me to just let her walk away, and I can't do that."

Liz straightened at the passion in his voice. "You really mean that."

"Of course I do."

"Look, I know you called and talked to her. Andrea and I have been hanging out since…the breakup. I know you have good intentions, but you being here is a *bad* idea."

"For her, or for me?"

"Both of you!"

Clay shook his head. "You walked away from Brady, and he let you do it. How often did you wish for him to just come back into your life and whisk you off your feet?" he demanded. "How often did you think he'd just show back up, but he didn't?"

Liz seemed to retreat into herself at the comment. It was as if she were going back in time and remembering something excruciatingly painful. She tried to clear her head from it, but the emotion was thick in her voice as she said, "More than I can count."

"And you're saying I can't do that? When it was all you wanted?"

"Clay…"

"Let him go, Liz," Brady said, resting his hand on her arm.

"What?" she asked.

"Just let him go. He's right. He deserves the chance to talk to her."

"Fine," she said slowly. "Just try not to mess this up for her. She's put a lot of time into the gallery."

Brady clapped him on the back and smiled. "Go get her."

"Thanks, man," he said with honest gratitude he thought he'd never feel.

Clay left Brady and Liz behind, ignoring Liz's words of warning. He just needed to find Andrea and invite her to the gala, and then everything would work itself out. They'd been through too much for the puzzle pieces not to fit back together again.

Then, he saw her.

She was standing in front of a trio of paintings of a landscape bursting in a rainbow of colors. It was a total contrast to the black lace dress hugging her frame and the stark honey color of her hair, which was hanging loose in waves down her back. The woman next to her was tall and lithe and kept gesturing to the artwork while shaking her head.

Clay had no intention of interrupting. It was just a marvel to see her again. His heart thudded, and something like panic flared in his chest.

Fuck.

He felt like a pussy.

There she was, standing like a sculpted goddess across the room. As if she herself were the artwork to be admired, not the paintings hanging limply on the wall.

How had he forgotten how beautiful she was in such a short period of time?

It was the longest they'd gone without the other. He was blinded by the sight of her. Her ass straining against the confines of her dress. The toned long legs he knew barreled through Pilates and yoga five times a week. The perky breasts that she complained were too small, but he'd always thought fit her. The slope of her neck up to her gorgeous face to that smile that would bring him to his knees.

They'd gotten so comfortable. So easily forgotten why they'd been together in the first place. He'd let it get that way. Taken that beautiful body for granted. Fucked up, like he always had.

Now was going to be different.

He waited until the other woman disappeared. The room was mostly empty anyway. This was his moment.

He had been hovering in the shadows, just out of her line of sight. Just when he moved toward her, pulling the invitation out of his suit pocket, another person entered the room at a near run and collided with Andrea.

Clay's feet stalled.

Bad Suit.

He wrapped his arms around Andrea's waist, hoisted her into the air, and swung her around in a circle. She laughed against him and clung on to keep herself steady.

Fuck, she looks fucking ecstatic.

Happier than Clay had seen her in a real long time.

Bad Suit set her back down on her feet, and she steadied herself against his chest. He was speaking animatedly about something. The grin on her face just grew and grew.

Clay heard her cry out, "Oh my God!"

And then her hands wrapped around his shoulders and clung on to him for dear life.

Pain like nothing he'd ever known stabbed him in the heart. He staggered back a step, unable to believe what he was seeing. He clutched the invitation tight in his hand, the paper crumbling in his death grip.

She'd moved on.

Stupid.

Stupid.

Stupid.

Liz had been right. *What the fuck am I doing here?*

He was just going to cause Andrea more trouble. Just going to fuck everything up for her. He wanted her to be happy. He wanted to go over there and punch the living daylights out of that guy. But he wouldn't be here if she didn't want him here.

He tortured himself, imagining her running back to him as soon as her things were out of their place.

Him helping her change the locks. Running through Europe together to find new art pieces. Fucking.

Fuck.

Clay took a step backward. Andrea turned her head in his direction, as if sensing that he was there. For a moment, he wanted to let her see that he was there…to let her know that he now knew. But he'd promised he wouldn't ruin this for her. And, before she could catch a glimpse of him, he darted out of the room.

His chest was heaving as he walked purposefully back through the art exhibit, through the crowds of people, and past the bar line that was still holding strong.

Just as he reached the exit, he realized he was still holding the invitation. The one chance he'd thought he had to win her back. Without another look, he tossed the invitation onto the top of the trash can before leaving the gallery and Andrea behind.

As soon as he got to his car, he headed straight to his favorite bar. *Forget giving up booze. Forget giving up women. Forget broadening my horizons and looking forward to a new life.* He just wanted to get black-out drunk and forget he'd ever been this much of a pussy.

He pulled out his phone and blindly dialed Gigi's number. He didn't even know why. He could have called the guys. They were his normal crew when he wanted to get hammered, but he wasn't feeling up to dealing with their idiocy tonight.

Gigi answered right away. "Hey, how did it go?" she asked on the other line.

"Like shit."

"Eesh. That's not good. Are you okay? What are you doing now?"

"Bar," he stated plainly, ignoring the other question. "You want to meet me?"

"That's not such a good idea."

"It's the only idea."

"Drunk in a bar in your current mood is bad news bears. Why don't you just come over here? We can talk about it."

"Don't really want to talk."

"Fine," she grumbled. "Then, I have alcohol here."

"Whiskey?" he croaked.

"Yeah. I have a bottle lying around here somewhere."

"All right. Where's your apartment?"

"It's near Dupont Circle. I'll text you the address, but be safe. You sound super pissed."

"That's one word for it."

Gigi's apartment was situated in the middle of a trendy neighborhood downtown. He could see why she lived here. Not too far from the office, but close enough to walk to anything she could really need.

He walked up the steps to the second-floor apartment and knocked on the door. She answered almost immediately. The place was extremely neat and tidy with a lot of clean, modern furniture. It was clear she didn't spend a lot of time in the place. The girl worked too much.

"Hey," she said, shutting the door behind him. "I found a bottle of Jack. Hope that's all right. I know you prefer Crown."

"That's fine," he said.

Clay turned around, and his stare pinned her where she was standing.

"What's up?" she asked cautiously.

But he didn't answer. He just walked her backward until her back hit the front door. He dropped his mouth down on top of hers and kissed her. Desperately, hungrily, with no thought for consequences or repercussions.

Gigi pushed hard against Clay's chest hard, and her breath was coming out in spasms. When he looked at her, her brown eyes were as big as saucers. His hands were on either side of her head, caging her in.

"What the hell do you think you're doing?" she shouted at him. "You can't just do that! That's not how this works. That's not how any of this works."

"Gigi—"

"No!"

She shoved him aside and started pacing the room in the same way he'd seen her do a hundred times while she was trying to work out a problem. Clearly, he was the problem.

"This is not who I am. And this is not what this is."

"Then, go to the gala with me."

"What? Ugh! No!" she nearly spit. "I'm not going to that stupid party with you."

"Why not?"

"Because you and I are bad news. We're way too goddamn similar in personality, and you'd drive me fucking crazy. You already drive me crazy. It'd never work. *Plus*," she cried, "you're still head over heels for your ex, who I happen to think is in the right here. You just went to see her, and it clearly didn't go well, so you're taking that out on me, which, I might add, is not fair!"

"She's with someone else," Clay admitted, finally letting the weight of what he'd witnessed settle on his shoulders.

"That doesn't mean that you need to be!"

"Come on, Gigi. Go with me," he prodded.

"No! Are you hearing yourself?"

"Come on."

"As a friend," she countered. "Just friends, Clay."

"You sure about that?" he prodded, still hoping to lose himself in the moment to forget the real issue. "I can be really charming."

"I am not one of the girls you meet at the bar with your stupid friends. This doesn't fix anything. Dealing with the issue fixes things." Gigi crossed her arms over her chest. "You need to deal with this, not try to forget it between a pair of legs or down a bottle. So, I'll go to the gala with you but only as friends."

"I'll have you know," he said, sinking into the chair next to the door, resigned and heartbroken, "I'm no good at that."

Gigi puffed out a breath and sat across from him. She tucked her knees up to her chest, resting her chin on top of them. "You've been doing just fine at it so far."

"Thanks," he said.

After a minute of silence, Gigi poured him a drink and took one for herself. She took a sip and then asked, "So, did she really turn you down?"

He shook his head. "No. I didn't even ask her. She seemed so happy with him. I just couldn't hurt her like that."

Gigi squeezed her eyes shut for a second. "Damn. I'm so sorry."

"Don't be." He leaned back and closed his eyes. "I was the idiot who thought it was a good idea. Didn't realize what I had until I lost it."

Chapter 16

CAREFUL WHAT YOU SAY

The annual Cooper & Nielson gala was in full swing by the time Clay and Gigi arrived. She'd shocked the shit out of him when she appeared in makeup that accentuated rather than masked her freckles and a floor-length burgundy dress that hugged the curves she normally hid in her work clothes. He approved.

He'd gone with a tailored Tom Ford tuxedo for the occasion. Though he felt it was wasted effort. He wanted to be in and out of the event as quickly as possible. It had been a month since he'd seen Andrea with Bad Suit at the gallery, and being here just brought up all the memories.

He missed her.

It fucking sucked.

Three fucking months without her, and he was still thinking about her. But he wanted her to be happy, and as much as he wanted to beat the shit out of that douche, he couldn't deny her the happiness she'd so obviously had. He just didn't want to see or hear about it either.

He worried that would be difficult with Brady and Liz's upcoming nuptials. He was in the bridal party, but with how close Liz had made it seem she and Andrea had gotten, he figured she would get an invite with or without him. That meant, going to his brother's wedding was feeling more and more like anticipating a funeral he'd dug his own grave for.

He and Gigi had just returned from the bar with drinks and were walking around and schmoozing with all the right people. Some of their colleagues kept giving them sidelong glances. He and Gigi had been spending a lot of time together. More and more, he was glad that she'd stopped him from pushing for a relationship…just like he'd stopped it from day one.

It was better to keep their relationship business professional. Plus, it was nice to have a real friend. Someone he actually felt he could rely on. Someone he wasn't trying to fuck. Well, at least not actively trying to fuck.

Gigi was going on and on with some guy beside Clay whom he had never met.

The man suddenly looked over at Clay and grinned. "Aha! A Maxwell. You were a lucky get for Cooper and Nielson!"

Clay laughed awkwardly.

"I'm surprised your brother didn't go this route first. Though it didn't seem to matter. He still got into Congress, didn't he? If by the skin of his teeth."

Clay decided right then he didn't like this guy. Whoever he was. "Brady has always been exceptionally lucky."

"He'd have to be to get reelected after that catastrophe."

"Careful," he said evenly. "That catastrophe is my future sister-in-law."

"Of course, of course. I didn't mean any offense. But what about you?" he asked, quickly changing the subject. "Do you have aim for the political arena? I wouldn't mind investing in a young face, if you know what I mean."

"No," he answered blandly. "I've never had an interest in politics."

For a moment, he wished that Andrea were here to navigate this situation with him. She knew what this kind of statement did to him...how manic it made him...how much he just wanted to lay into this guy.

"Come on, Gigi."

Gigi hurried after him. She grabbed his arm as they veered toward a table for the dinner and silent auction portion of the event.

"Man, you were short with him," she said.

"He shouldn't talk shit about stuff he doesn't understand."

"I think he was totally harmless. If anything, it was a compliment that he wanted to back you if you ran. He's a huge donor, you know?"

"I didn't. Though I guessed. And it's not a compliment," he told her, staring her down. He'd forgotten how little people knew about the system when they hadn't been in it their whole life. "He just offered to buy me for his interests, which means he's already associated the Maxwell name with sellouts."

Gigi gave him an uneasy look. "That's not what he meant..."

"Yes, it is."

"Okay. Well, even if it was, you clearly didn't take his offer, so just ignore it."

He shook his head and took his seat. He couldn't explain to Gigi how much it bothered him. His father's approval had always hung just out of his grasp. Brady had always had it, of course. But Clay had always been determined to get it outside of the political arena. To be good enough for dear old dad without the backing of political supporters and a carefully planned election. He'd keep on dreaming for that day to come.

Dinner seemed to take forever. Clay wasn't in a mood to entertain, but he smiled and talked with the people they were seated with for the event. Soon enough, plates were cleared, and the silent auction began, raising money for the local orphan charity that Cooper & Nielson sponsored. At this point, people could walk around and mingle.

Clay was itching to be back on his feet and away from these people. "I'm going to get us drinks. Vodka?" he asked, resting his hand on the back of Gigi's chair.

"Please." She looked up and him and smiled.

He returned with drinks in hand and extricated Gigi from the conversation she had been having.

"Thank you for saving my life," she said. "Those women were so annoying. Is it about time that we can leave?" She teetered in her high heels.

"One more sweep, and then we'll go."

They were walking a circuit through the room during the silent auction. A man pressed pieces of paper in their hands so that they could bid on items. Gigi tried to cajole Clay into putting money down for the seats behind home plate at the Washington Nationals baseball game. He laughed and added a sticker to the list. He was more of a basketball person himself, but any sports were entertaining to watch from the best seats in the house.

Gigi was still laughing when Clay stopped dead in his tracks. The next thing displayed for the auction was artwork with a sign next to that read, *Donated by Billings Gallery*.

"What?" Gigi asked, reading the sign.

But it wasn't the sign that kept him from answering. It was the stunning blonde standing in front of him in a long black evening gown.

"Andrea," he whispered in shock.

Gigi squeaked next to him.

"Clay," she responded.

The energy between them crackled. He hadn't been face-to-face with Andrea in three whole months. Three very long months. While he'd seen her beautiful face a month ago, it was different, looking at her. It was worse, knowing she was with someone else and whatever was passing between them didn't matter.

"What are you doing here?" he asked immediately.

"As you can tell, I donated some paintings for the auction. You know I support the orphan charities. This felt like too good of an opportunity to pass up," she said softly. Her words seemed to hold two meanings. As if she were here to see him, as if this were her opportunity, but her eyes told a different story.

"I'm just going to…" Gigi muttered behind him.

"Oh, sorry. Where are my manners? Andrea, this is my date, Gigi. Gigi, Andrea."

"Hi," Gigi muttered, politely extending her hand.

Andrea took it and shook it firmly. "Have we met before?"

"I don't think so."

"You look very familiar."

Gigi retrieved her hand and smiled warily. "I'm sure I would remember you if we'd met. If you'll just excuse me, I'm going to, uh…go get another drink."

Both of them glanced down at her still full glass, but she disappeared without another word.

"Charming," Andrea said.

"Yeah. Gigi's great," Clay said, not letting himself fall into the trap she was laying. "We work at Cooper and Nielson together. When did you start your own gallery?" The words tumbled out of his mouth before he could stop them.

"It's recent. Still in the works," she said vaguely. "Look, I really hoped I'd run into you tonight."

"Really?" he asked.

"I just wanted to apologize for hanging up on you."

"Oh."

"I know it was a while ago, but I just thought…we could still be civil to one another…even if we've…" She cleared her throat and glanced behind his shoulder. "Even if we've moved on."

Clay clenched his hands at his sides. *She'd come all the way here and cornered me to tell me that we should be civil? Is this about the wedding? Is she worried I'd do something stupid?*

Well, he'd been the one to walk out of that art gallery. He wanted her to be happy. If she needed him to say that all of this was fine, that her being with someone else was fine, to get through a whole day at the wedding, then he'd do that.

He held his hands up to stop her from continuing. "It's fine," he said roughly. "I get it. You and I are…civil. If you'll excuse me."

Before she could say anything else, he turned and walked back toward Gigi, seething all the while. Worry creased her brow as he approached.

He took her arm and guided her toward the exit. "Time to go."

"What happened back there? She looks really upset," Gigi said.

"Nothing. She confirmed she's with someone else and wanted to make sure I wouldn't make a scene. That we'd be civil when we next saw each other at Brady's wedding," he ground out. "Fuck."

"Clay, there's no way that's what she meant," Gigi told him. "You didn't see her face when you walked away or when she saw you with me, for that matter. She was totally jealous…totally devastated."

"I think you were seeing things."

"I was not," she snapped.

"Why would she look devastated when she's the one who is seeing someone else?"

"Look, I don't know. But you should go talk to her. Figure it out."

Clay shook his head. "There's no chance of that happening. She made her point clear."

Gigi grabbed his sleeve and stopped him in place. "Are you sure?"

"Positive. Are you coming or not?"

Gigi hazarded one more glance over her shoulder, taking in the sight of his ex-girlfriend talking to other people about the paintings, and then she nodded. "I'm coming."

The cab back to Clay's place was silent. Gigi seemed to be brooding, and all Clay wanted was to get his hands on the scotch in his liquor cabinet. Seemed fitting to crack it open tonight since Andrea was the one who had given it to him.

~

They went through half the bottle before Gigi looked like she was about to fall over at every turn. Clay was still pretty coherent, but the liquor was potent. They had been guaranteed the rest of the weekend off because of the event, which thankfully meant neither of them would have to see the office tomorrow.

"Oh my God, I need to go home," Gigi croaked. She stumbled toward her bag and then tripped over her own feet, landing hard on all fours. "Shit!"

Then, she burst into giggles.

"There is no way you can go home right now. I don't trust a cab for this," he said.

He helped her to her feet, and she swayed.

"I can't stay. I'd feel bad," she slurred.

He laughed at her. "It's not a big deal. I'll just...take the couch," he offered.

"You're serious?"

"Hey, you said we're just friends," he reminded her. "And I think you're right. It's a good idea. Plus, you're trashed. Just crash here."

She giggled again as she tried to steady herself. "Okay, maybe you're right." She held her hands out. "But I can take the couch."

Clay shook his head. "Even if I'm an ass, I'm a Southern gentleman at heart. You take the bed. I'll take the couch. End of story."

He climbed the stairs to the second floor and helped Gigi along the way. He fished out some clothes for her to wear, and she changed in the bathroom, somehow managing to get out of her dress. He grabbed a few blankets and a pillow just as Gigi crawled into his bed and promptly passed out. He sniggered at her and shut out the light.

The couch wasn't half as comfortable as his awesome fucking bed upstairs, but this was safer than letting her drunk ass take a cab home. He had just stood up to turn out the lights when a knock came from his door.

He yawned and went to check to see who the fuck would be here at two o'clock in the morning. He stumbled into the doorframe, ran a shaky hand back through his hair, and then straightened himself before opening the door.

His eyes widened when he saw who was standing at his doorstep—Andrea.

Chapter 17

WHAT DREAMS ARE MADE OF

Clay just stared at Andrea in disbelief.

She was here.

He couldn't seem to process this fact fast enough. Her being here this late at night…her being here at all made no sense to him. *Why is she here?*

But he realized then that it didn't matter.

Here was everything that he wanted…that he'd been dying to have for the last three months. She was standing right in front of him, and all he had to do was reach out and take it.

"Do you want to come in?" he asked, pulling the door open wider.

She seemed just as shocked to be on his doorstep as he was that she was here. But she gathered herself together, nodded, and crossed the threshold into his townhouse without a word.

He shut the door behind her, wishing he were a little less wasted for whatever was about to happen. He was regretting that bottle of scotch right about now. But whatever she had to say must be important or else she wouldn't be here. All he could fixate on now that he had her in his place was the way her hips moved in the silky black dress and the peek of leg from the slit.

Then, all he could think about were those lips as she whirled back to face him. Uncertainty rippled through her body. Her gorgeous blue eyes were wide. Her soft pink lips parted, as if to speak at any moment. Worry lines hit between her eyes as her brows drew together.

"Clay," she whispered.

And she sounded different than he'd ever heard her.

Helpless.

Something shifted in that moment. He didn't care if she belonged to someone else. He didn't care if she had walked out on him. He didn't care about the last three months of torture. All he cared about was that the woman he'd spent damn near fifteen years in love with was *here*.

A tear trickled down her pale cheek, unchecked and uninhibited. Her eyes were raw with emotion. Her body was tense yet vulnerable.

He couldn't help himself. He cleared the distance between them in one easy stride. She barely breathed when he reached up and wound one hand up into her hair while sweeping the loose tear from her cheek with the other. She just tilted her face up to look at him, to judge and weigh him.

"Why are you crying, baby?" he finally asked, breaking the weighted silence.

She swallowed hard but kept their gazes locked. "I don't know why I'm here."

Clay leveled her with a disbelieving look. She had a reason for being here. And she had a reason for crying. Andrea did nothing without a purpose.

"Yes, you do."

She shook her head but didn't dislodge his hand from where he still held her. "No. I just know that I shouldn't be here."

"But you are." He kept his voice firm.

She was here. He couldn't leave her standing there, crying in his apartment, without an answer…some kind of reason. He needed to know what this all meant. He couldn't read her mind. If he'd been able to do that, then they wouldn't have been in this mess to begin with.

"Yeah." She breathed out heavily. "I'm so stupid."

"You're many things, Andrea, but stupid is never one of them."

Andrea's eyes filled with surprise at the comment. She seemed to be debating with herself as to what else to say. He just wanted to push her. To make her admit why she had come crawling to him in the middle of the night…why she was letting him touch her so affectionately when she had ended it all.

"I ruined everything," she whispered.

Clay stilled completely. "You think so?"

"We…we were fine before, right?" She seemed so hesitant, like she needed confirmation for all the questions she had in her head. Like she had no clue what *he* was thinking when he was sure it was clear on his face.

But before what? Fuck. He just wanted her to be clearer. Before Bad Suit? Before the attack? Before *what?*

Yet he couldn't say any of that. He couldn't voice the ugly thoughts that crept into his head, at how cruel he wanted to be with her. He should send her home, send her packing right now, like she'd done to him. Give her a taste of her own medicine. But he couldn't do it.

Andrea was a hard woman. He'd always loved her for it. He'd thought that her tough exterior meant that she didn't care about anything. Thought it meant she didn't want a diamond ring and a happily ever after. He'd been wrong about a lot of things.

So, he just shook his head. They hadn't been fine before. If they'd been fine before…they wouldn't be in this spot right now.

Confusion seeped into her features at his denial that their relationship had been all right before she'd left. Before…before…

God, he desperately wanted to know what was going on behind those eyes. Learn all the secrets left buried in this woman. Lay her bare before him until nothing could tear them apart again.

"I tried to stay away," she said. Her voice shook, and her hands reached out to fiddle with the hem of his shirt. "I promised myself that, after you left the gala, I'd just let that be it. The end."

"So, why are you here?"

"I mean…I can't change how you reacted," she said, ignoring him. "How you just walked away. I deserve it, right? After I just walked away."

She retreated from his gaze, letting his shirt go and taking a step away from him. She hugged her arms around her waist and shivered. He could see that something was eating her up from the inside out. Maybe this whole time, she'd been suffering as he had. Maybe they could just fix this…here and now.

No.

Fuck.

What the fuck am I thinking?

Am I that stupid to see her sad eyes and think that everything could change in a matter of minutes? Did I just forget the gallery so easily?

She had Bad Suit.

He'd seen them together.

He couldn't just give in to this. But, fuck, he wanted to give in to this. Hear her moan his name, hear her beg for his kisses, hear her ask for him again and again. To put the broken pieces back together with such ease.

But that ease was an illusion. A dirty illusion he'd conjured up due to the blistering silence. That would never happen while she had someone else. This was just old memories floating up to the surface…that was all.

For three long months, he'd been waiting, just like Brady had said, for her to make a move. He'd gotten the courage to do it himself anyway. He'd chased her. And, each time, she'd slapped him in the face.

If she were here on misguided terms, he wasn't here to help.

"I don't know what you want me to say."

She swung around to face him again, her face open and stark. "Anything."

"Why are you here? What do you want from me?"

"Isn't it obvious?"

"I'm not a mind reader. Be more specific."

"I miss you. God," she said, dropping her head back to look up at the ceiling, letting the weight of her words sluice off of her. "God, I miss you. Against all fucking logic. And watching you walk out with her tonight was pure torture of my own devices. I just had to see you. So, what do I want from you?" She splayed her hands out in front of her. "This."

Hope zapped through him, and he tried to squash it. No, God, he couldn't just give in. He needed answers. "And what about Bad Suit?"

Her focus snapped. She stumbled back a step in surprise. That reaction nearly stole his breath. He considered forcing her out of his house right at that moment. *What more did I need to know?*

It had been mostly a joke when he'd tried to steal Liz for his own. It was quite another thing to think he'd survive doing that with Andrea.

"What about Asher?" she asked.

"Does he know you're here? Does he know that you've missed me? That you showed up at two a.m. to see me instead of returning to his bed?" he asked the words that were cold and dark on his tongue. "Tell me, is he not giving you everything you'd hoped for? Or are you really just a masochist?"

"What?" she stammered out. "Clay…that's not…"

He shook his head. "Fuck. Do I even want to know?"

"Asher and I aren't together!"

"Don't lie to me, Andrea," he said with pure venom in his voice. "I saw you two together."

"I don't know what you think you saw, but we're not together," she insisted.

"Really?" he asked in disbelief.

"Yes. We're…we're just friends."

"Right." He couldn't bite back the sarcasm that was heavy in his voice.

Andrea glared at him. "How dare you stand there and lecture me, Clay Maxwell! How dare you talk to me like that and accuse me of things you know nothing about when *you* were the one who showed up to the gala with a new girlfriend!" she cried. "Not to mention, the exploits I've heard about since you've been single."

"Girlfriend?" Clay asked. He didn't bother refuting the revolving door he'd given in to, starting with the idiot Snowball girl.

"Gigi," she accused. The old familiar flare of anger shot through her.

"She's not my girlfriend. We work together. I told you that at the gala."

"Is *that* what you're calling it now?"

"Look, I don't have to fucking justify anything to you!" he shouted, towering over her. "Don't throw accusations in my face, at my house, in the middle of the night when *you're* the one who left."

"Fine," she spat in his face.

Oh, shit.

That's not good.

Brady had said that was not good. That was not the way to end an argument. It only meant she was pissed, and things most certainly were not fine.

"Clearly, coming here was a mistake." Andrea stalked back to the front door and yanked it open.

But before she could take a step outside, Clay kicked it shut. She yelped and took a step back.

"Fuck that," he growled out.

He grabbed her wrist, swung her around, and slammed his mouth down on hers. It was like coming home. He kissed her relentlessly. Their tongues volleyed for position. Their hands roved each other, as if discovering new territory all over again. The pent-up anger and frustration coursing through them only fueled them onward. A hunger so fierce gripped him and nearly knocked him off his feet. This was what he wanted.

Fuck. This was all he ever wanted.

She had been pushing him away for months, making him ache for her. He wanted nothing more than to correct this shit. To just bury himself so deep in her that she never came up for air. Never saw sunlight again.

He wanted to remind her whom exactly she belonged to.

Mine.

No one else.

Ever again.

He'd dreamed about this moment. With his fucking cock pounding into her pussy and driving it all home. Reminding her what she was missing. Reminding her that this was all she was ever going to have again. Making sure, from this day forward, she always remembered. Now, he was finally going to get to show her just what she had given up.

They were a tangle of limbs as their bodies collided together. He pushed the slit of her dress aside and hoisted her legs around his waist, never breaking their kiss. He purposely walked them over to the couch, threw them both down onto the leather, and then covered her body with his own.

His touch was greedy and demanding. This was what he had wanted for so long. He had every intention of taking it all until they both had nothing left to give.

Her hands were grasping at his shirt, desperate to have it off. He obliged her. He pulled back just enough to rip it over his head and throw it across the room. He gave her a full view of the six-pack abs and bulging biceps he had developed in her absence. He might have been an alcoholic, but he'd made up for it with his time at the gym. He'd spent enough time in there between work and boozing to blow her mind when she got a good look at him. She raked her fingers down his stomach. He just smirked.

Then, he lifted the slit of her dress, letting the material bunch up around her waist. To his delight, he found that she was wearing his favorite undergarment—nothing at all.

He was yanking his shorts off just as he heard footsteps on the stairs.

Andrea stilled beneath him. Her eyes went wide. "What was that?"

"Fuck."

Fuck. Fuck. Fuck.

He was such an idiot. *How the fuck did I forgot about Gigi? How did I forget that I'd let her crash upstairs?*

"Clay…" Andrea said. She was pulling her dress back down and staring up at him, as if he'd betrayed her beyond measure. "You have got to be fucking kidding me. Please tell me you're joking, and that's not what I think it is."

"Andrea, no…it's not."

"Clay?" Gigi's voice rang from the top of the stairs. She stumbled down a few and then came into sight, wearing nothing but one of his T-shirts and a pair of boxers. Her hair was a hot mess from taking all the pins out of it. It had looked like that when she'd come out of the bathroom earlier.

But he knew.

He fucking knew.

It looked like sex hair.

Shit.

Fucking. Fuck.

"I heard the door slam. Is everything okay?" Gigi slurred.

Andrea jumped up off the couch and glared at him. "You are the scum of the earth. You know that?"

"Andrea, come on," he pleaded, racing after her.

She yanked the door open, started down the stairs, and ran out to her car.

He just went ahead and followed her. "This is not what it looks like. I can explain!"

"Don't bother. I don't want to hear it."

"We are not together. We didn't sleep together. I was taking the couch. I swear to God."

Andrea screamed, actually screamed, at the top of her lungs before glaring at him from the driver's side of her car. "I don't want to hear it! I can't listen to it any longer. You had another girl in your bed while you were trying to have sex with me!" She shook her head. Her eyes were glassy. "I truly am a masochist. I must be. Why else would I ever want to love someone who constantly hurts me like this?"

She threw the question at him, leaving him standing there, stunned, as she drove away. Gigi stepped outside a few minutes later, but Clay just stood there and watched his last chance disappear into the distance.

Chapter 18

HOME SWEET HOME

The weeks up to Brady's wedding passed by in a blur. Andrea refused to take Clay's phone calls and never returned any of the long voice mails he'd left. She probably deleted them before listening to them, which was for the better since they were pretty embarrassing, all things considered. His text messages were never opened, and he'd officially been blocked from her Facebook account. She had clearly decided that the night of the gala was a mistake. He was a mistake. And she was moving on.

Things were just as weird with Gigi for the next week. No matter how many times she'd apologized for walking downstairs that night, he couldn't convince her that he didn't actually blame her for anything. She'd done nothing wrong in his eyes.

He'd been so wrapped up in the moment that he'd just forgotten she was upstairs. That was on him. It wasn't like Andrea wouldn't have found out anyway. He would have asked her to stay, if they'd gotten that far. Having Gigi stay the night, what had happened with Andrea afterward…it was all on him.

But, for at least a week afterward, Gigi walked on eggshells around him. It was ridiculous, coming from the girl who gave him more shit than anyone else he'd known. She acted as if he were going to dissolve their friendship on the spot. Whatever had happened in her past to make her edge around him like that was a story he couldn't get out of her.

But he wasn't going anywhere.

"If I ask you to go to Brady's wedding with me, will you stop acting like a lunatic? This isn't your fault. Stop punishing yourself. I'm punishing myself enough for the both of us," Clay told Gigi.

"Will Andrea be there?" She chewed on her bottom lip and looked like she wanted to start pacing.

Clay shrugged. "It doesn't matter. I fucked up too bad. She'll never talk to me again."

"It totally matters. She might be pissed at you, but she's going to *hate* me."

Fair point.

She probably would hate Gigi on principle.

"I'm sure she'll be there. She's friends with Liz, and my family has always treated her like family."

"Bad idea."

"Otherwise, I don't have a date."

"That's probably good for you."

"Just as a friend, so I don't look like a loser, showing up alone?" he prodded.

"You could never look like a loser."

Clay glared at her. "You're going with me."

"I can't find a dress," she said, trying to dig in.

"Then, I'll get you one. Christ, just go with me."

"All right, all right," she groaned. "I'm so going to regret this. I'll be there for moral support, but if she is there, I'm finding someone else to dance with."

"Deal."

With all the manic rush of last-minute preparations underway, it was the weekend before the big event, and the moment Clay had been waiting for finally arrived—Brady's bachelor party. Clay had volunteered Las Vegas as the best possible location for this event, but Brady had vetoed that suggestion. He'd claimed he wanted something low-key. No casinos. No strippers. No strip clubs. Basically, he wanted to take all the fun out of it.

But Brady's best friend, Chris Atwood, was the best man and thus in charge of the party. He lived in New York right now, but he and Brady had been best friends while growing up and played basketball together at the University of North Carolina for four years in college. Chris knew Brady like the back of his hand. Clay was pretty sure that Chris was the only person who had been in Brady's shadow more than Clay had, but Chris didn't resent him in the same way. He was his best friend, not his little brother.

Since Chris was in charge of the weekend, he had decided to go to the Maxwell's house in Hilton Head for the beach, scotch, and cigars. It wasn't exactly Vegas, but it was going to be a great weekend regardless.

The day before he was supposed to be in Hilton Head, Clay had taken the extra day off work to drive to Chapel Hill to visit his mom and Savannah and breathe in some much-needed *home* time.

"Mom?" Clay called into his parents' mansion when he entered through the garage.

"In here, dear," Marilyn called back.

His mother was a law professor at UNC and extremely well established in her field. He had always looked up to her even though he knew he could never teach like that. It would drive him mad. But he had always been closer to his mom than he was with his dad. With his mother, there was none of that need to please.

He entered his mother's office on the first floor, which looked more like a library with a large wooden desk and two giant iMacs hooked up as dual monitors. Clay bent down and gave her a kiss. Then, he slumped back onto the only available space in the otherwise cluttered room.

"How was the drive down?" Marilyn asked. She peeked at him over her rather chic burgundy-rimmed glasses.

"Not so bad. Glad to be out of the city though."

"I know just the feeling," she said with an easy smile. Her blonde hair spilled over one shoulder. It was longer than it'd been in a while. Normally, she kept it in a bob. "I love coming back for the semester to teach and escape the oppressive D.C. hustle. But I have a feeling it's more than the city you're trying to escape." She shot him a knowing look.

"You got me. Who told you?"

"The walls bleed secrets." She winked. "Now, tell me what's going on with you and Andrea."

So, he did. She listened all the while, nodding with some of his points and shaking her head at all the others. He left out some of the more…repugnant details, but she had raised him after all. She could piece together what was missing.

By the end, to his surprise, she was smiling.

"What?" he asked warily.

"I'm not sure you've gone after anything this hard since you decided you wanted to be a lawyer. I still don't know where that drive came from…"

"Runs in the family," he muttered under his breath. He'd never acknowledge he'd only done it because he wanted to become attorney general and win his father's approval. Somehow, all the lines had blurred anyway.

"But I know where this drive comes from." She tapped her heart twice with a red lacquered nail. "You love her very much, and you always have."

Clay sighed. *How did she see what I hadn't for so long? How could she see what even Andrea couldn't?*

She just smiled and stood. "Come on. Let's get out of this stuffy office. Savannah should be here with Easton at any moment. No need to dwell. I can see you came home to avoid that."

Clay followed his mother out of the office and into the kitchen. He leaned against the counter as she poured him a glass of sweet tea. God, he'd fucking missed home.

"Mom?"

"Hmm, honey?"

"What do I do?"

She set the glass of lemonade she had just poured for herself on the counter in front of him and then set a reassuring hand on his shoulder. "I know this will come as a surprise, but I don't have all the answers." She chuckled softly, her eyes crinkling at the corners. "But what you have with Andrea is special. You wouldn't have made it this long otherwise. Don't give up on her just yet. When we were at the hospital after you'd been…attacked, I sat with Andrea for a very long time. You don't know it, but you both changed that night. Looking in her face was like seeing a new woman. She couldn't bear the thought of losing you, so she latched on at the very moment you needed space to breathe…to heal—physically and emotionally. If it's meant to be, it'll happen."

Clay swallowed back the lump in his throat and nodded. Just then, Savannah bounded into the kitchen from the garage, her long brown hair swinging, with her boyfriend Easton in tow.

"Hey!" she cried. "I didn't know you'd be home already."

"Well, I'm not Brady, so no city parade to announce my arrival," he joked.

Savannah snorted. "Jerk."

Easton laughed. "Hey, man. Good to see you again."

They shook hands.

"You, too," Clay said.

"Good to have two out of my three children home," Marilyn said, pulling Savannah in for a hug. "Good to see you, Easton."

"Good to see you, too, ma'am."

"Can I get you two a drink?"

"Sweet tea," Easton agreed.

"Me, too," said Savannah.

Marilyn poured out the rest of the drinks, and then they all crowded in at the small breakfast bar in the kitchen.

"You just graduated, right?" Clay asked Easton.

He had an arm wrapped around Savannah and nodded. Clay dimly remembered Easton was a year ahead of Savannah in school. Savannah had posted pictures of them together with Easton in a cap and gown just last weekend.

"Any big plans for the future?"

"I'm taking a year off. Actually working in Brady's Raleigh office for the year while I apply to law schools."

Clay raised his eyebrows. "That so?"

"Yeah. It's a great opportunity. I'm really lucky that Brady gave me the job. It's definitely something I want to do before I decide to run for local office," Easton said.

Clay's gaze shifted to Savannah. If he knew anything about his little sister, he knew what she thought about politics. They were good for the family, but she wanted to stay as far away from them as possible if she could help it. She was proud of their dad and Brady, but she didn't want that for herself. She'd even dated some tatted up douche on a motorcycle once to prove her point. He'd thought she'd run headlong in the other direction from someone like Easton. But it seemed even Savi could change.

"Cool, man," he finally got out.

He silently asked Savannah with an arched eyebrow, *Politician?*

Her eyes rounded out with a warning, *Don't you dare mention it!*

All right. Off-limits.

"So, where do you want to go to law school? Just served my time. It's the worst three years of your life, and then there's clerking."

Easton laughed, but Clay really hadn't been joking. He'd been lucky to have Andrea through it. Easton would be lucky to have Savannah.

"Don't listen to him. It's not all that bad," Marilyn said.

"We'll see how the LSAT scores come back, but I'm pretty open to anywhere. Ideally, top ten."

Clay had wanted Yale and only Yale.

"Good luck with that. Glad it's not me again. It's cutthroat, but if you have the right woman at your side, it's all worth it."

Savannah coughed and then stood. "Hey, baby, since Clay is here, I think I'm due some sibling time. I'll see you later?"

"Damn," Easton said, rising to his feet. "I lose you all weekend and then tonight, too?"

"All weekend?" Clay prodded.

"I'll tell you on the way to Franklin," Savannah said to Clay.

"All right." Clay bent down and kissed his mom. "Love you. Be back in an hour or so."

"Y'all have fun," Marilyn said. "I have so much work to do anyway."

"Bye, Mom!" Savannah yelled from the doorway.

Clay wandered out after Savi and Easton. Savannah gave him an exaggerated long kiss at his driver's side door and then waved as he got inside and drove off.

She sighed and then trotted over to Clay's hybrid. He'd driven it to Chapel Hill since the gas mileage was so much better, but he already missed his Porsche and her pickup.

"So," he said as they started toward Franklin Street in downtown Chapel Hill, "where are you going this weekend?"

"No one told you?" she asked, shifting awkwardly in her seat.

"Told me what?"

"You know…that Liz's bachelorette party is this weekend, too."

"Right. No, I did know that. Forgot about it, but I knew. Where are you going? Vegas?" he asked hopefully. He could just envision Liz at a strip club. He found it both highly amusing and extremely provocative. He would need that image for his fantasies later.

"Um…no. Hilton Head."

Clay slammed on the brakes at the red light, and they both rocked forward. "What?"

"Jesus, Clay. Easy on the brakes."

"Sorry. But…what? Did Brady set this up? Are y'all going to be at the house?"

"No. No. Um…it was actually Andrea's idea," she said softly.

"Andrea's idea," he repeated hollowly.

"She offered her parents' house for the beach weekend when our house was taken by you and the guys."

Clay was reeling. He floored it when the light turned green and got into a parking spot before he found words again.

"So…Andrea is going to be there?"

Savannah nodded as she climbed out of the car, and they started up the street. "Yeah. She's coming with the bridal party—me, Victoria, and Massey."

Fuck.

Andrea was going to be at Hilton Head this weekend at her place where they had first met, just down the beach from where he was staying. That was a world of possibilities.

"Just don't tell anyone I told you," Savannah said. "I didn't know that you didn't already know. I probably wasn't supposed to say anything."

"Don't worry about it."

They entered Sugarland, a small cupcake and gelato shop on Franklin Street that was everyone's favorite dessert place in town. Savannah got pink champagne gelato, and he got a double-chocolate cupcake. They took their desserts to go and wandered the all too familiar streets.

"Oh, by the way…can I drive down with you since you're here?" Savannah asked.

"You're a hellion, Savi."

She nudged him. "Pretty much. Learned it from my big brother."

"Which one?"

"Well, we both know I didn't learn to be a hellion from *Brady*. He doesn't even know what that word means," she said with a giggle. "I doubt you're going to have any fun at this bachelor party. He's probably going to have one drink, declare his love for Liz, and go to bed by ten."

Clay snorted. "Oh, joy."

Savannah giggled and then they headed out to walk around campus situated just off of Franklin Street. Savannah stopped in front of the Old Well for a picture with her half-finished gelato. Clay snapped one with his phone and then they took a selfie.

"Send that one to me!" Savannah said.

Clay shook his head, but did as he was told. "So…you and Easton, huh?"

"Uh…yeah."

"Seems pretty serious."

"Ew. Are you going to have a birds and the bees talk with me?"

Clay laughed. "Definitely no. I'm just curious. Politician?"

Savannah groaned and looked away. "I can't help it that the profession he's interested in happens to coincide with something I detest."

"True," he admitted. "Just doesn't seem like you."

"Maybe he'll change his mind," she said hopefully. "Law school changes people right?"

"That's a fact." Clay was thinking about all the couples who broke up and got divorced while he was in law school. He didn't wish that on his sister and hoped she knew what she was getting herself into.

"Hey," she said as they veered back toward the car, "can you try not to fuck it up this weekend?"

"Language, Baby Maxwell," he joked.

Savannah punched him. "I mean it!"

"Yeah," he agreed. "I'll give it a try."

Chapter 19

BACHELOR PARTY

Savannah piled into Clay's car the next morning for the drive south. If he'd been in D.C., he would have just flown, but it was good to spend the time with Savannah. They'd argued more than gotten along while growing up. It was weird sometimes to think she was of legal drinking age and would be graduating from college in a year. He still saw her as that little kid, but she clearly wasn't that anymore.

They spent most of the drive arguing over what music to listen to, debating which nineties band was the best, and dissecting Savannah's misguided love for One Direction. She insisted that Harry Styles was the best, and Clay could only agree because he'd banged Taylor Swift.

Due to frequent pit stops for snacks and the fact that it was Memorial Day weekend, so traffic was atrocious, their five-hour drive turned into six, and they rolled into Hilton Head Island in the middle of the afternoon. It was already boiling hot, and the air was so humid that he could practically drink it. The smell of sea salt was in the air, and both he and Savannah were jittery while driving through downtown toward the sandy beaches.

Truly, Memorial Day weekend was the worst possible time for them to be here, but it meant they would get to stay here on Monday before driving back home. Traffic was bumper-to-bumper on the little island, and they inched along, fighting to get to their beach house.

Clay had been to Andrea's beach house nearly as many times as his own. Every summer since he was twelve, they'd skirted the beach that occupied the short distance between their two places, disappearing in and out of each other's houses, making the other a part of their family, no matter how messed up it became.

Andrea's mom, Cathleen, had gotten the house in the divorce, and when she'd remarried a year after divorcing Andrea's father, Rupert, Andrea and Clay had had to deal with her two younger stepsiblings. The only person in her family whom she still talked to was her mother, and Clay knew that was only on her terms. When Cathleen called, that usually meant trouble. Her father had remarried a few years later to someone roughly Andrea's age, and they'd never reconciled their differences. From the start, she had said that the only thing she got from her dad was her last name.

Having Hilton Head dredge up all these old memories made him uneasy. And miss her all the more.

While he'd always felt like he was in Brady's shadow, he had never thought about how *he* had been the one to really give Andrea a family. No rings or big wedding plans, but she had clearly become a Maxwell long before that thought had ever entered her mind.

He pulled into the driveway to Andrea's whitewashed beach house and parked the car.

"Thank God we're here," Savannah said, hopping out of the car. She grabbed her purse, slung it over her head, and then started collecting her backpack and bag of snacks from the backseat.

He unbuckled his seat belt and popped his own door open. It felt like a lifetime ago since he had last been here. If only he could go back to that time when he'd been so naive and tell that little kid not to be such an idiot when it came to this beautiful girl...

Nah, it wouldn't have mattered. He hadn't been that jaded yet...and neither had she.

Clay pressed the button to pop the trunk and helped Savannah take out her giant suitcase. "What do you have in here?" he asked with a grunt. "Bricks?"

"Just the essentials!"

Clay closed the trunk, and when he glanced back up at the door, two beautiful blondes were staring back at him. Liz was in nothing but a red string bikini and white cutoff shorts that made her curvy body look fucking amazing. But Andrea was what stole his breath.

Fuck.

She had on a hot-pink strapless bikini. Her blonde hair rippled down over one shoulder. Even from a distance, he couldn't help but admire every inch of her milky-white skin. And it took a lot of self-control not to storm right over, throw her over his shoulder, and take her upstairs to fuck her brains out until she forgave him. The caveman inside him begged to be unleashed.

Fuck it.

Savannah put her hand on his arm and shook her head almost imperceptibly. *How the hell did she know what I was thinking? Is it written all over my face?*

Because, right now, all he could think about was Andrea. All the old familiar emotions and memories sprang up between them. He didn't understand how she could just stand there and not feel the heat radiating between them. It was like a ticking time bomb just waiting to explode.

Their eyes met and, fuck, if he didn't want to make things right with this woman. He'd been sure that all was lost. *But how could it be lost? How could all this history just disappear?*

He hadn't slept with anyone the night of the inauguration, and he hadn't slept with Gigi. He didn't know what he had to do to prove to Andrea that he was the man for her…but he'd do it.

Andrea seemed taken aback by the intensity of his gaze, bit her lip, and then slipped back into the house. He deflated, but Liz was already barreling down the stairs toward him.

"I'm getting married next weekend. I'm getting married next weekend!" she cried.

"So I've heard," Clay said, pulling her in for a hug.

Savannah started wheeling her massive suitcase over to the front of the house, leaving Liz and Clay alone to talk.

"Gah, how excited are you for the wedding?" Liz leaned back onto the trunk of his car and tapped the back twice. "Kind of a downgrade from your normal ride, isn't it?"

Clay laughed. "The car is for trips. Better gas mileage and good for the environment. I heard you're big on that."

Liz brightened. "That's true. Good for you!"

"And, to answer your question, it's clear I'm not as excited as the bride."

"Bride," she breathed. "That word. Can you believe Brady and I are tying the knot?"

"Nope. Not at all. Pretty sure I tried to prevent that at every turn."

Liz laughed and just shook her head. "So, what are your plans for Brady? You'll watch over him, right?"

"Yeah, yeah. He'll be fine. We don't really have plans."

"Strippers?" she asked curiously.

Or was it interest in her voice? He never could tell with Liz. Things that might piss off most girlfriends would go over her head. And then, sometimes, things that didn't bother anyone else would piss her off.

"You volunteering?"

Liz rolled her eyes. "You wish."

"Got me there."

"It would be Victoria, if any of us," Liz said about her crazy voluptuous best friend whom he'd heard was wild in bed.

"I'll have to give that a go." He winked at her.

"One, she's taken, and two, you couldn't handle her."

"We'll see about that. I bet I could give her a run for her money."

"Hmm…" she said, assessing him, "Maybe."

"I gave you a run for yours," Clay joked.

Liz shook her head and bumped him with her hip. "You're ridiculous. Get out of here, and take care of my fiancé."

"I'll do my best."

She followed him back to the driver's side and gave him a pensive long stare. "Hey, Clay?"

"Yeah?"

"She misses you," Liz said quietly.

Clay frowned. Andrea missed him. It was like Liz was offering him a small sliver of hope. Andrea had said she missed him at his house, but then he'd fucked it up. If Liz was telling him again, it had to be because she thought he still had a chance.

"I love her," he told Liz.

She immediately broke out into barely suppressed laughter.

"What?" he demanded.

"Clay Maxwell…in love." Liz shook her head. "When I first met Andrea, I thought you two hated each other. But I was so wrong. You just hadn't realized how much you loved each other yet."

"You think I still have a shot?" he asked.

She bit her lip and then glanced back up at the house. "You just might."

"Thanks"—he brushed a kiss on her cheek and laughed—"sis."

"Oh, get out of here," she said, shoving him into the front seat of his car.

He revved the engine at her as she walked back toward the house. As he drove the short distance to the Maxwell property, he had a smile plastered on his face, and a plan was forming in his mind.

He could win Andrea back.

He could be the man she wanted.

He could make her see how much he loved her and that flushing fifteen years of history down the drain was the worst idea she'd ever had.

He could do it…

He had to do it!

~

Brady, Chris, and Lucas were already outside at the pool, decked out in swim trunks and drinking beer, when Clay finally made it to the house. He'd dropped his stuff off in his room and changed into a pair of Carolina blue swim trunks before entering the pool deck.

"The party has arrived," he said, walking out to them and grabbing a beer off of Lucas.

"Hey, man," Lucas said. He extended his hand, and Clay shook it.

Brady and Chris nodded their heads at him and said, "Hey," at the same time.

"Had to drop Savi off with the girls," Clay said. He sank into a chair and took a long swig of his beer.

"How was the drive down?" Brady asked.

"Yeah, I can't believe that you actually drove," Chris said. He had his ever-present smile plastered onto his face.

The dude was as tall or taller than Brady but lacked all the seriousness of his brother. Brady finally relaxed when he was around Chris. He was actually able to kick back and have a good time rather than always acting so uptight.

"Well, I wanted to visit home first. Then, Savi forced me to drive her." He shrugged. "It was all right even though she's a fucking handful."

Lucas snorted beside him. "That's the truth."

Clay wondered what the fuck was up with Lucas and Savannah. Andrea had mentioned that they had been a thing at one point, but it couldn't be the case if she was attached at the hip with Easton.

"How's Vanderbilt treating you?" Clay asked instead.

Lucas had just finished his junior year, like Savannah, and played on the Vanderbilt basketball team.

Lucas swiped his shaggy hair out of his eyes and grinned. "Pretty epic. We made it to the Final Four this past year. I can't believe I only have one more year."

Brady raised his beer to him. "Enjoy it while it lasts. Nothing else like it."

"That's right, man. I'm *definitely* enjoying it."

Clay had a feeling he knew *just* what Lucas meant by that.

"What about you?" Clay asked Chris. "How is New York treating you?"

Chris worked at some marketing firm in New York City. Clay wasn't exactly certain what he did, but he must be making bank because he had a nice apartment in Manhattan even if he couldn't seem to hold down a girl to save his life.

"Didn't you hear?" Brady asked.

"What?"

"I got a promotion," Chris said with a slightly delirious laugh. "I got a job in D.C."

"Fuck, tell me you're not working with this dipshit," he said, pointing at his brother.

"Nah, the company is expanding. They want me to head the new office in D.C. Offered it to me, knowing I had connections on the Hill, of course." Chris shrugged. "It's a great opportunity, and I get to be near you two assholes more. Plus, higher pay in a city with lower cost of living."

"Who are you trying to convince?" Lucas joked.

"Hey, hey!" Chris said, holding his hands up. "We're here to celebrate Brady getting hitched, not ragging on me!"

"The old ball and chain," Clay said.

Brady leaned back in his chair with a smile that Clay could only call dreamy. Normally, Brady was so reserved that there was nothing to see beyond the politician's mask he always wore, but this weekend, it was gone. He was ecstatic.

"Hottest ball and chain I've ever seen," Brady said.

"I'll toast to that," Chris said, holding his beer up.

The guys spent the rest of the afternoon lounging around the pool and drinking. When dusk hit, they changed into more suitable clothes, had dinner at a local restaurant, and then retired relatively early, for all of them were worn out from traveling.

The next day convened like the last. Innocent jabs, lots of poolside beer, and a whole lot of brotherly camaraderie that Clay found he'd actually missed. He didn't know the last time he and Brady had just hung out like this without him always being wary of the political arena. For once, the politics were off his back, and he was just a man about to marry the woman of his dreams.

At one point, Clay pulled Chris and Lucas aside while Brady had disappeared upstairs, presumably to talk to Liz.

"I know we agreed to take it easy," Clay said, holding his hands up, "and we're doing that. But I gave up Vegas for this. The least we can do is get him shitfaced in his last hurrah."

Lucas just nodded. "I'm down. I'd love to see Brady get turnt."

"Oh God, the slang just keeps getting worse and worse," Chris groaned.

Lucas clapped his brother on the back. "Come on! Don't you remember what it was like in college? I know it was a long time ago for you, but you have to remember—the booze, the women, basketball. Let's bring that back for him."

"Minus the women," Chris clarified.

Clay shrugged. "There are some very hot women right down the beach."

"It's a bachelor party. We're not bringing Liz over here. If we get him sloppy, it's on us. No one else has to know."

Clay and Lucas exchanged a glance that said they would both be taking videos of this shit later and then nodded. "Deal," they said at the same time.

That was how Clay and Lucas piled into his hybrid and rolling to the liquor store later that day. They'd given Brady some bullshit excuse about going to pick up lunch. Guess they'd have to do that now, too.

He and Lucas grabbed some more beer, a handle or two of tequila, a few bottles of whiskey, and some mixers. They hauled it all back out to his car and deposited it into the trunk.

"So," Clay said as they walked to the sandwich place next door, "are you and Savannah a thing?"

Lucas grunted and shrugged.

"What does that mean?"

"Dunno. Where'd you hear that?"

"Someone mentioned it once. That the case?"

"Look, man, it's not a big deal. We were kind of an on-and-off-again thing. But, now, Savi and I are ancient history." Lucas looked up at him and seemed really unconvincing. "She has a boyfriend, you know?"

"Yeah, I know. I know that don't mean shit though if you really like her. Or if she really likes you. Didn't matter for Brady and Liz."

"Hey, I tried with her. If she really likes me, then she has a funny way of showing it." He rubbed his jaw, like he was remembering a particularly painful memory.

"Well, that's good for your health."

Lucas cocked an eyebrow. "That so?"

"Yeah, because, as her brother, I have to let you know…I'd kick your ass."

"Cool, man," Lucas said with a stiff laugh.

They returned to the beach house after picking up enough sandwiches that it looked like they could feed a small third world country rather than four guys all over six feet tall.

Brady took one look at their liquor loot and shook his head. "What's all this?"

"The party!" Lucas cried, pulling out the tequila and pouring it into the small shot glasses they'd picked up.

"Drink up, big brother." Clay patted him on the back.

Lucas passed Brady a shot.

"I promised Liz no strippers, but if we don't finish all this booze, I can't guarantee I'll hold to that promise."

Brady laughed, raised his shot of tequila into the air, and said, "Bring it on."

Chapter 20

BOOZE & CIGARS

Several hours and a shit-ton of alcohol later, Brady Maxwell was hammered. It was easily the drunkest Clay had ever seen his brother. Not that he had seen Brady get drunk all that often, but Chris had seen him drink all through college, and even *he* swore, he had never seen Brady like this. Claimed he'd never gotten this wasted at school. Clay thought that just meant Brady had been way too uptight in college.

They'd lit cigars at some point, and the air was still perfumed with the scent. Brady's was half-discarded in an ashtray they'd found in their father's office. Clay had felt like a proper gentleman, smoking his cigar with the guys, but the very idea of it made him laugh.

"I just…I just love her," Brady slurred. He smiled dopily before taking another shot on the table.

"I'd hope so. You're marrying her," Clay told him.

He rolled his eyes at Brady, who just smiled back at him. He was so wasted. It was hilarious to see him try to hold on to the vestiges of his political self even now.

"You're going to find this…this one day," Brady began. He swung his beer around, trying to aim at all three of them. "All of you."

"That's right, man," Chris said, trying to hide his laughter.

"Giving speeches, even when he's drunk," Clay said. He shook his head.

"It's who he is." Chris just shrugged one shoulder and waited for whatever Brady was saying to make sense.

"You're going to find…it. And when you do…" he said, taking a sip of the beer. "When you do, I'm going to be…there."

"What are we finding?" Lucas prompted. He was beyond wasted all on his own, kicked back in the lounge chair. His eyes were glassy.

Clay was pretty sure, at some point, he'd gone down to the beach to smoke a blunt because he'd come back smelling like it. No one else had seemed to notice or care.

"Her. The one," Brady told them.

Clay and Chris cracked up at him spouting his unconditional love. Neither of them had gotten as drunk as Brady. Chris had had more than Clay though, as he was under orders from Liz to take care of Brady.

"And I'm getting y'all this drunk when it happens!" Brady yelled.

"Done!" Clay agreed.

"I just want you to all be as happy as I am. She's a fucking incredible woman." Brady started wandering around, teetering and nearly falling over.

"Oh, there. Hold on. Don't fall over," Clay said. He put his hand out to steady Brady.

"I'm fine. I'm fine," Brady said, shaking him off.

"I don't think so."

Brady patted him on the cheek and laughed. "Look at you."

Clay shook his head in despair. *What the fuck?*

Brady stumbled and fell into the chair next to Lucas.

"Fuck, is this what it's like, dealing with me?" Clay asked as he helped Chris haul Brady back to his feet.

"Worse," Chris told him.

"Ass. That was rhetorical."

"Call 'em like I see 'em."

"No wonder I don't have any friends," Clay said.

"I need to take a piss," Brady announced to the room before pushing past them, making his way toward the bathroom.

"Oh, Jesus. He's going to drown, and we'll never deliver him whole to Liz," Clay groaned.

"Don't worry. I got him," Chris said, fending him off. "He's probably about to pass out, and then I'm following him."

"You know," Clay called to Brady down the hall, "if you practiced drinking more, this wouldn't happen!"

Brady flipped him off and Clay just laughed.

God, his brother was a fucking wreck. And it was awesome. He hadn't known what to expect, coming to this bachelor party, but it was better than anything he could have anticipated.

Lucas staggered out of his chair and nodded his head toward the stairs leading to the beach. Clay followed him right out to the beach. He'd been right. Lucas pulled a joint out of his pocket, rolled it between his fingers, and then lit it. He took a drag between his thumb and forefinger and gradually released the smoke.

"You in?" He passed it to Clay, who shrugged and took a hit off of it.

"Fuck," Clay said. "I haven't done this shit since college."

"Haven't had one since basketball season started," Lucas admitted.

Clay passed it back to him. "You smoke regularly otherwise?"

"Nah. Just at parties and shit." He took another hit and then offered it to Clay again.

"I'm good. I think I'm going to go for a walk."

Lucas's eyebrows rose. "Yeah? You going to see the girls?"

Clay shrugged. "Might just do that."

Lucas smirked at him. "Let's do it."

"Don't forget what I said about how I'd beat your ass," Clay told him.

But there was mischief in Lucas's eyes that Clay recognized, that reminded him a bit of himself.

So, they walked down the beach in silence.

It was better not to know.

The night air was cool, a total contrast from the oppressive heat that hit them during the day.

The stars were just visible on the horizon, and the moon was nearly full to bursting.

If not for the nearly full moon, Clay would never have noticed the blonde girl seated on a blanket on the beach. Lucas bumped him in the shoulder and then disappeared into the night. Whatever he planned to do, Clay no longer cared.

He was just drunk enough to actually go through with this. Andrea was sitting there, just like the lost twelve-year-old girl she had been that day he'd found her crying on the beach because her parents were arguing. The same day they'd shared their first kiss.

He hadn't walked away then.

He couldn't walk away now.

"Hey," he said softly as he approached.

When she heard his voice, she jumped and glanced up at him. He could see tears brimming in her eyes. She looked as if she had been sitting here, crying, for a while. He hated that.

"What are you doing here?" she asked. She hastily wiped at her cheeks.

"Thought I'd walk on the beach. Want to walk with me?"

She shook her head. "I'm just going to sit here. You go ahead."

"Mind if I join you?"

"If you must."

Clay sank down onto her blanket and stared out at the ocean. The waves were nearly black in the dark. Watching them crash evenly was melodic and comforting.

"Going to tell me why you're crying?"

"No," she whispered. The wind carried it away, and he barely heard her.

"All right."

They sat there like that listening to the waves crash against the sand. Clay didn't know how much time had passed. But he just sat there with her. She needed someone, no matter if she would admit it or not, tell him what the issue was or not, allow herself to be comforted or not. She clearly needed someone.

And he was her someone.

He was her person.

"Tell me about the gallery," he finally said into the stillness.

She stirred next to him. He could feel her eyes on him. He turned to face her and saw that she seemed startled.

"What about the gallery?"

"Everything. How did it start? Where have you been getting the paintings? How much do you love it?"

Her face changed in that instant, as if a weight had been lifted and she was thinking about the happiest part in her life. "I'd never wanted to open my own gallery. It felt really…constricting. I'd thought for a long time that it was just a hobby, you know?"

"I do."

She smiled and glanced away, as if admitting that she couldn't face that he'd been there for all of that. "Then, I sold that French piece for over half a million dollars."

"The one of the woman looking out the window when it was raining?" he asked.

Her mouth opened slightly in surprise. "Yes, that one."

"And that changed the game?"

She winced. *Wrong choice of words.*

"It made me realize that my collection could become a career. One that I enjoyed." Andrea crossed her feet and turned to face him. "After that, I had a few people contact me about opening my own place. I was kind of floored. I didn't know what to do. I didn't want to just work with anyone, and I needed the perfect space."

"And you found it?"

She winced slightly and nodded. "Asher actually found it."

Clay tried to play it cool and not let her know how much that actually hurt. He just kept trudging forward. "Oh, yeah?"

"He'd heard that I was in the market for a space. He had a space. He kind of knew what I was looking for. And then I just kind of acquired it. I mean…it's not even officially open yet," she told him.

"When does it open?"

"I don't know," she said with a sigh. "I have the artwork for the space, but it has to be perfect to have an official grand opening, and I don't have that piece yet."

"You'll know when you're ready."

"Yeah," she murmured. "I think you're right."

She fidgeted and leaned back on her elbows. She shifted her legs out straight in front of her in the sand.

"Why didn't you date Asher?" he asked finally.

"What?" she asked, startled by the question.

"You broke up with me. You…you left me," he said, unable to keep the waver from his voice. "Why aren't you dating him?"

She sighed again, heavier this time. "It was never about dating someone else, Clay. It wasn't like I wanted to leave you to run into someone else's arms. That wasn't my idea of moving on. Maybe it's yours."

"Maybe," he said uncertainly.

"And I did date Asher." She looked at him and frowned. "Before you were attacked, we dated for weeks."

Clay swallowed hard. He'd known this. It was what had sent them into disarray in the first place. "Right."

"It didn't work out then. *He* wasn't what I wanted. And then, after what happened…" She looked away again, shaken all over by the attack. "Did they ever find those bastards?"

He shook his head. "No, the police called off the search. Wrong place at the wrong time."

"So, it was all just bad fucking luck?" she asked in dismay.

He shrugged. "I'd say it put a lot of things in perspective. Showed me what was important and what wasn't."

Andrea frowned again and then glanced out at the water. "You want to know why I was crying when you found me?"

"Yes."

"I was thinking about the first time we met. You remember?"

"Of course. It was right here on this beach."

"I thought you were so cute. I was so young and naive, and I just wanted the cute boy to like me. Because, if the cute boy liked me, then maybe it wouldn't matter that my parents only spoke when they argued. Maybe it wouldn't matter that they hated each other. That they hated me," she said in a mere whisper.

As she leaned forward, her blonde hair fell forward into her face and over her bare shoulder.

He carefully pushed her hair out of her eyes. "Your parents didn't hate you. They still don't hate you. But you just deserved so much more than what they gave you. Do you know what I think about that first day we met?"

"What?" she whispered. Her eyes were glassy, and she looked frightened of the answer.

"I remember falling in love for the first time with this beautiful girl who was giving me the time of day. *Me* and not my brother. Who cared about me and kissed me. You're so beautiful," he said, drawing her closer to him. "You always have been."

"Clay…" she whispered.

He bent down and placed the softest, lightest kiss on her lips, just like the one they'd shared all those years before. She leaned forward into him at the touch, asking for more, but he pulled back. He didn't want to push her.

"I won't," he said huskily. "I want to, but I won't."

Andrea looked like she wanted to say something more, but whatever was on the tip of her tongue, he never found out. In the distance, they both heard voices coming from the direction of her house and stomping in the sand nearby.

"What the…" Andrea muttered.

"Savannah," he muttered, jumping to his feet.

"Why is she out here?"

"Um…shit. I think she's with Lucas."

"Together?" she asked, her voice panicky.

"Yeah."

Andrea swept to her feet. "That can't be good."

"Let's go," Clay said.

He took her hand in his without asking permission, and they loped across the beach. Few things pissed him off more than something hurting Savannah. When she was upset, he automatically went into big-brother mode.

Savannah's voice carried louder and louder as they approached. "God, why do you always have to do this?"

"Do what?" Lucas drawled. "Love you? Not sure I've ever been able to help that."

"Ugh, Luc! That's not enough. It's not."

"It could be."

"You're drunk and high and being a total asshole," she cried. "When you sober up tomorrow, you're going to regret this."

"I'd never regret you." Then, he grabbed her by the back of the head and kissed her.

"Shit," Clay groaned, picking up his speed.

Savannah hesitated for a moment and then pushed him backward. "What are you doing? Why do you only want this, us, when I'm with someone else?"

They never got an answer to that because Clay and Andrea had finally reached them.

"All right, all right," Clay said, "break it up."

Andrea wrapped an arm around Savannah's shoulders and hauled her back a step from the guys.

"I'm fine," Savannah muttered.

"You're not," Clay said. He turned his gaze to Lucas. He grabbed him by the front of his shirt and got in his face. "Let's go. Get out of here. Didn't you listen to me earlier when I said I'd kick your ass? Fuck!"

"Whatever, man," Lucas said, wrenching himself from Clay's grip. "We were fine."

Lucas started walking away, unprompted, and Clay sighed and followed him. He glanced over his shoulder just once, and he and Andrea locked eyes for just a second. When they looked at each other, in the midst of taking care of their friends, a small smile tugged on her lips before she turned back to keep walking.

It was a step.

A tiny step.

Chapter 21

WEDDING DAY

"You can still change your mind," Clay said.

Liz rolled her big blue eyes and laughed at him. "Are you trying to convince me to be a runaway bride?"

"I'm just saying…I have a car out front. We could make a break for it. Just think about it. You'll be tied to my older brother forever."

"That's kind of the point."

"We could always run away together." He winked at her and waited for another laugh to split the air.

"What you've always wanted."

"I'm not denying it if you're not denying," he said.

"Oh, Clay…" She patted the shoulder of his black suit. "Whatever will we do with you?"

"Whatever you want."

Liz exploded into laughter once more, and Clay followed suit. He was joking…mostly. He was glad that Liz and Brady were happy. They had something special. Something he now knew he desperately wanted. And he didn't think she'd really split anyway.

They had just spent the better part of the last three or four hours taking pictures in the gardens around the Biltmore Estate in Asheville, North Carolina, on the intense June morning. The high was in the eighties, and already, it was blistering hot. Halfway through the ordeal, Clay was glad when they ventured inside to take indoor pictures.

Clay had always thought Liz was more of a traditional girl, but the number of pictures she wanted seemed to outweigh her desire to wait until the wedding to see Brady. Instead, they had done a very private outdoor First Look with just the photographer present. Savannah and the girls had all been bursting at the seams to see how it had all turned out.

But, thankfully, now, they were all cooling off inside before the main event that afternoon. Brady had left when the wedding planner had scurried into the room and asked for him. Liz had looked worried, but he had assured her that he was a politician, so he could handle anything.

But Clay never did hear what had happened because when Brady returned, he nodded at the guys. "Let's go."

"Is it time already?" Liz asked, her voice rising an octave.

Brady smiled at her and looked like he wanted to vault across the room. "Soon."

"See you there," she whispered.

"Airplanes, baby."

She giggled and bit her lip.

Whatever that meant. Clay just shook his head and followed Brady, Chris, and Lucas out of the room.

Brady directed them to another smaller room that faced the front of the estate. There, on a long wooden table, was a bottle of the most expensive scotch Clay had ever heard of.

An older waiter walked in behind them with a tray full of crystal whiskey glasses and poured the scotch for them.

Clay sniffed the scotch and nearly came in his pants from lust. This was like heaven in a glass. Pure sinful heaven.

"I just thought we could have one last drink before we went out there," Brady said.

Clay held his glass up. "To Brady and Liz."

The guys followed suit, and then, they all dropped back the expensive liquor like a shot. They poured another round and drank that one slower, savoring the taste and enjoying each other's company.

If Clay didn't know his brother better, he would have thought Brady was nervous. He kept walking back and forth in the room, muttering to himself, as if he were reciting a speech he had memorized, and Clay swore, he saw a slight tremor in Brady's hand.

But no way. Brady Maxwell was never nervous. That was a fact.

The wedding planner appeared then and stuck her head into the room. "Showtime."

Brady nodded and set his drink down, and then they filed back out of the room. They exited the estate, single file—Brady, Chris, Clay, and then Lucas—and then lined up behind Brady in front of the flower archway that had been erected at the front of the lawn.

Rows and rows of white wooden seats with blue satin cushions were filled with guests. Baby-blue and white flowers were knotted to each of the chairs at the end of every row. Enormous bouquets marked the end of the aisle that had formed for the girls. Not much else was needed since they had chosen the most gorgeous outdoor venue possible.

A string quartet was playing soft music for the guests. Just as the music shifted, Clay adjusted his Carolina blue tie one last time and then clasped his hands together in front of him.

Massey appeared first with her blonde hair braided into a bun at the back of her head. She wore a strapless knee-length baby-blue dress and was holding a bouquet of white flowers. Savannah followed next, beaming up at the crowd, taking measured steps forward. Then, it was Victoria's turn. She didn't walk so much as saunter. He wasn't sure if she could even help it.

Then, once all three girls were in place, the minister asked the audience to rise, the quartet shifted to an instrumental version of Rachael Yamagata's "Be Be Your Love," and everyone seemed to still.

Liz appeared at the end of the aisle, like a dream wrapped in lace. It didn't matter that they'd just spent the last four hours staring at her dress; the entire wedding party gasped at her entrance. The entire audience sucked in a collective breath.

She was stunning. Breathtaking. The most beautiful person there. Just as she should be.

Her dress was simple but elegant with thin multi-straps and an all-lace bodice that was entire see-through in the back. The bodice hugged her chest and then flowed out in a wave of lace to her feet before trailing behind her in a long train. A long veil was pinned into her hair. But the most beautiful part of all was her smile, filled with pure joy, as she walked down that aisle on the arm of her father.

Clay glanced to Brady and saw him swallow hard. He seemed to be fighting back tears, and his eyes were solely on his bride.

Liz finally reached them, her train swishing the rose petals down the aisle. Her eyes were bright but dry. She looked excited and ready…so ready. Like she was born for so much more than this moment yet exactly where she was supposed to be.

Clay's eyes drifted from the bride as her father kissed Liz's cheek and handed her over to Brady. Instead, he looked out at the crowd. He found Gigi seated alone, near the back. She wore a plum-purple sundress and smiled when his gaze landed on her. She had agreed to go to the wedding with him, even when he'd told her he had plans. He was glad they were just friends and had remained that way, despite both their idiotic attempts to move forward.

Then, his eyes swept from her to Andrea. She was in the second row, seated next to Bad Suit. Clay's jaw clenched, but he reminded himself that she'd said they weren't together. If she wasn't claiming him, then that meant she was single and open and available.

Mine.

That was the only thought that clawed its way out of his mind.

His eyes locked with hers for a split second before she quickly averted her gaze back to the wedding.

Clay tuned back into the ceremony.

"Today, we have come together to witness the joining of two lives. The extraordinary has happened. They met each other, fell in love, and are finalizing it with their wedding today. Romance is fun, but true love is something above and beyond. It is their desire to love each other for the rest of their lives, and that is what we are celebrating here today. Repeat after me."

"I, Liz, take you, Brady, to be my husband and my partner in life. I will cherish our friendship and love you today, tomorrow, and forever," she said in barely a whisper as she repeated the words. "I will trust you and honor you. I will laugh with you and cry with you. Through the best and the worst. Whatever may come, I will always be there. As I have given you my hand to hold, so I give you my life to keep."

Brady swallowed and repeated the words next.

"Brady, do you take Liz to be your wife?"

"I do," he said.

"Do you promise to love, honor, cherish, and protect her, forsaking all others and holding only unto her forevermore?"

"I do."

"And do you, Liz, take Brady to be your husband?"

She hiccuped. "I do."

"And do you promise to love, honor, cherish, and protect him, forsaking all others and holding unto him forevermore?"

"Yes. Yes, I do."

Brady and Liz squeezed their hands together. Chris presented the rings next, and they sealed their love together with the binding of the unbroken circle of love. Liz slid a wedding ring onto Brady's ring finger, and tears brimmed in her eyes. Chris passed Brady Liz's wedding ring, and then he slipped it onto her finger.

The minister smiled. "By the power vested in me, I now pronounce you man and wife. You may kiss your bride."

Brady chuckled. "Finally."

Liz gasped. Then, he pulled her toward him and passionately kissed her in front of the hundreds of people in the audience. Everyone applauded. People rose to their feet. Clay was even sure that he'd heard someone whistle.

Brady finally released Liz. Her cheeks were pink with excitement and embarrassment and joy.

"I would like to introduce you to Mr. and Mrs. Brady Maxwell III."

Everyone else leaped to their feet, cheering and applauding. The string quartet picked up again, playing "I Won't Give Up" by Jason Mraz. Brady and Liz took two steps down the aisle before he scooped Liz up into his arms and marched her down the aisle, as if she weighed nothing. Her train dragged behind them, but all Clay could see was Liz's elated face staring up at Brady, as if he were her world.

Clay was dimly aware of taking Savannah's arm and following them down the aisle and past all of their friends and family. He caught one glimpse of Andrea with tears in her eyes. She looked both happy and terribly sad, and he swore that he'd figure out how to fix it.

As soon as they were past the rest of the audience, the wedding planner ushered them away from the party and to a secluded area. Brady and Liz were in a daze, gazing up at each other, as if it were the first time they'd ever seen the other. It was contagious. Clay couldn't stop smiling.

"Will you help pull aside all the family that we need for the pictures?" the wedding planner asked Clay and Savannah when she caught up with them.

"More pictures?" Clay asked.

"Just with the families, and then we'll head over to the reception. I wanted to give them a moment though," she said.

"Good idea," Savannah said. "We'll cover it."

They spent the next twenty minutes herding together all of their family and trying to figure out who belonged to Liz's family out of the nearly eight hundred people in attendance. They were almost done when Savannah nudged Clay.

"What?" he asked

She nodded her head off in the distance, and he saw what she was getting at.

He smiled. "Thanks, Savi."

"Well…I owe you for the beach," she said quietly. "Thanks, by the way."

"That's what big brothers are for."

He wandered away from Savannah and went directly to Andrea, who was speaking animatedly to Bad Suit. She was waving her arms around a lot, and that normally meant bad news.

"Mind if I cut in?" Clay asked, as if this were a dance.

Andrea immediately dropped her arms and turned to face him. "Clay…"

"Why don't you just turn around and walk away like you did last time?" Asher said.

Clay raised his eyebrows. He was not going to get into a fight at Brady's wedding. He was not going to punch this douche bag in the face. He was not going to do it. Even if the guy deserved it.

So, instead, he just smiled neutrally, letting the cocky attitude return with ease. "You think so?"

"What are you talking about, Asher?" Andrea asked, whirling on him.

Clay realized what was going on and almost laughed. "You saw me there. That's why you did it."

"Did what?" Andrea asked.

"He saw me at the gallery. That's why he picked you up and twirled you around. Why he acted like your boyfriend. Isn't that right?"

"You were at the gallery?" Andrea asked, confused. "What is he talking about, Asher?"

Asher shrugged. "So maybe I saw you there. She wouldn't have reacted that way if she wasn't interested in me."

Clay laughed. "You did it so that she wouldn't show you how interested she still was in *me*, right?"

"Can someone *please* tell me what's going on?"

"I came to your gallery opening. Brady and Liz were there. They can corroborate my story. I came to invite you to the Cooper and Nielson gala, but when I showed up, he picked you up and twirled you around. You looked so happy, so I walked out and never invited you."

Andrea's mouth dropped open. "You were there? I swore, I saw you, but...I just thought I'd been seeing things."

"And he did it, hoping I'd walk."

"Just like you did," Asher said with a sneer.

"I can't believe you didn't tell me that you saw him after I *swore* to you that I saw him that day. You made me feel like a total crazy person, as if I were the one chasing ghosts."

Asher shrugged, slightly uncomfortable. "I just knew Clay was no good for you. If you'd just give me a chance, you'd see how right we are."

"You had no right to do that," Andrea snapped. "As I was so eloquently saying before Clay showed up, we're not together. Stop trying to act like we're together. I invited you to this as a friend. Clearly, you don't know the meaning of that…so you can leave." She twirled her fingers at him in a dismissive manner.

"Andrea—" Asher said.

"No. Good-bye."

Asher opened his mouth, like he wanted to say more, but Clay got between him and Andrea. "As much as I'd love to hear what you have to say…oh, wait, no, I don't. I have to take Andrea for pictures anyway."

"Pictures?" she asked in surprise.

"Family pictures."

Her eyes rounded. "I don't…I mean…I don't know."

He took her hand. "You've always been family. Not going to change now, Andrea."

"You're just going to take him back like that?" Asher asked in disbelief.

"That's none of your business," she snapped. "I said good-bye. You can get off the property before I ask someone to have you removed."

"Fuck that," Asher said. Then, he turned and stormed away like a thundercloud.

"Shall we?" Clay asked with a self-satisfied smile on his face.

"This does not mean I'm taking you back," she said, pointing her finger in his face.

"Of course not," he said. He brought her hand up to his lips and placed a soft kiss there.

"It doesn't."

"We'll see about that."

Her mouth dropped open, and he just smirked, gesturing for her to head over to the rest of the party for family photos.

Chapter 22

OUT IN THE OPEN

"So…did you really show up at the art gallery?" Andrea asked.

Clay nodded. They'd just gone through an incredible amount of pictures, and soon, the bride and groom would make an appearance at the reception. The rest of the family who weren't in the bridal party were making their way inside to find their seats, but Clay had held Andrea back a minute.

"I was there. I came to see you."

"I still don't understand why you walked away. That doesn't sound like you at all." Her blue eyes searched his with a mix of fear and curiosity.

"You don't know now…but you will." He took her hand and kissed it. "I've done a lot wrong by you,

Andrea. But, in the four months since we've been apart, you're the only person I've been thinking about."

"That's not exactly what I heard," she grumbled.

"Anything that happened was to try to forget. And I couldn't. I can't. I won't. I refuse to. You're my past and present, and I am damn well going to fight to make sure you're my future."

"Clay…" she whispered.

A flicker of hope dashed across her face, like the guttering of a candle before it was quickly extinguished.

"I'll believe it when I see it. I'm going to go find a seat." With that, she turned and departed.

This time, when she walked away, he didn't feel downtrodden. In fact, he felt quite the opposite. She had wanted to hear those things. And if she needed to hear them every day, then he'd figure out how to make her come around. Because he wasn't going to let her get away. Not when he could see how hurt and alone she was without him.

"Come on, lover boy," Savannah said. She latched on to his arm and dragged him back toward the bridal party.

The wedding planner was speaking hurriedly and rearranging the bridesmaids and groomsmen into order with Brady and Liz at the back. Clay was standing with Liz's friend Massey, who looked giddy at the prospect of the reception. Clay was pretty sure Massey was dating one of Liz's other friends, Justin. They'd met at school at UNC before Justin had been kicked out for a DUI. Afterward, he'd started his own tech company.

"Ready?" she breathed. She was practically bouncing up and down.

"Yeah. All good to go."

The DJ called their names as music played in the background, and Clay and Savannah walked into the entrance hall behind Massey and Lucas, who he watched like a hawk. Chris and Victoria followed behind Clay and Savannah. Then, the music changed, everyone rose to their feet, and in walked the bride and groom. The floor cleared completely, and then the DJ announced their first dance. "Everything" by Michael Bublé filtered in through the speakers.

"Don't you dare," Clay heard Liz warn Brady.

Brady raised his eyebrows and smiled down at her. "You just need the right partner, baby."

Then, Brady swept her around the room. All the Maxwell children had taken dance lessons when they were younger. Their mother had thought it a necessity for formal occasions, and Brady was proving that they'd paid off. Liz tilted her head back and laughed as they moved gracefully to the song playing. As it came to a close, Brady dipped Liz until her long blonde hair nearly grazed the floor, and he kissed her to raucous cheer.

When he righted her, Liz pointed her finger at him and said, "You owe me cheesecake, mister."

Brady kissed her hand. "Oreo it is, my love."

Brady and Liz encouraged the rest of the bridal party to join in on the next dance. Clay drew Massey out onto the dance floor and regrettably let Savannah dance with Lucas. But Clay was only dancing with Massey for a total of ten seconds before her boyfriend, Justin, appeared out of nowhere to cut in. He was glad to see Easton cut in in almost the same amount of time. Maybe he was smarter than Clay had given him credit.

Clay's eyes sought out Andrea, but she was nowhere to be found. He found Gigi instead and helped her to her feet.

"Everything okay?" she asked once they were dancing in the center of the room.

"Yeah. Everything seems to be going as planned. Thanks for coming with me to this, Gigi."

"What are friends for but to endure really awkward occasions with each other?"

Clay laughed. "I hope you're okay with being introduced to Andrea."

"Again?"

"This time, as my friend and not my date and preferably not in my clothes."

Gigi's cheeks reddened. "I'm still so sorry about that."

"Hey, it's all right. All's well that ends well."

"Well, speaking of things ending well…maybe it would be better for me to dance with someone else until things *do* end well."

She nodded her head to the side, and Clay turned her to get a clear image of Andrea. She looked nervous. He only knew that because of the way she was standing, as if nothing bothered her. She only needed that strength when she was about to go head-to-head with someone.

"Good idea," he said. "Hey, Chris!"

Chris was standing a few feet away, still dancing with Victoria. "Yeah, man?"

"Hand her off to Duke Fan and dance with my friend Gigi."

"Friend?" Chris asked with raised eyebrows. Then, he caught sight of Gigi, and his entire body stilled.

Victoria laughed and shook her head. She was already searching for her boyfriend, and Chris was still standing there, tongue-tied.

"Yeah," Clay said, releasing Gigi and holding her hand out to Chris, "we work together."

"Uh, Gigi," she said, reaching her hand out to Chris. "Giana, uh…De Rosa. I mean, Giana De Rosa, but my friends call me Gigi."

"Chris, uh…Atwood. My friends call me…Chris."

Clay cocked his head to the side with a satisfied smirk. He seemed to be helping out more than one friend today.

"Wait, I didn't know your name was *Giana*!" Clay said indignantly.

"That's because you don't pay attention to anything," she said.

"Fair."

Chris and Gigi were still standing there. Clay kept waiting for Chris to reach for some of that Maxwell charm that he'd been surrounded by his entire life, but he seemed completely mesmerized by Gigi.

"Go on," Clay urged, pushing her toward his friend. "I'm going to go find Andrea."

"Don't forget your toast," Chris muttered, not taking his eyes off of Gigi.

"Oh, I won't."

Clay laughed and then headed across the room where his beautiful girl was standing near the dessert area. People had already gotten up and started getting food from the various buffet areas filled with different kinds of Southern food. Liz had insisted she didn't want a stuffy sit-down meal for the occasion but rather something fun and festive. There were even games set up outside for when the real party began. Already, the line for booze was long. But Clay didn't care about any of that right now.

"Hey," Andrea said warily when he approached.

"Hey."

"So…you brought *her* to the wedding," she said with disdain.

"Course I brought her. She's probably my best friend."

"I didn't know we all slept with our best friends."

"I'm pretty sure we don't," he said with an easy smile. "Since I haven't slept with her."

Andrea rolled her eyes. "Let's not do this at the wedding. Brady and Liz deserve a good time."

"And you deserve the truth, which I'm giving to you right now." He stared into her eyes. "I've never slept with Gigi. I have no interest in Gigi. In fact, I hope she hooks up with Chris because, when I left them, they were making goo-goo eyes at each other."

Andrea giggled at the comment and then tried to cover it up.

"No, don't do that, baby," he said, trailing his hand down the side of her jaw. "Don't ever hide that beautiful smile."

"Clay, stop…we can't do this."

"Why not? We've been doing it for fifteen years. I fell in love with you on that beach all those years ago. Can't expect me to change now."

"Look, this all sounds…great," she said, stepping away from his embrace. "But the truth is, you can't be serious. You can't take us seriously. You don't want the same things I want anymore. When we started this, I just wanted an out, a way to escape my family. Now, I know that I need more than that. I can't expect you to change with me, Clay. I can't expect for you to want more when you've never wanted it before."

"So, have you found it elsewhere then?" he asked gruffly. He hated the way she'd said that like he couldn't change. She could change, but he was incapable? The past four months, he had proven to himself just how much he could change when he really wanted something.

"No," she admitted, "but I deserve the chance to try."

"Try then. Try with me."

She closed her eyes. "Let's not do this. Please. Another day. Another night."

Clay shook his head. "No, I'm not backing down. I'm not walking away, like last time. You've had space. You've been away from me. I *know* you miss me, Andrea. And, fuck, have I missed you. Walking away is out of the question. Try with me."

Andrea's eyes darted up to his. Whatever she was thinking, none of it was on her face. If he didn't know she hated the idea of politics, he would recommend her for the job. She was better at hiding her emotions than Brady.

"Fine," she snapped. "Right here? Right now?"

It was time for his eyebrows to shoot up. "Yes?"

She took his hand in hers and then dragged him out of the reception room. They walked outside to the empty green space near where the games had been set up. Everyone was inside, eating and dancing, so they hadn't yet ventured outdoors. Andrea pulled him past the games and around the side of the building. It wasn't exactly secluded but close enough.

"Talk. Why the hell should I give you another chance? After the inauguration, you slept with someone else, which was specifically against the rules. And, beyond that, we were at a function together, as a couple, with your *family*. Then, you went and slept around afterward. For all I know, you're with that Gigi girl," she cried. All of her anger from the past few months seemed to pour out of her at once. She was waving her hands around and practically growling at him. "You don't want what I want, Clay. I want this!" She gestured back toward the reception. "Love. Marriage. Kids. Things I *never* thought I'd want. Things I *know* you don't want. We're not right for each other, and I've spent the last four months trying to tell myself that."

Clay stood there for a second in silence. "How did that work out for you?"

"Horrible. Just fucking horrible." She pushed her platinum blonde hair off her shoulders. "Why is it that I want the one thing that I shouldn't want? Why do I want you so fucking bad?"

"Because those things you said aren't true."

"What part?" she demanded.

"Most of it."

She narrowed her eyes and huffed. "Don't bullshit me, Clay."

He strode toward her. She stumbled backward and straight into the side of the building.

"Don't presume to tell me what I want, Andrea. If you'd let me talk to you that night after the inauguration, you'd know by now that I didn't sleep with anyone. I went to bed, alone, and I woke up that way."

She snorted, but he just slammed his hand down onto the wall behind her head.

"I'm fucking serious. I was an idiot. I wanted to hurt you after you'd hurt me with Bad Suit…with Asher," he ground out the name. "*You* hurt *me*. I told you I wasn't jealous, that I didn't care, and it was a bold-faced lie. I was blind with jealousy that you'd gone home with someone else when you could have been with me. I wanted you to feel that. It was wrong. I get it now. All right? I get it."

"That doesn't change anything though," she said, but the venom had left her voice. "So you were jealous? Mission accomplished. Didn't change shit."

"You haven't been around. You don't know whether or not I've changed."

Andrea rolled her eyes. "Yeah. Okay."

"So, you can change, but I can't? You can want love, marriage, and kids after ten years, but I can't? Somehow, I'm standing still, the same guy you went to Yale with, but you get to grow up?" he demanded.

"I didn't say that…"

"You did. And I'm here to tell you, that's bullshit. I've been standing in Brady's shadow for a long fucking time. But, watching him with Liz, I feel more like I'm on the sidelines of something great. It never felt like a difference to me before now. But he's happy. She's happy. They're so in love that it's practically sickening," he admitted. "Yeah, I'm happy for them. Not jealous or angry about Brady getting everything he's ever wanted. All I know is that…what I've always wanted is standing right in front of me. And I'm not letting you walk away again."

Then, before she could say another word to contradict him, he dropped his mouth down on hers, kissing her with every ounce of passion flooding between them from four months of missing her and fifteen years of being desperately in love.

Chapter 23

THEN TAKE ME

Andrea gasped against his lips.

She tasted like heaven and smelled even better. It was as if Clay had spent the last decade with her, yet she had just reawakened all of his senses. His hand ran down the side of her body. It ignited something between them, and soon, she was clinging to the front of his suit.

His tongue ravaged her mouth, taking everything she was giving back. It had been so damn long. The way he'd had her back in his townhouse just hadn't been enough, and it had been interrupted way too soon. There was no way he was going to let that happen now.

"I need you," he groaned deep in the back of his throat.

"Then, take me."

That was all the confirmation he needed.

Clay grasped the backs of her thighs and hoisted her legs up and around his waist. She made the most amazing squeak he had ever heard. He could die a happy man with that noise.

"Fuck, that's sexy."

He started walking them farther away from the party, and Andrea's head popped up. "Where are we going?"

"Who fucking cares? I need you. Right now."

She had never cared about public fornication before…and, technically, it was a private event.

She ran her hand down his cheek, scraping her nails across the soft stubble that had come in along his jawline. "Dirty boy."

He grinned and kicked open the door to the waiting area they had used earlier. The girls' stuff was still scattered across the room, but his mind was set on the large black couch along the windowed wall. If it had been up to him, he would have fucked her right there against the wall of the Biltmore mansion. But he didn't want to disrupt Brady's wedding. He owed his brother that much.

But not enough to stop.

He needed to be in his woman. He needed her with a fiery passion that he hadn't even known existed. He just needed her.

All of her.

He didn't want there to be anything left hanging between them by the end of this. She needed to know how he felt about her. No more games. No more miscommunication. No more fucking time apart. Just him and her in this moment.

Without preamble, they crashed back onto the couch. Andrea still had her legs wrapped around his waist, and he bucked against her as they fell. She moaned with her head back on the cushion. Then, she grasped his face and brought his lips back down on hers. He wasn't complaining.

He couldn't get enough of her. Four months had been an eternity. Not from the lack of sex. He'd had some of that, and it hadn't mattered. It hadn't quenched a damn thing inside him. It hadn't released him from this thing eating away at his insides. For those months, all he had wanted was one thing. One thing to fix him.

Andrea.

And, now, she was here.

His hands ran down her dress. Fuck, he had missed her perfect body. All lithe and bendy. Gorgeous. Just for him.

He slipped a finger inside the top of her dress and flicked it across her nipple until she gasped again.

"Don't you dare tease me," she told him.

"I'd never dream of it."

But he didn't stop. She liked it. She was practically writhing beneath him. Without another thought, he yanked the material aside completely and brought the erect nipple into his mouth. Her legs tightened around his waist. A whimper escaped her lips but no words about stopping him.

He flicked his tongue across the sensitive skin while he worked on the other one, fiddling with the bud between his fingers. He gently drew it between his teeth while he pulled the other one, being less than gentle. And her entire body tightened around him.

"Clay," she whispered, "I can't…I can't wait."

He continued to hold one of her nipples between his fingers while his other hand trailed between them. He pushed up the skirt of her dress and found her without panties again.

Fuck.

He would never buy her panties again if this was going to keep happening. As much as he enjoyed ripping them off of her…the thought of her never wearing them was just as appealing.

"Is this what you want?" he asked, slipping a finger between the folds of her body.

"Oh God," she murmured.

She clearly did want him very bad. She was soaked, and all he wanted to do was bury himself deep inside her and never leave.

But this wasn't only about him. He wanted her to get off, too. More than once if he could help it.

He circled two fingers around in her wetness until her hips started bucking against his hand, demanding him to enter. He ran his thumb across her already sensitive clit, and she shivered all over. It was goddamn sexy as hell. Not that he had her in submission, but that she was allowing him to give her this pleasure. That he could bring this out of her. That they could bring this out of each other because, frankly, he was as hard as a rock beneath this goddamn suit.

When he felt her already on the verge of collapse, he thrust his fingers into her, drawing out the waves of pleasure he could feel rocketing through her body. He wanted nothing more than to get down on his knees and eat her pussy, but considering the time constraints, he just worked her into a frenzy.

"Fuck me," she pleaded. "Get inside me."

He kissed her lips once, softly, tenderly. Met her dazed blue gaze and smiled. She smiled back, slightly lopsided and sated. He loved it.

He swiftly released himself from his suit pants and let them fall into a heap at his feet. Then, he grabbed her legs and brought them back around his waist before driving into her.

"Oh, fuck," he groaned when he bottomed out inside her. "Fucking hell."

"God, I have missed you," she said.

"You have no idea."

"I think I do."

He brushed her platinum hair out of her face, placed another tender kiss on her lips, and then moved. Not slowly. He could hardly contain himself. The way she was looking at him. The complete adoration on her face. The mask dropping and the desire evident. The way she breathed in short sputters. The way her eyes glazed over. The way her acrylic nails dug into his back.

It was like coming home.

This was where he was meant to be and whom he was meant to be with.

He'd been an idiot for thinking he could ever get it from anyone else. Sex. Fucking. None of it was the same compared to how it felt to be inside the woman he loved.

His thrusts picked up tempo until they were both panting with exertion. He slammed into her body. Owning it. Their bodies came together over and over again. They both knew exactly what made the other tick, and with so much practice over the years, it was like playing a well-tuned guitar. He could pluck just the right string. Strum just the right melody. Play the perfect song of her body.

Harmony.

Perfect fucking harmony.

Andrea fiercely kissed him once before he felt her walls contract all around him. He saw stars as his orgasm rocked through him with the same ferocity.

He collapsed forward onto his forearms and rested his forehead against hers. Their breaths came out in gasps in the mingled air. The space felt very small. Like it was just the two of them and the rest of the world didn't exist. Nothing could come between them in that moment.

Not after sharing that.

"Clay…"

"Andrea…"

"I love you."

He breathed out heavily and looked down at her to see she was smiling. "I love you, too."

After a few minutes of being wrapped together, they both straightened out their clothes. Andrea located an adjacent restroom and came back looking only slightly flushed with her hair tamed and her smile beaming. He didn't even care about what he looked like, but she insisted he take a look in the mirror.

It was for the better that he straightened up some since…he still had a speech to give.

He took Andrea's hand when he came back out. "You said that I couldn't change…that you didn't expect me to. I'd love to imagine that this right here could put all the past behind us, but I know that sex doesn't heal all the old wounds. As much as I want it to. I'm just asking for a chance…a second chance. I've changed."

"That's wonderful to hear."

He smirked. "I mean, honestly, I'm still the same asshole that you fell for, but I want to be with you. If I have to grovel…I can work on my groveling skills."

She laughed, and it was a beautiful sound. God, everything about her was beautiful.

"We'll see about groveling. That would seriously be a sight. Clay Maxwell…groveling." She looked away from him, as if she were imagining him on his hands and knees, pleading.

He sank to his knees then and there, still holding her hand, and kissed it. "We both made mistakes. We both hurt the other. The only way we'll know if this is real is to give it a real shot. If it's not enough for you after that…then you can walk. I won't keep coming back for you. I'll let you go."

"Clay," she whispered. She bent down and brushed a kiss on his forehead. "I do like you on your knees, but get up. You don't have to grovel to me. I messed up, too. I'd like another chance. I don't know if it will work," she admitted. "But I'd like it to."

The pair returned to the reception to find that dinner was over. Champagne was being passed around to all the attendees. Brady and Liz were standing at a side table, cutting into the cake, while everyone snapped shots of them.

Chris appeared in front of Clay, looking frantic. "Where the hell did you go? Toasts were supposed to happen at the end of dinner, but we couldn't do that without you. They just moved on to the cake."

"No one seems to mind," Clay pointed out.

Chris shook his head. "Well, we're about to do that, so I hope you're ready."

Cake was passed out to the attendees, and then Chris and Victoria gave their speeches before the rapt crowd. Chris joked about Brady's rise to fame at UNC and then into politics. He talked about the first time he had met Liz—when Brady had brought her over to his apartment—and how he had known that first day that she was the one for Brady. Victoria was a little more…colorful. She made several inside joke references that made Liz turn scarlet. But, by the end of it, Brady and Liz were laughing so hard that each had to clutch their sides.

Clay knew it was his turn then. He left Andrea with the cheesecake she had gotten from the dessert table and walked to the front of the room. He took the microphone from Victoria, who flashed him a grin.

"Beat that," she said with a wink.

"Challenge accepted."

He ran a hand back through his disheveled hair, not giving a single fuck about what he looked like after what had just happened with Andrea.

"Hey, everybody!" Clay said, straightening his tie as all eyes turned to him. He glanced over at Brady and Liz.

Brady looked a bit worried and Liz even more so. *Did they think I'm going to throw them under the bus?*

"Ever since I was told I was supposed to give a speech at Brady's wedding, I'd been planning out something horribly embarrassing to say about Brady. I mean, really, it's the first time where I'm behind the microphone and not him, so I should use this to my advantage right?"

The crowd laughed, and a few people in the back cheered, egging him on.

"I'm sure everyone would like to hear a few horror stories about my brother, the perfect Brady Maxwell," Clay joked. He even managed a grin. "But, truth be told, I couldn't find any of those stories to share with you. Because that man who married Liz Dougherty today—" He laughed softly. "Liz Maxwell, excuse me—is the luckiest son of a bitch alive."

Everyone burst out laughing again. But he was damn serious.

"When I first found out that Brady and Liz were a couple, my first thought was, *How the hell had he gotten that lucky?* I mean, Liz is even more perfect than my perfect brother. Smarter, prettier, maybe even *more* ambitious than Brady, and I never in a million years thought that would be possible."

He ran a hand back through his hair again and winked at Liz. "Then, as I've watched them together for the past year, it was plain to me and everyone else who knew him that my bachelor brother had fallen in love. Head over heels, risk-his-career, risk-the-public, risk-his-world in love with this woman." Clay pointed at Liz. "And it was the best decision of his life."

Brady's smile was magnetic in that moment. It was like he had never known Clay could say something this nice about him. Could say something this nice about anyone.

"As the younger son, you can only imagine what it was like, living in the shadow of a legend. But since he's been with Liz, it hasn't felt like a shadow. It's felt like being on the sidelines of something incredible. Of something worth believing in. Brady and Liz are the kind of couple that makes everyone in the room demand to find their one true love." His eyes searched out Andrea. "To find something so magical that nothing and no one could stand in the way of it. And I'm so happy and proud to be standing here today, delivering a congratulatory speech to two of the best people I know."

Clay raised his glass in the air. "To Brady and Liz. To a lifetime of happiness, good cheer, endless sarcasm, and great sex!"

Everyone burst out laughing again and raised their glasses, too.

Someone from the back yelled out, "Clay Maxwell for president!"

He laughed and said, "Cheers!"

He downed his drink and went over to give his brother and new sister-in-law a hug.

"That was great, man," Brady said. "I appreciate it."

"Do what I can."

"Clay," Liz said, throwing her arms around his neck, "who knew you could be so kind? I love it."

"Easy there, sis. You just got married. Wait to ravage me later."

"Looks like someone already did," she said as she nudged him.

He shrugged and nudged her back. "Can't help it, you know."

"I do."

He shouldered his way back through the crowd toward Andrea. Victoria glared at him as he passed her.

He winked. "Challenge completed."

"Ass. You weren't really supposed to outdo me. Why didn't I think to raise a toast to good sex?" Victoria grumbled.

"Great sex," he corrected. Then, he scooped Andrea into his arms. "Speaking of great sex…"

"You just had some," she said with a shake of her head.

"Yeah…but I have a room." He produced a key out of his pocket and dangled it in front of her eyes.

"Later," she said, swatting at him. "Let's celebrate with them first."

"You're right. You're always right."

So, they spent the next few precious hours enjoying Brady and Liz's epic party. Clay didn't know how much of this time with Andrea would change what was between them. He could still feel some distance from her. He was sure it was borne out of fear of the unknown between them, but for this one night, he wasn't going to think about it. They could deal with the real world tomorrow. This truly was their element after all—a big event with his entire family around them.

Maybe tomorrow, when it was just the two of them, they could figure out how to move forward.

Brady and Liz finally proclaimed that they had to leave the party for the night.

"We'd love to stay and party all night," Brady said, wrapping an arm around Liz's waist, "but I *have* to be alone with my bride."

Clay snorted. He couldn't blame the guy.

They set up for the send-off, and soon, Brady and Liz were running through a line of people, waving farewell, climbing into a limo, and riding off into the sunset.

Chapter 24

OUR DECISION

Waking up next to Andrea the day after Brady and Liz's wedding was the best thing that had ever fucking happened to Clay. He'd forgotten what it was like to have her warm body curled into his side. To have her fan of platinum hair splayed out across the pillow, some strands so light that they blended into the pillowcase. To have his hands running down her sides, his lips pressed into her shoulder, his dick against her tight little ass.

Naked.

Completely one hundred percent naked.

That was how he liked her here with him.

His cock was already hardening and lengthening at the feel of her. He'd had all night with her, and it hadn't been enough. Not even close. He wanted inside her all over again.

"Baby," he whispered against her skin.

She groaned. He kissed across the rise in her shoulder and slid his hand forward over her hip bone and down between her legs. She stirred at the first gentle touch to her clit. He pulled her leg over his hip to spread her open to him and gently coaxed life back into her. It took a minute or so before she seemed to really realize what was going on.

"Clay?" she whispered.

"That's right, baby." He kissed her shoulder again.

Then, he dipped his fingers inside her, wetting the tips of them and going back to her clit for more.

"God, that feels good," she purred.

"Good morning to you, too."

She sighed pleasantly as she reached her hand back and wrapped it around his dick. His eyes rolled into the back of his head as she started stroking him with the leisurely pace he was applying to her.

It was intoxicating, this buildup between them. It didn't matter how many times he'd had her last night or over the years before this; it felt like the first time all over again.

New explorations. New sensations. New orgasms.

Yet the same fucking desire. The same way he knew her body—every noise, every squirm, every breath. The same way he knew that the soft sputters coming from her meant his baby was getting damn close to an orgasm.

"I need you to come for me, love," he whispered.

"No," she breathed.

"Oh, yes."

Andrea rolled away from his hand. For a second, he was left there, bereft, wondering what the fuck she was thinking. They'd been together all night. Of course, things weren't magically better between them, but it didn't fucking mean she could run away in the morning.

Then, she grinned at him and pushed him backward onto the bed with his dick protruding upward, as hard as a rock and ready for her.

"I want to be on top, and I want you to come with me," she demanded.

He relaxed back into the bed. "Whatever you want."

He realized how terrified he'd been there for a second, worried that she had wanted this to stop. He couldn't remember ever being frightened about a woman like that before. If that made him a pussy, then fine. He'd gone crazy for months over this woman…just add it to the list.

Andrea hooked her leg over his hips and eased herself down on top of him. The smile on her face was euphoric. She rested her hands on his chest and started to move up and down on his cock. Her tits bounced wonderfully with the movement, and he nearly forgot to meet her thrusts as he stared at the sight. In the early morning light shining in through the windows, she looked like a goddess. And as she made herself come on his dick and he followed along with her, he truly believed he would worship her.

They took a long shower, soaping each other up and remembering the ease of being together. Then, after he gave her one last kiss, he left her in the bathroom, as he knew she liked to spend ample amount of time in there, getting ready.

Clay grabbed his phone out of his hastily discarded suit pants and checked the messages. He had one from Brady.

You just had to trash the car, didn't you?
Dick.

Clay laughed heartily. He, Chris, and Lucas had *decorated* Brady's Lexus the day before with wedding slogans painted on the windows, flowers over every conceivable space inside and out, and cans hanging off the back of the bumper on strings, so they'd rattle when he pulled away.

They'd all gone in on the event and probably gone a little overboard. But Brady was only going to get married once, and it was fun to get at him like this. Plus, he couldn't be that upset. He and Liz were on the way to the airport to go to Bora Bora for three weeks and stay in some private overwater bungalow where Clay suspected they would just fuck the entire time. Though Liz had sworn she'd bring enough books with her to fill a library, Clay doubted she'd have any time to read.

The second text was from Gigi, who he guiltily remembered kicking out of their room. He'd gotten a suite with two rooms for them since, obviously, they weren't sleeping together, but since things with Andrea had worked out even better than he'd imagined…he'd asked Gigi not to come up.

She hadn't seemed to care. In fact, with the way she had been eyeing Chris all night, Clay wondered if that was where she'd ended up anyway.

Whenever you come up for air, I kind of need my stuff. Clothes or something. Let me know when it's safe. Otherwise, I'm just sitting here, smelling like vodka and looking like the walk of shame. So, you know...normal for me.

Clay snorted and messaged her back.

Going to be a while.

Fuck.

Maybe if you came up right now, it'd be fine.

If this is awkward, I'm going to hate you forever.

Clay figured Andrea had at least another forty-five minutes before she would be done in the bathroom anyway. And, if last night wasn't proof that she was the only woman he wanted in his life, then he wasn't sure what else he could do to convince her right now. Though he had some ideas for later.

Using her key card, Gigi came in through the door and practically tiptoed over to the second bedroom where she had been planning to stay. Clay had been sure to put some actual clothes on—a teal polo and khakis—before she got there. She waved at him as she grabbed clothes out of her suitcase and then zipped it closed once more.

"Thanks," she whispered.

"So...where were you last night?" he asked, following her to the door.

"I got a room."

Clay narrowed his eyes. "Bold-faced lie, De Rosa. The Biltmore was booked up for the wedding."

She rolled her eyes. "And?"

"You couldn't have gotten a room, which sounds to me like you stayed in someone else's room." He leaned against the doorframe and watched her squirm.

"Doesn't matter where I was, Maxwell. All that matters is, you got your girl back."

She gave him a quick hug and then opened the door.

"Um…what's going on?" Andrea asked.

She had appeared silently into the bedroom. He was shocked as shit, considering she'd only been in there for fifteen minutes, and she came back out with pencil-straight hair and only light makeup. She was goddamn stunning. It was like looking into the sun.

"Hey, baby," he said casually. "Gigi just came to pick up her stuff. She was trying not to disturb us."

Andrea wrinkled her nose. He knew that she still wasn't over what she thought had happened with Gigi…even though nothing had happened. He certainly didn't consider the ill-conceived kiss he had given Gigi the night he thought he'd lost Andrea for good anything for her to worry about.

"I see," she said, crossing her arms and eyeing Gigi.

"Yeah. So sorry. I wouldn't have bothered you at all, but well…I don't have any other clothes," Gigi said hastily.

Clay gave Gigi a sympathetic look. This was so awkward for her.

"Just really glad to see you two back together."

"We're not back together," Andrea said frostily.

Clay's head whipped back to face her. "*What?*"

"Um…I didn't mean to cause any trouble." Gigi held her hands up. "I'm not into Clay at all. He's like a brother."

"What do you mean, we're not back together?" Clay asked.

"It's pretty obvious, isn't it?" Andrea said.

"I don't think it's fucking obvious at all. What was all of this, if we're not getting back together?"

Gigi backed up a step. "Fuck. I'm sorry. I shouldn't have come to get my stuff. I'll just, um…go back to Chris's or something."

Clay heard her in a fog. He wanted to feel triumphant that he'd been fucking right about Gigi and Chris, but all he could hear was buzzing in his ears. Gigi backed out of the room, and the door clicked shut behind her.

"Why are you freaking out?" he demanded. Without another thought, he strode across the room and got in her face. "We go from fucking this morning to you pissed at me all over again?"

"Do you expect me to be happy when I see her in your hotel room while I'm off in the bathroom?" Andrea asked. She crossed her arms over her chest. "I'm not going to let that shit slide. I can't do it anymore, Clay."

"There is *nothing* going on with me and Gigi!" he bellowed. "Nothing!"

"Then, why were you hiding her? Then, why was she sneaking around?"

Clay grabbed his phone and shoved it in her face. "Read. She didn't have any of her shit and was staying in Chris's room because I booted her yesterday so that we could be alone. She had her own room. We weren't even going to be sleeping in the same *room*, Andrea."

Andrea scrolled through his phone and then seemed to crumple under the weight of the messages. "You're…you're really not with her?"

"I'm really not," he told her firmly.

"I don't understand how you can just be friends with another girl," she said uncertainly. "You've only ever had that relationship with me."

"I didn't either. Honestly, I had no idea what the fuck I was doing. But it's never been like that with me and Gigi. We're too much alike. We spend too much time together. And she gives me shit for everything." He shook his head. "I actually think she's more on your side than anyone else is at this point. She thinks I'm a big fucking idiot forever letting you get away."

"Well…you are," Andrea said.

"Yeah, you're right. And I've been regretting it every day for the last four months." He reached out for her, and this time, she let him take her hand. "I know it's not going to be perfect. I know we both have issues with moving forward. We both fucked around on the other for ten years and that was fine. Then when we were coming to terms with the fact that it wasn't fine to do that anymore then, we acted like idiots. But I'm here, and we're going to have to trust each other. I'm trying, and there's no one else here for me but you. Do hear me?"

She nodded. "Yeah. I just…I guess I need to see this in action before I can start to move past those issues."

"That's fine by me. I think we both will have to work through it. I mean…" Clay scratched the back of his head. He hated admitting how fucked up he'd been about the break up, but he had been a total maniac. Andrea walking out on him had been one of the hardest times of his life. "You walked out without a word, Andrea. No matter what you *heard* while we were apart, that wasn't easy for me."

"I know," she whispered.

"But I made up my mind in our time apart that we'd do things differently if we got back together. After last night, I thought that's where we were headed. So, I don't want to hear you saying that we're not getting back together again."

Her eyes narrowed when she looked back at him. "That's my decision."

"No, it's not. It's *our* decision, and I don't want you to go and make it without me again."

"I just…" She swallowed and dropped her hands. "I just don't know how to do this."

"Yes, you do. We do it together."

"Who are you, and what have you done with Clay Maxwell?" she asked lightheartedly.

"I've been here all along. Right here. I just…I don't know…grew up?"

She laughed. "Who would have guessed?"

"Probably no one. Ever."

"Yeah." Andrea brushed her hair off her shoulders and sighed. "So, where do we go from here?"

"Well, we should probably start with Gigi."

Andrea clenched her jaw. "Do we have to?"

"We already dealt with Bad Suit. I don't want Gigi to be between us."

"Ugh. I just don't like her, okay?"

Clay nodded. "You don't have to. But she's going to be around, Andrea. We work together, and we're friends."

"Friends," she said dryly.

"Yes. Just friends. I'll tell you as many times as you need for it to sink in."

"Why didn't you just *tell* me that she was coming to get her stuff? Why did you have to hide it?" she asked, her voice small. "I understand she had to come get her stuff and that you weren't going to be sleeping in the same room, but did you really have to sneak around?"

Clay ran a hand back through his hair and shuffled on his feet. This had been him for so long that some habits die hard. He knew from now on that he was going to have to be careful. "I don't know. Maybe I was a little worried about ruining the peace we'd established."

Andrea blew out a shaky breath and shot him a hesitant smile. "I was kind of a bitch, wasn't I?"

"You were…less than pleasant," he said carefully. "But I should have warned you that she was coming to get her stuff."

"Yes, you should have told me. But I guess I get why you didn't," she said finally. "I just don't want you to do it again. If Gigi is forced to be in our life, then I don't want to be second-guessing everything between you."

Clay bent down and placed a soft kiss on her lips. "Done."

"And I guess I'll try to be more…pleasant. Maybe we should…see if she and Chris want to get brunch?"

She chewed on her bottom lip after she'd said what he was sure was a really hard thing for her to ask.

"I'm sure they would like that."

~

Twenty minutes later, the four of them were seated inside the Estate's restaurant for a champagne brunch. Gigi looked supremely uncomfortable. Andrea downed her first glass of champagne in two point five seconds and had already requested another one. Chris just kept looking up at Clay and snickering under his breath.

Yeah, this was his doing. And he had to admit…he was a total idiot.

This was not going at all how he wanted it to go.

"So…should I address the elephant in the room?" Clay asked.

Gigi and Andrea both looked up at him with strained eyes. Chris looked like he was trying not to laugh still.

"Did you and Chris fuck?"

"Oh my God!" Gigi cried. She buried her head in her hands.

Andrea swatted at him. "Ass."

Chris actually did burst out laughing. "Why am I not surprised?"

"But come on! Everyone is wondering it," Clay said. He waved his hands between them. "She said she stayed in your room. You guys hung out all night. Just tell us."

"You are such an insufferable ass," Gigi cried. This time, she smacked him on the arm. "I cannot believe you brought that up."

"Really?" he asked, honestly surprised.

"Okay, no, I can. But thank you for one of the most awkward weekends of my life."

"Anytime, De Rosa." He grinned at her, and she just shook her head.

"Well, I'm glad we can all agree on something," Andrea said airily to the table.

"That Clay is an idiot?" Chris joked.

"Precisely."

It was his turn to be affronted. "Hey! I was just trying to break the mood. You two looked like you were either going to gouge each other's eyes out with forks or never make eye contact with anyone else again. If it takes a few laughs at my expense, it seems worth it."

Chris grinned. "That's the spirit."

"And, anyway, you guys should probably get used to hanging out together," Clay said, "my best friend and my girl."

"Which one is which?" Andrea said under her breath.

He gave her a long, level look. Then, he reached for her hand and kissed it. "You know the answer to that."

"You're right," she said with a sigh.

"I'm the best friend, in case anyone was wondering," Gigi said.

Chris chuckled. Clay looked relieved. Andrea seemed unconvinced.

"Yeah. I guess I still can't get over you coming downstairs in his boxers at his townhouse," Andrea said. "Sue me."

Chris's eyes rounded as he looked between Clay and Gigi.

"That's actually what we do," Gigi said with her own tentative smile.

Andrea cracked up. "True."

"But really…that wasn't what it looked like. We didn't have sex and never have." She shuddered. "I still feel really bad that you assumed otherwise."

Andrea gave her a curt nod.

"Man, Clay," Chris said, cutting the tension, "you sure know how to keep things interesting."

"I do what I can. Now that we've gotten all of that out of the way, do you think we could eat?" Clay asked.

"Food would be excellent," Chris agreed. "Though I don't mind more awkward conversations, if that's necessary."

Both girls rolled their eyes at the same time. Then, when they realized the other had done it, they burst out into laughter.

"Men!" Gigi said.

Andrea nodded. "Right?"

Clay didn't understand it, but at least they were getting along. That was all that mattered to him.

Chapter 25

BIG SURPRISE

Two weeks later, Clay and Andrea landed at LaGuardia Airport in New York City. Clay had managed to get the weekend off and had this whole vacation planned out.

After the wedding weekend, he and Andrea had been on good terms. It wasn't exactly like everything was suddenly all better. They weren't living together again. She stayed at her apartment. He stayed at his townhouse. Their house in the suburbs was basically abandoned. He hated her absence when he didn't get to see her, and even more so because they'd had endless sex the wedding weekend and that had since come to a standstill.

She had been more selective of her time and body with him since coming home and returning to reality. He didn't like it. He had every intention of changing her mind. At least, that was the plan this weekend.

They spent the better part of the next two days relearning how to be a couple. In so many ways, it felt the same as it always had. They had always been good together. They'd traveled together so often that it was easy to slip into a simple routine. But still, it was as if Clay had this awareness of her that he couldn't even explain.

He'd reach out his hands to keep people from drawing near her. He'd open car doors for her, pulling her in for kisses before letting her sit down. They'd enjoy wine and whiskey together—not to numb the pain, but to remember the taste with the other. In some ways, it was just incredible, being with her and remembering all the things about her that he'd fallen in love with in the first place.

They'd just left the Metropolitan Museum of Art after spending several hours observing the paintings. A display had recently come in from The Louvre, and they'd spent so much time in there, discussing the pieces that Andrea adored. She'd been an art history major at Yale, much to her father's chagrin—not that she had ever needed his approval for anything.

He'd made a reservation at Tavern on the Green, a historical Central Park fixture, so after the museum, they sat outside under the Chinese lanterns in the gardens, enjoying a decadent dinner and polishing off their second bottle of wine. An excellent vintage.

His head felt as light as the clouds, and a lazy smile rested upon his face. Andrea looked quite as relaxed as he felt. All in all, he thought the evening had been a success. And it wasn't over yet.

Clay paid the tab and then took Andrea's arm.

"A walk through the park?" she asked when he drew her away from the open cul-de-sac where the cab had dropped them off at the restaurant. "Isn't it a bit too late for that?"

"Indeed."

He kissed her hand but kept walking away from the restaurant. She didn't protest, even in the mile-high heels she always wore. He was looking forward to fucking her in just the heels later tonight.

Her mouth opened slightly in surprise when she saw the horse-drawn carriage waiting for them. Her eyes glittered. "For us?"

"Anything for you."

"This is…romantic, Clay."

He chuckled. "You seem surprised. I told you I wanted this to be about us."

"You did," she whispered, as if finally realizing it.

Clay helped her into the carriage and then sat down next to her. He wrapped one arm around her shoulders and then laced their fingers together. She nuzzled into him as they set off to trot around the park at twilight.

"Clay…" she said after a few minutes of silence.

"Mmhmm?"

"This thing with us…it's real?"

"Very."

"And…we're starting over?" she murmured.

"I don't want to start over. Starting over means we forget everything we went through to get to where we are, and I won't do that. We had an unconventional relationship for a long time, and it worked for us."

She tensed under him.

"But that doesn't mean we didn't have a relationship at all. You were always important to me and always my girlfriend. It just took our unconventional relationship not working anymore to really show me how much you mean to me."

"So…we're *not* unconventional anymore?"

"Does this look unconventional to you?" he asked, sweeping his hand out at the park before them.

"No," she said. "I just mean…there aren't any other girls?" Her eyes widened hesitantly, as if she hated asking it and hated even more how much she feared his answer.

Truly, he just couldn't believe that she didn't believe him. He stared at her in surprise and bewilderment. Of course, it made sense for her to question him. She probably wanted it all in writing. And he'd be happy to put it on paper for her.

But his hesitancy was a bad idea. She seemed to have misread where his thoughts had drifted.

"I see…so not that different," she said, dejected.

"No." He grasped her chin and made her look up at him again. "There is no one else for *either* of us."

"You sure about that? You didn't seem so sure."

"I'm sure. I just couldn't fathom how I'd want anyone else."

"Well, you wanted someone else all the time before. So, why is now different?" She straightened. "Why should I believe that it's not going to be a game or a revolving door of women like it was before?"

He blew out harshly and ran a hand back through his hair. "I can tell you over and over that it's just you and that I don't want to be with anyone else, but you won't believe me until you realize it's not happening. I haven't been with another woman in months. I stopped sleeping around when I realized that sex wasn't enough."

Her mouth popped open, and she quickly tried to hide it. "What do you mean?"

"I mean…what I want is you. I don't miss the nameless sex. I want the connection that I have with you, and I am no longer satisfied without it." He brushed her hair off her face and dragged her closer to him once more. "I don't want what we had before. I want more. I want you."

"You figured all of that out in a few months?" she asked breathlessly.

"Yes. Didn't you? You started dating Bad Suit looking for a relationship. The relationship you wanted with me. Have you been satisfied without that connection?"

She shook her head. "No, but I didn't go looking for it between someone else's legs."

Clay rasped a frustrated sigh. "No, you didn't have to. You already *had* before we broke up. Come off of your high horse, Andrea. Our relationship spun out of control partly because of your actions. You left me that night, breaking the rules."

"As if you ever cared for the rules," she said, crossing her arms.

"You know I did."

"God," she groaned. She leaned forward and braced her elbows on her knees, covering her face with her hands. "I don't want to argue about this. I'm ruining the perfect weekend."

"You're not ruining our weekend." He rubbed gentle circles into her back. "We have issues. We're going to need to talk about them at some point."

She peeked up at him through watery eyes. "The day I saw you in the hospital, I wanted to die. You brushed it off so easily that I'd had nothing to do with it, but I completely blamed myself. I shouldn't have left with Asher. I shouldn't have been doing any of that shit I was doing, but I was scared that you'd freak out…that we'd shatter. I should have just talked to you."

"Hey," he said, pulling her back into his arms. "First, you know that wasn't your fault. No need to keep beating yourself up about ancient history. Second, you could have talked to me about what you wanted until you were blue in the face, and I wouldn't have listened. In one ear, out the other. As much as I hated the time apart, we needed that to recover and to figure out what we wanted. I was and am a total ass." He chuckled. "That hasn't changed. I just decided I couldn't be me without you."

Tears glistened in her eyes, and she nodded. "I love you."

"I love you, too."

The carriage dropped them off in front of the Plaza hotel where Clay had booked one of their more extravagant suites. He helped Andrea out of the carriage and held her all the way upstairs. He knew they had more to talk about, but it would happen over time. He never expected everything to resolved overnight.

They took a private elevator to their suite and entered the incredible space. The decor looked as if they had just stepped into the royal court of

Louis XV with gilded frames, chic furniture, a grand piano, and crystal chandeliers. It had a state-of-the-art kitchen and a dining room to seat a dozen.

There were three-bedrooms and three-bath including a library with hand-selected books, an en suite gym, cherry-red wood office, and a white marble bathroom with a two-person walk-in shower and Jacuzzi tub. But the master suite was stunning with a walk-in closet big enough to hold Andrea's clothes back home and a massive bed that they'd already spent a considerable amount of time in.

Clay took her hand and pulled her toward the balcony. His favorite part. Before them was the most coveted view of Fifth Avenue and Central Park. He could even see the famous Pulitzer Fountain from where he stood. It was one of the most expensive views in the city.

Clay wrapped his arms around her waist and rested his chin on the top of her head. She leaned back into him. Their earlier conversation forgotten in the moment.

"You didn't have to do all of this," Andrea admitted.

"Yeah, I did."

"The Maxwells and their big gestures."

"It's not just that. Though…it is that," he amended carefully. "I just wanted it to be real for you. I wanted us to be real to you."

She sighed. "It's always been real for me, Clay." She turned around and faced him, wrapping her arms around his neck. "I wasn't pretending to enjoy your company. I wasn't pretending to love your family. I wasn't pretending to love you."

"I wasn't pretending any of those things either. Well, except for your family."

She wrinkled her nose. "You know what I mean."

"I do. I just want to make things right by you, Andrea." He bent down, so his lips were nearly brushing hers. "I want to make you remember all the good times and forget all the times we fucked up."

His tongue darted out and traced a line across her full bottom lip. She shivered in his arms.

"But our ten-year relationship is just the foundation to the building I plan to raise."

He pulled her flush against him now and let his lips fall down onto hers. She didn't resist. Not one bit. Her fingers tangled up through his dark blond hair as he tasted her sweet lips.

They had kissed since the wedding, but it was nothing like this. She hadn't been this open or vulnerable. She certainly hadn't been needy or demanding with her kisses, like she was rushing toward now. And he didn't mind in the least.

Her hand slid down the front of his shorts, and he stiffened under her eager touch.

"Fuck, woman." Clay reached out and roughly grabbed her shoulders. "I'm trying to be all romantic here, and you're making me want to just fuck you into next Tuesday."

"At this point, I wouldn't mind either," she said, her voice breathy and seductive.

Fuck. Fuck. Fuck.

He'd brought her here to seduce her, but somehow, the tables had turned, and she was fucking seducing him. It was hot as fucking hell.

Her hands went to work, unbuttoning his pants and sliding them to his ankles. Then she pointed to the chair overlooking the park.

"Sit."

He obeyed and, without preamble, she climbed on top of him. She settled herself against his cock and then sheathed herself around him. He wrapped his arms around her waist, bringing her closer.

"You're perfect for me."

She smirked lazily as she started riding him. "And don't forget it."

Chapter 26
FIX IT

The next few weeks, Clay was intensely overworked.

He'd barely had time to breathe, let alone see Andrea. He'd almost forgotten what it felt like to be this overworked and not enjoy it. He wanted to be working a nine-to-five, getting off and heading over to Andrea's to spend time with her. Instead, he was lucky if he could leave by midnight.

Andrea seemed understanding, but he worried that his past actions would be his downfall. Would he ever be able to escape that look in her eyes, the one that showed that he might be doing something wrong? Wondering if he was he at the office late for some other reason?

She never said those things. But it was like he could see her hesitancy.

Before, they had never had any of this doubt because they'd had an understanding. Now, she was suspicious because, without the understanding, she had nothing to guard her heart with. He would see it all over her face when he came over to her place at night.

It was almost the end of July when he finally left court at a semi-decent time and realized quite unexpectedly that he had the rest of the evening to himself. He drove to Andrea's gallery, parked in the back lot, next to her Mercedes, and then he took the stairs to the back door. He entered her office. It was immaculate. Basically, the opposite of his space—all soft, floral, and girlie but still modern and chic. It had Andrea written all over it.

"Hey," she said, coming out of the door that led to the gallery space. "What are you doing here?"

She was smoothing out her navy pencil skirt when she entered, but all he could focus on was the white V-neck shirt she had tucked into it. She must have been wearing one killer push-up bra because her tits looked amazing.

She snapped her fingers at his face.

He blinked and then grinned. "I came for a tour."

She shut the door in his face. "You can have one when it's open."

He grabbed her around the middle and planted his lips on her. "How about now?"

"Nope."

He sucked on her bottom lip, dragging it into his mouth. His hands slid to her ass. "How about now?"

"How about…the night I open?"

"I'll see it first?" His lips went across her cheek and ever so slowly down her neck.

"Mm…hmm."

"Okay," he said, abruptly pulling away and leaving her standing there with her mouth slightly open, looking dazed. He smacked her ass. "I'm taking you out. Let's get going."

"You're trouble, Clay Maxwell," she growled.

"That I am."

He grabbed her hand, and then they walked back out to his Porsche. He held the door open for her, and she slipped into the passenger's side. Then, he jogged back to his side, sat down, and revved the engine.

"Where are we going?" she asked.

"You'll see. Have you decided when you're opening?" he asked, deftly changing the conversation, as he drove them away from the gallery.

"Labor Day weekend."

"So soon? That's only a month away."

"I know. But I think I have everything I need. I hired an event planner for the occasion, and we just have to make it happen."

"You will. I know it."

He pulled off the main road, wove through a few back neighborhoods, and then stopped in front of a historic brick townhouse.

"What's this?" Andrea asked.

"Just something I'm looking into. I thought, since I finally had some time off, I could take you with me to come look at it."

"You're thinking of moving?" she asked. Andrea cautiously exited the car.

"Something like that," he muttered.

She stilled. She had a half-smile on her face, but there was clearly something wrong. "What? Looking for a new bachelor pad?"

The joke was there, but it was riddled with underlying truth. "Why don't you take a look inside?"

"What's wrong with your other place?"

"Besides the fact that you won't step foot in it?" he countered, walking around the car to her.

And she hadn't. Not one foot. He'd even gotten new sheets. Not that she seemed to care. She hadn't been there since she had stormed out on him the night Gigi had come downstairs.

"I…would. You haven't asked."

"You would, but you wouldn't like to," he corrected her.

"There are a lot of memories there," she said. "Not all of them are that pleasant."

"Like Gigi coming down the stairs?"

She closed her eyes and blew out through her nose. "Like Gigi coming downstairs."

"Are you ever going to forgive me for that?"

She opened her eyes and answered, "I do. I do forgive you for that. I know nothing happened, but it's hard, Clay. It's hard when we had ten years of a relationship that was based on an understanding…not trust. I want to trust you. I want to go back to your place. I want to accept Gigi as your friend. I just…I'm not entirely there yet."

"Okay," he said, not pushing her. "Well, maybe this will help. Maybe if we have a place without memories, it'll help."

"You're probably right. I'm just letting my own insecurities rule me. I'm working on it."

He kissed the tip of her nose. "It's okay. We'll figure it out. Can I show you the place now?"

She nodded. "Please."

Clay punched in the code that the real estate agent had given him into the lockbox. The key dropped out of the bottom, and he let them both in.

Andrea walked in first to the partially furnished townhouse. The agency liked to put enough furniture into the space so that people could get a realistic view of what it looked like. Or at least that was what the realtor had told him when he asked.

"Hmm," Andrea said. She turned in a circle in the foyer and looked three stories up to where a skylight cast afternoon light into the room.

"Well, what do you think?" he asked, closing the door behind him. "Give me the rundown."

"All right," she agreed.

Then she started telling him everything she liked about the space starting in the living room, moving to the dining room and then the kitchen. Her eyes lit up.

"Wow," she breathed.

"You like it?" he asked, following her inside.

"Like it? No. I love it." In awe, she ran her hand across the granite countertops and to the large center island. Her eyes flickered up to his, and then she bent forward at the waist. His eyes landed on the ample amount of breasts spilling out of her top and then to her ass that was perfectly level with the counter.

"Good, sturdy island. Good size. Good height."

"Fuck," he breathed. He strode toward her and grabbed her hips. Yeah, perfect fucking height. He was definitely going to have to break this in.

She straightened, sliding her ass against his dick, and he just gripped her tighter. *Fucking hell.* He wasn't going to get through the rest of the tour.

She giggled and then started toward the stairs, leaving him alone and horny.

Goddamn it. He loved this woman and all her torture.

He followed her all the way up to the top of the steps. She skipped the second floor and went straight to the third.

"Most important things first," she told him over her shoulder.

Then, he followed her into the large master bedroom, which she observed with little interest. Then, she strode right on into the walk-in closet, just like he'd known she would. It was huge, and by her gasp when she entered, he was pretty sure she hadn't seen anything like it, except for in one of those *Sex in the City* movies.

"What the hell would you need all this space for?" she asked, looking around, her eyes as wide as saucers. "Your suits will only take up this much space."

Clay shrugged, his eyes alight with mischief. "Always room to grow."

She furrowed her brows and then strode out of the room and scrambled down the stairs to the second floor. There were two bedrooms and a third room, which was clearly meant to be an office. It had a large bay window with a window seat.

Her lips trembled slightly for a second, and then she gave her opinion of the room. "You'd put in built-in shelves for your law books, of course.

A mahogany desk about yea high," she said, gesturing to just above her hip.

She turned to face him, and he could see she was wary. Very wary. Confused and excited and cautious. She couldn't seem to decide what to do with her hands, but she didn't break his stare.

"I had other plans for this room."

"Oh?" she whispered.

"This room has the best view and the best light." She swallowed hard as he approached her. "I thought it should be your studio."

Andrea stilled entirely. "What?"

"The walls are empty. I want you to fill them. I know you love painting just as much as you love collecting even if you pretend like you have no interest," he told her. "You'd put your easel there." He pointed at a corner. "The light reflects there best in the morning, which is when you'd work. I'd bring in a long table to fill some of the space and a settee for you to work on when you can't sit at a stool any longer."

Tears brimmed in her eyes. "How did you know?" she whispered.

"Because I know you. I know every little thing about you, and I love you for it all. I'd love you if you never once let me see your paintings. If you kept them hidden away in that spare room in your apartment. Locked away and contained, like you've always treated the rest of your life, Andrea. I'd even put a lock on this door for your privacy. I know you, love. You must realize this by now."

She nodded softly but didn't say anything. She seemed struck with awe.

"Move in with me," he said softly.

"What?" she asked.

"Move in with me, Andrea."

"You're serious?" Her mouth was hanging open. She seemed shocked that this was what he wanted.

"I've never been more serious. You said that I needed to prove that this was what I wanted. Well, this is what I want." He gestured around the space. "I don't need another woman in my life. I don't want you second-guessing our relationship. I don't want you worried about anything. I just want us together."

"You don't…you don't think this is too soon?" she asked.

"Maybe it is," he said with an easy shrug. "Maybe we're moving too fast, but we spent so much time at a standstill that I don't want to do it anymore."

A tear slipped down her cheek, and a smile spread across her face. "So, this really isn't a new bachelor pad for you?" she joked through a hiccup.

"No, it's really not," he told her with a kiss to her stunned lips. "Move in with me. I want to come home from a long day at work to find you sprawled in our bed. I want to wake up every morning with your body curled around me. I want us to share a space, as I have shared my life with you. I want you here. With me. Always."

"Clay," she gasped. "I…I can't believe this is happening."

"Believe it. I want to get rid of our apartments and sell the house." He drew her even closer. "Make new memories, happy memories, here with me."

"Okay," she said finally as if she had finally realized that he was completely serious.

"Is that a yes?" he joked.

She stretched up onto her tiptoes and kissed him full on the mouth. "Yes, I'll move in with you. There's nothing else I want more in the world. Let's do it."

Chapter 27
THE ISLAND

"No! No! Be careful with that!" Andrea shrieked. "Do you know how much that cost? I'll sue you for everything you're worth if you drop that."

The mover stared at her, as if she were insane. Clay just chuckled. Andrea was a little obsessive when it came to moving.

"Now, put it over there." She flung her hand to the side and pointed at the wall. "And hang it *neatly*, please."

The guy trudged into the room, and Clay followed him as Andrea flounced back out to harass the rest of the movers.

"Hey, man, sorry about that. She's just really particular," Clay said after the man had settled the artwork down on the floor, as if it were the most precious thing he'd ever held.

"No offense, but your wife is a little crazy," the guy said.

Clay smiled and didn't correct him. "That she is. But we all love them that way, don't we?"

The mover shrugged and nodded. "Sure. Makes them good in bed."

Clay pulled out a hundred-dollar bill and passed it to the man. "Just do whatever she says."

"Sure thing. Priceless artwork hanging on the wall—*neatly*."

"Thanks, man."

When Andrea set her mind to something, everything had to be done exactly the way she wanted. He'd known as soon as she had agreed to move into their new place together that the move-in job was going to be one hell of a ride. She couldn't even go to sleep unless all of her artwork was unpacked and hanging on the walls.

It didn't help matters that she'd decided they needed to move in within the week. Nor did it help that he'd been so swamped at work that he couldn't be there to pack. She'd hired someone to do most of the work, of course, but she also didn't trust anyone with half of the things in her house, so she'd stormed around in a rampage, making sure people were properly storing everything in sight.

Most people would find it annoying.

He found it adorable.

They spent the better part of the day arranging, rearranging, and unpacking. It was grueling but worth it. When he surveyed the place at the end of the long day, he saw how it had transformed from a house to a home before his eyes.

"What do you think?" he asked.

Andrea was coming down the stairs in nothing but a pair of skintight workout shorts and a tank top with the hem tied under her tits. Her hair was in a messy bun at the top of her head with wisps floating all around her face. At that moment, he'd do anything to get his hands on her.

"It's a work in progress." She stopped at the foot of the stairs. "But it's ours."

"Very fitting then. I'd say we're a work in progress." He reached out and pulled her into his arms.

"Ugh! I'm so sweaty and grimy." She tried to wrestle away, but he just lowered his lips to the crook of her neck and licked up her skin. She shivered in his arms, and he watched her pupils dilate with desire.

"Perfect then."

"You're ridiculous. We should go shower."

"Oh, we will." He gave her a mischievous look. "After we christen that kitchen island you've been teasing me with all week."

She arched an eyebrow, but he didn't wait for her to respond. He hoisted her up into his arms and carried her into their kitchen. *Their* kitchen. He deposited her on her ass onto the kitchen island. *Their* kitchen island. His fingers brushed across her knees, spreading her legs open as far as they'd go.

"I hate to break it to you, lover," she whispered, her voice breathy, "but I'm actually wearing something under this."

"Well, I'll just have to fix that, won't I?"

She grabbed him by the collar of his T-shirt and yanked him toward her. She'd been right. The island *was* the perfect height. He pressed himself hard up against the front of her shorts and was rewarded with a moan of pleasure from Andrea. He pushed her back flat against the kitchen island and then buried his face into her thin workout shorts. He breathed heavily against the material until she was squirming against his face.

"We're going to need to get rid of these."

"Definitely."

She hopped off the counter and removed all her clothes at once. Then, without warning, she grabbed his shorts and dropped to her knees, dragging his shorts to his ankles. Her hand grasped his dick, and he had to reach forward to hold on to the counter as she massaged him up and down.

Her tongue licked around the head of his cock, and he closed his eyes to keep from coming all over her face. She lavished his cock, wetting the entire head, before popping it into her mouth and playing with it, as if it were a Popsicle. His jaw clenched as he strained for control.

Fuck, she was going to work him so hard that he wouldn't be able to get her off.

He needed to hold out.

FUCK!

She rocked forward toward him and got half of his dick in her mouth before sucking backward to the tip. Then, she pushed forward again. He knew she had an almighty gag reflex, and he didn't want to push her, but, fuck, did he thrust his dick further into her mouth the next time she took more of him in.

Her fingers dug into his thighs, and it took all his strength not to grab her head and bottom out in her mouth. He let her do the guiding even though it was sweet, blissful torture. She drew back and forth, in and out, until he thought he might fall apart at her ministrations. His cock was thickening, lengthening still. He could feel the veins throbbing as he fought not to come yet.

Fucking hell, the woman could she suck a dick.

She didn't do it often, but, damn, when she did, he was a goner.

"Andrea," he growled, "I'm going to come all down your throat if you don't stop, baby."

She didn't stop.

"Baby," he moaned, fisting her hair. "Baby…I need to fuck you."

She looked up at him with those big blue eyes, and he had to really tense up not to pop out and come all over her face.

Clay pulled out of her mouth, lifted her up off the ground with ease, and then bent her over, ass up on the counter. Her pussy was pink and gleaming at him, totally exposed in that moment. He ran his fingers through the wetness just once before prodding her opening with his dick and ramming forward into her.

He knew he had zero chance of lasting long, so he needed to make this good for her. He slammed into her brutally, unrelenting. His balls smacked against her clit as he pushed all the way inside her. He could already feel his release threatening to take him, but he needed her to come with him.

"You close?" he asked.

She moaned loudly. He pounded inside her a few more times, grabbed her hips hard enough to leave indents, and then came like a torrent inside her body.

She let out a piercing scream as he felt her walls contract all around him. Her body shook. Her legs gave out, and he had to hold her up to keep her from falling over.

"Damn," she murmured, resting her cheek against the cold counter. "What a way to break the house in."

"We're not done yet," he told her.

She laughed as he pulled out of her. "We still have a lot of rooms to break in," she agreed.

"We do."

"Shower first?" she suggested.

"Mmm…wet and naked. I approve."

"I have an idea," she said a few minutes later while under the hot stream in the shower.

"I like ideas."

He ran his hands up and down her body, unable to believe that all of this belonged to him. That he had earned her back. That this was his reality. He'd thought Brady was the luckiest son of a bitch alive. Now, he was pretty sure that title went to him.

"How about a housewarming party?"

His lips found hers once more as he slipped his fingers between her legs and pressed her back into the shower wall. "Anything you want."

~

Clay could tell right away that Andrea was completely in her element as a hostess for their housewarming party and that she was also scared as hell about what was about to happen.

"It's going to be fine," he told her again.

He ran his hands up and down her bare arms. She was in a sleeveless, short floral dress and heels that kept clicking all over the hardwood floor as she paced.

"I know. I know. I just…"

"It's okay. You want to make a good impression, but…these are our friends and family. It's not going to be any different."

She nodded. "It's just…it's the first time we're doing something like this and as a couple."

"We've been doing things together as a couple for years. The only people who know that it's different this time are you and me. The only people's opinions who matter here are you and me."

She straightened her back and nodded. "I know. I don't know why I'm nervous. Silly, really."

He smiled at her just as the doorbell rang.

"I'll get it," she squeaked, rushing to the door.

Brady and Liz entered the room, and then there was a chorus of cries from the girls.

Liz pulled her into a hug and squeezed her tight. "Ahh!" she yelled again, bouncing up and down on her own high heels. "This is so awesome."

Andrea laughed and then tried to wriggle out of Liz's embrace. "Thank you. Y'all come in. Come in."

Once Brady and Liz were inside the foyer, Andrea shut the door behind them and teetered back and forth in anticipation. "What do you think?" she asked.

"It's beautiful!" Liz gushed. "Oh my God, show me everything!"

And then they dashed away for Andrea to give Liz a tour.

Clay just shoved his hands into the pockets of his shorts and rocked back on his heels. "At least the squealing is gone," he said to his brother. "Drink?"

Brady put his finger in his ear, as if he were trying to hear again. "Absolutely."

Clay led him into the dining room where he had a full wet bar set up on an antique cabinet Andrea had insisted they purchase for the room. He poured out some scotch for both of them and handed off one crystal tumbler to Brady. They each took a swig from their glasses.

Then, Brady extended his hand to Clay.

For a moment, Clay looked at it in surprise and then shook Brady's hand.

"Congratulations," Brady said honestly. "I'm proud of you."

"I…well…thanks."

"I know what it means for the both of you to be here right now and how hard it's been for you the last few months. Wish I could have been around more."

"Yeah, well, I doubt I would have come to this conclusion without your help," Clay admitted.

It was strange really, to have this heart-to-heart with Brady. The one person he'd always envied…always despised…and always looked up to. His emotions about Brady had always been so unclear. Like looking into lake water to try to find the bottom. Murky and diluted with darkness. Yet things had cleared up between them. Gradually, over time, he had stopped hating Brady, stopped envying him, and just let the past go.

"Look," Brady said, scratching the back of his head, "that stuff you said at the wedding during your speech. We haven't really had a chance to talk since then. You didn't really mean that you thought you'd been living in my shadow, did you?"

Clay scoffed and shook his head. "It was hard, being your younger brother, Brady. I meant every word, but I'm cool with it now. You do your thing, trying to take over the world or save it or whatever. I'll do mine."

"From what I hear…you're doing some good yourself," Brady said.

"Where I can," he said honestly, thinking of the side projects he'd been working on with Gigi.

"That's the Maxwell way."

"What are you boys getting on about in here?" Liz asked, coming down the stairs again just as the doorbell rang.

"Nothing, honey," Brady said.

Andrea rushed to open it as Liz joined them. Chris walked through the front door, and Brady walked over to greet his best friend.

"*Nothing, honey*," Liz repeated with a roll of her eyes. "Why do I feel like you're up to something?"

"Because we usually are," Clay said with a wink.

Liz poured herself a drink from one of the bottles on the table and took a sip before eyeing him carefully. "I do have one thing to say about all of this."

"And that is?"

"Maybe you're not as big of an idiot as I thought you were."

He sputtered and laughed. "That right?"

"I mean, I know you're an idiot but maybe not *as* big as before."

"Oh, I'm as big as before."

She rolled her eyes again. "You know what they say about the ones who brag about it."

"Last I checked, you knew firsthand."

"You're a scoundrel," she said with a laugh.

He touched her shoulder and stared into her baby-blue eyes. "It would have never worked out with us, love."

She rolled her eyes again.

"I know you're still beating yourself up about it."

"Oh, yeah, totally," she said sarcastically. "Those three weeks in Bora Bora…really upset."

"I'll always be the one who got away."

"Obviously," she said with a giggle. "Now, tell me everything about how this happened."

So, Clay launched into the story with Liz as his house slowly filled up. At some point, Gigi, Ethan, and Cash all showed up and stopped in to say hi. Andrea actually pulled Gigi aside to give her a tour. Gigi looked frightened as shit but went regardless. She was still wary of Andrea after the two times she'd thought she'd fucked things up for them. Clay just hoped Andrea would push Gigi in Chris's direction now that he had moved to D.C. Andrea's friend Jamie showed up with her husband, and she and Liz traipsed off to discuss the artwork all over the house. And then a bunch of Clay's coworkers at Cooper & Neilson and people Andrea knew through her art business all filled the space.

Andrea looked way more relaxed now that everyone was here than when they'd first started arriving. She was mingling in the living room with a group of her coworkers whom she'd introduced to him, and he left her to it. He wandered into the kitchen and over to Ethan and Cash. He hadn't had much time to see them lately…not since he hadn't been boozing it up like before.

"Hey, guys. Glad you could make it," Clay said, shaking hands with first Ethan and then Cash.

Ethan held up his beer. "Wouldn't have missed it."

"Yeah. Never thought we'd see the day when Andrea actually pussy-whipped you quite this bad," Cash said.

"He has a point," Ethan said with a laugh.

Clay went still. Rage filled him from head to toe. He'd always gotten along with the guys. They'd had their differences, and he'd grown tired of them over the last couple of months, but he couldn't handle this shit any longer. They'd always talked shit about Andrea before, and he just couldn't allow that anymore.

"It was *my* idea to move in together actually," Clay said. His tone was dangerous and filled with warning.

Ethan seemed to get the message, but Cash had always been an idiot.

"Man, she even has *you* convinced that you want this shit. That old ball and chain. Hope you're still fucking some hot pussy on the side." Cash took a huge swig of his beer.

It took everything in Clay not to punch Cash in the face. It had been a while since this anger had filled him so completely, but he wasn't going to brutalize his own friend.

"Don't fucking talk like that in my goddamn house," Clay growled.

"What the fuck, man?" Cash asked.

Ethan smacked his arm. "Dude, I think he's serious."

"Yeah, I'm fucking serious."

"Aw, come on," Cash said with a laugh. "I am just joking. Weren't we just joking, Ethan?"

"No, you weren't," Clay said. "And you're not going to joke about Andrea anymore. I'm putting my foot down. You have *always* treated her like shit and talked shit about her, and I will no longer fucking tolerate it. You don't know the woman that she's become. You clearly don't know shit," he said darkly. "So, fucking think before you talk like that again about my girl. If it's you or her, I'm choosing her. Every time. So, get fucking used to it."

"Hey, I'm sorry," Ethan said quickly. "I hope you don't think we're serious about Andrea. We always knew she was your girl. Just…thought things were back to the way they were."

"Well, they aren't."

"Don't get all uptight about it, Clay," Cash said quickly. He seemed to have realized that he'd actually gone too far. That was a real feat. "We get it. You're a one-woman man now. We'll back off."

"Good."

Clay took a deep breath and then reached his hand out to his friends. They each shook his hand again, and then the conversation shifted to the law jobs that Ethan and Cash had at the same firm uptown. It was easy to fall back into that conversation with them, but he was glad he'd laid down the law. Things had changed, and they needed to know talking about Andrea that way wouldn't be tolerated, but he didn't exactly want to give up his friends. They were idiots, but they were *his* idiot friends. Every group had at least one.

The night slipped away, and soon, their party guests were saying good night and congratulations. As people filed back out of the house, Andrea and Clay each hugged and shook hands with them.

Gigi squeezed him extra tight and said into his ear, "That wasn't half bad. I'm really glad you're happy."

"Thanks, Gi." He released her. "So…how about you and Chris?"

"And, suddenly, I hate you again."

He laughed. "So, there's hope."

"I'm not going to talk about this with you. He and I are just friends, all right?"

"'Just friends,'" Clay repeated, using air quotes. "I bet."

She punched him roughly on the arm. "Stay out of it, Maxwell."

"Can't do that, De Rosa."

"Good night," she said firmly before following the other guests out.

Andrea finally closed the door and leaned back against it with a sigh. She closed her eyes. "That was great."

"A lot of fun," he agreed.

"No…"

"No?" he asked, confused.

She opened her eyes and looked at him, fiercely, possessively. "The way you spoke to Ethan and Cash."

"What? You heard that?"

"Yeah. I kind of accidentally stumbled into you telling them off."

"Well, I just…" He scratched the back of his head. He hadn't known he'd had an audience. "I wanted them to know that you were the most important thing in my life. They couldn't talk shit about you anymore. That you were it for me."

She smiled, like the sun filling the room. "You have no idea how much that means to me. I've dreaded their presence all week."

"Why didn't you tell me?" He closed the distance between them and ran his hands up and down her arms.

"They're your friends," she said simply.

"They are, but they won't be if they can't respect you."

"I was just worried. That's all. I know how they influence you. I know what's happened with them in the past." She dragged her lip between her teeth. "I was just…worried."

"Well, no more worries any longer," he told her simply.

"None at all," she agreed. "Things are different now."

She ran her hands up his shirt and brought his lips down to meet hers. The kiss was sweet and filled with promises of a bright future, hope-filled days ahead, and all of her dreams come true.

Chapter 28

ALL ABOUT YOU

Clay stepped out of the enormous waterfall shower. Steam filled the bathroom so densely that he could barely see the mirror across the room. He reached for a plush white towel and wrapped it around his waist. After a long day at the office, he'd been dying to come home and wash the day off. Plus, Andrea had her art gallery opening this evening, and he wanted to be presentable by the time she got home.

Just then the door to the bathroom burst open, releasing the steam.

"Oh!" Andrea squeaked. "Shit."

"Hey, I didn't think you'd be home already."

"I didn't think you'd be…" She trailed off as the steam cleared, and she got a good look at him.

"Yes?"

"Whoa," she breathed. "You look sexy as fuck."

He laughed and ran a hand back through his wet hair. "Thanks, babe."

"No, seriously." She entered the bathroom and then ran her nails down his chest and over the washboard abs. "You're fucking delectable."

He reached for her hips and dragged her closer. "In that case, if you're hungry…"

She wet her lips. "Always, around you."

"Well, I can arrange for you to be well fed."

She groaned. "As much as I want you to fuck me right here and now," she said, taking a tender step backward, "this steam is killing my hair for the opening."

Clay laughed and smacked her ass as she hurried out of the bathroom. He changed into the requisite tuxedo for the evening, and Andrea reappeared from their closet in a red dress with tiny straps and a narrow slit down the middle to her navel. She paired it with shimmery gold heels.

Andrea had arranged a driver for the evening so that they could enjoy themselves without having to worry about getting home. Especially if they wanted to stay after and celebrate what he knew would be an incredible success for her.

She threaded her fingers together and then apart, back and forth.

He reached out and took her hand. "You're going to be wonderful tonight. You don't have a thing to worry about."

"You're right." She sounded hollow.

"Look at me," he told her.

She turned her face back toward him.

He tilted her chin so that she looked up into his eyes, and he smiled. "We're together, and nothing can stand between us when we're together. This is just another gallery opening. You blew the other ones out of the water. You have *nothing* to worry about."

"Okay," she whispered.

He leaned down and kissed her lips. "Nothing," he repeated.

"I'll just be better when it's over."

"I know. You worry too much. I'm just ready to finally get to see this gallery of yours."

A real smile cracked her lips. "I hope it meets your expectations."

He smirked. "I have faith that it will exceed them."

The driver pulled up in front of her gallery, and Andrea once again let them in through her back office door.

She took a deep breath with her hand on the door to the studio and looked up at him with eyes full of hope. "Ready?"

"Very." He could hardly control his excitement as he waited for her to show him around.

She pulled the door open, reached inside, and flicked on the lights. Then, she gasped. Standing in the center of the large gallery room was a painting on an easel, covered with a white cloth.

"What the hell is this?" she asked. "Sorry, Clay. This isn't…this isn't how I wanted you to see it. I don't know who put that there." She blew out a frustrated breath. "I cannot believe I left people here when I went home to change. When I find out who did this, it's going to be their head."

Clay laughed. "Andrea, it's fine. It's just one piece of artwork."

"It's not just one piece of artwork! I've been working on the arrangement for weeks. Everything was in order. Now, *this*."

"We can move it. It's all right," he reassured her.

She sighed. "Fine. Let's figure out where it belongs before I have a fit and start throwing things."

Her heels clicked against the hardwood floor as she raced across the room. He was right behind her with his hands behind his back and a huge grin on his face. She yanked on the sheet, and as it fell away, she gasped even louder than before. Her hands flew to her mouth, and she seemed to be stuck in place.

"Clay…" she murmured.

"Surprise!"

"You couldn't have," she said, staring up at the painting of the woman looking out the rain-splattered window with tears running down her face. The very painting Andrea had been obsessed with for so long and had sold for over half a million dollars—his entire year's salary.

"Oh, but I could."

Tears welled in her eyes as they turned to face him. "How?"

"Does it matter how? Just know that I got it back for you."

"It absolutely matters how. I mean…this painting…this…" She couldn't seem to speak. "It was highly sought after. I know who I sold it to. I know what he was willing to spend to get it. He *never* would have sold it back to you."

He grinned. "Well, that's obviously not true, is it?"

"How?" she repeated.

So, Clay launched into the story. "It took a hell of a lot of backroom dealings to even freaking figure out who you'd sold it to. I didn't want to invade your privacy, so I didn't go through your things. But I eventually found out who you'd sold it to and confronted the couple who had purchased it. They point-blank refused to sell it back to me, no matter my sob story."

Andrea chuckled. "I bet they did."

He took a deep breath. This was the part he wasn't fond of. "So…I went to Asher."

"You did what?" she stammered.

"Well, he seemed to know the art industry, like you do here. I had to use all my resources. Let me tell you…he wasn't exactly happy to see me."

"After what happened at Brady's wedding, I'd think not."

"But he ended up helping me."

"Why the hell would he do that?" she demanded.

Clay scratched his head and looked at his feet. "You, Andrea. He hates me, but he still cares for you enough to help me keep you happy."

"Oh, Clay, you didn't have to do that," she whispered.

"Course I did. Anyway, we tracked down an art dealer who was selling another painting that the couple wanted even more than this one. I put the bid in on it and then went back to the couple and offered a trade."

"They didn't…"

"They didn't want to. They offered to buy the piece from me. I told them what they told me…it wasn't for sale. I think I ended up charming them though because here's the painting I wanted, and they have the one they wanted on their fireplace mantel."

Andrea leveled him with a look that he couldn't read at first. It was part, *You're an idiot*, and part, *I'm going to fuck you on the spot*. He was pretty okay with that.

"Well, do you like it?"

She shook her head. "I love it. I cannot believe you right now."

He wrapped his arms around her waist and brought his lips down on hers, slowly and gently. "You make me crazy, Andrea. All I want is for you to be happy. I would do anything to make you happy."

"Can't you see?" she whispered, tears brimming her eyes again. "You make me happy. It's always been you that makes me happy."

"Now, don't mess up your makeup," he joked, clearing his throat. A lump was growing there, the more choked up she got. "You still have a gallery to open."

"Thank you. For this. For everything."

"Thank you for giving us a second chance. I never knew that this was what I wanted all along. But I'm never going to forget it now."

She kissed him then, ceaselessly, drowning out the rest of his words. They stayed like that—flat-out making out—until someone cleared their throat behind them. Apparently, the staff was here and ready to prepare the gallery to be opened.

~

When the gallery officially opened an hour later, Clay was at Andrea's side for the entire thing. He greeted her customers and directed people to the various displays, and overall, he enjoyed her success.

The last art gallery she'd had...was horrible for him. One of his lowest points during their breakup. Now, he was here with her, watching her brilliance close up.

At one point, Asher turned up. He looked anxious about being there, but Clay stuck out his hand. Asher had helped him when he needed it. As long as Asher stayed far away from his girlfriend, then he could move past what had happened. Clay had won after all.

More people he knew filed in. All of their friends and family, who had recently been at their housewarming party. His boss, Ted Cooper, showed up with his wife. And then, just as it was thinning out and it was about time for Andrea to return to the crowd to mingle and wheel and deal...his parents appeared, as if out of thin air.

Andrea smiled brightly. "Mr. and Mrs. Maxwell," she said formally, "I had no idea you'd be in attendance this evening."

Clay's mother went straight up to Andrea and pulled her into a hug. "Andrea, call me Marilyn. We've known you since you were a kid."

Andrea laughed softly. "Of course, Marilyn. You know how I am. It's so good to see you. Are you here for anything in particular?"

"Just to see my son and his very successful girlfriend," Marilyn said with a smile. "Isn't that right, Jeff?" She nudged Clay's father.

"That's right," he said. "Congratulations, darling." He gave Andrea a peck on the cheek and a big politician's smile. "We're both proud of you."

His father reached out his hand, and Clay shook it. He was slightly flabbergasted that his father was here. He knew that they were on the invite list for the opening, but they hadn't said whether or not they would be coming. His parents spent most of the summer in Chapel Hill and away from D.C. if they could at all help it.

"I was glad to hear that you two had finally moved in together," his father said. "None of that separate housing situation."

"It was about time," Andrea said, jumping in.

She knew that he had never really gotten along with his father.

"That's right," Clay said. He wrapped an arm around Andrea's shoulders. "It was about time. Should have done it a long time ago."

"Well, we're just so happy for the both of you. After Brady and Liz's wedding, we hoped you two would settle down next," Marilyn said.

Clay coughed, and Andrea's cheeks heated.

"Don't get ahead of yourself now," Andrea said with a laugh.

"We're just happy to be together again," Clay told him. "Take things as life throws them at us."

"That's the way to do it. You're only young once," Jeff said. "I always knew you were the smartest of all my children."

Clay nearly staggered backward.

What?

His father had never said anything like that to him before. He'd never even hinted that he thought Clay even deserved to stand in Brady's shadow.

Attorney general was as good as it would get for Clay. But no recognition until he was there. Top of his class at Yale. Top of his class at Yale Law. Supreme Court clerking. Best law job in the nation…and still nothing.

Now, all of a sudden, because he seemed to be settling down with Andrea…he was enough.

"Thanks, Dad," he said with genuine surprise.

Andrea squeezed his arm. She knew what this meant to him.

"Can't get to where you are today without brains and a tough work ethic," his father continued. "It's the Maxwell way. You're doing great, son. Both of you."

He smiled at them, and then Marilyn ushered him away to check out the rest of the gallery. Clay was left reeling.

"Are you okay?" Andrea asked.

"I just…I never expected his approval," he admitted.

"You never needed it. You have always been amazing, just the way you are. You walked out of Brady's shadow. Maybe it's time to let go of the things that your father said to you when you were just a kid." She brushed her fingers across his cheek. "You were just a kid."

He nodded. "You're right. It's…it's time to let them go. Focus on what's important. What's right in front of me. And that's my successful girlfriend."

She giggled. "This isn't about me."

"Oh, Andrea"—he swept his hand out to the incredible gallery opening—"this is *all* about you. Just as it should be."

Chapter 29

MY SOUL TO TAKE

"Are you sure you're ready?" Gigi asked.

She was anxiously biting her nails. It was a habit he had been noticing more and more over the last couple of weeks.

He grabbed her hands and forced them still. "Stop biting your nails. You're making *me* anxious."

"Sorry. I just want everything to be right for you."

"It'll be fine. I mean…" He ran a hand back through his hair. "I think it will be fine. Just have everyone there at the right time, and it will all go as planned."

She beamed. "Excellent. I can do that." Then, she launched herself at him and squeezed him tight. "Oh my God, I'm so excited for you."

Clay gingerly patted her shoulder, laughing all the while. "You're so excitable."

"Not every day this sort of thing happens," she said, releasing him. "I mean…once in a lifetime, really."

"Let's hope."

"And she really has no idea? I mean, you told her that we were all going out to celebrate Chris moving to town. Big party and all. She hasn't suspected a thing?"

Clay grinned. "Not a thing. Though…I suppose that's my fault."

His face fell. Tonight was the big night. He was getting all of his friends together. He'd made sure they had the room reserved at Andrea's favorite restaurant. He was going to take her on a moonlit stroll, the whole shebang. And then he was going to pop the question. He could do it.

But, of course…Andrea never would suspect it. Because he had made it so damn clear to her over the years that he never, ever wanted to get married. That wasn't his future. In fact, the mere thought of marriage had made his throat swell up, his hands sweat, and a sudden fever come on. Marriage had felt like a trap. One woman forever. He'd shuddered at the very thought. And Andrea, of all people, knew that. She'd always known that.

No…there was no way she would see tonight coming. Not at all.

"It's not your fault. You've changed," Gigi said at once. "And, anyway, her not knowing is a good thing. Every girl wants to be surprised by a proposal! You're doing the right thing. She'll never guess!"

"Right. The right thing," he muttered.

"Oh my God, do *not* get all freaked out on me now! You have the ring. You have the setup. You have all your friends in place and even a freaking photographer to capture every moment. Clay, all you have to do is ask her."

"Yeah…"

She put her hand on his arm. "And she's going to say yes."

"Well, we'll see tonight, won't we?"

"Yes, we will. Eep! I'm so excited that I get to see it all happen!" she nearly shrieked. "Okay. Go home. Get your girl. I'll see you at the restaurant, and I will have everything in place! Don't worry about a thing."

"Got it. I'll see you soon."

Clay fingered the box in his pocket, opening and closing it obsessively as he walked out to his waiting Porsche. He couldn't believe how much he was freaking out. His stomach was in knots over this. He didn't think she'd say no. *She wouldn't say no. Would she?*

God, stupid insecurities.

He drove back to their place without really even realizing where he was going. But, suddenly, he was parking and walking up the steps. He needed to get his thoughts in order if he was going to get through the next couple of hours without her suspecting anything was up with him. He wanted this to be a total surprise.

Clay unlocked the door and slipped inside. "Andrea?"

"In here," she murmured from another room.

He followed the faint sound of her voice and found her curled up on the back patio with a book open in her lap.

"Hey, babe." He kissed her cheek, pulled off his suit jacket, and started loosening his tie.

"Mmm…hold on. Let me finish this chapter."

Clay laughed. "I've heard that before."

"Just one more," she told him, not looking up.

"All right. Well, I'm going to go change for dinner."

"Oh, right," she said absentmindedly. "Chris's thing is tonight. I'll be up in a minute."

"Okay. Enjoy your chapter."

She made some noise of assent but still didn't look up at him. Whatever she was reading must have been engrossing. Though that was Andrea. All or nothing.

Clay changed into a pair of dress khakis and a thin button-up that he rolled the sleeves up on. He put on brown boat shoes. Then, he added the jewelry box to his pocket. It bulged slightly, and he frowned. He didn't want her guessing what he had in there.

With a sigh, he pulled out a light jacket. The nights were already getting kind of cool, so it wouldn't look too strange. Then, he stuffed the box into his jacket pocket.

Unsurprisingly, Andrea had never appeared to change.

When he walked back downstairs, she was still lounging around in a tank top and teal cuffed shorts. Her feet were bare. She twirled her long blonde hair over one shoulder, completely fixed on the book in front of her.

"I thought you said one more chapter," Clay said. He leaned down and kissed the top of her head.

"I did. But the last chapter ended on a cliffhanger, so I needed to know what happened next. I mean…their entire relationship was in peril."

"Every chapter ends on a cliffhanger. That's how they get you to stay invested."

"Shh," she said, waving her hand at him. "One more chapter."

He slouched into the chair next to her without complaint. If she wanted to sit around and read, then that was fine by him. So long as they got to the restaurant in time, he didn't mind.

After another twenty minutes, she finally sighed, stuck a bookmark into the book, and closed it. "They worked it out. I can move on with my life."

Clay chuckled. "You realize they're fictional, right?"

Andrea gasped. "What? They're fictional? No way! They are real, damn it!"

"You kill me."

"Yeah, well, you're the one trying to shatter my dreams with your 'truth,'" she said, using air quotes around the word *truth*.

"Fine. They're real, and they're all going to run away and live happily ever after."

She shrugged, stood, and stretched. "For now at least. I'm sure they have to suffer a little more first."

"Don't we all?"

"Come upstairs with me." Andrea took his hand, and he stood, giving her a long, slow kiss. "Mmm…definitely come upstairs with me."

He laughed. "All right, but let's not be late for dinner."

"Just a teensy bit late?" she encouraged with another kiss.

"You might be able to convince me."

She dragged him off the patio and then up the stairs. They were on the second landing when Andrea stopped abruptly. "Actually…I have another idea."

"What's that?" he asked.

His eyes cut to her studio. As promised, he'd put a lock on the door for her, and since they'd moved in, he hadn't been inside. He was curious, of course, but he would never invade her privacy. This was important to her. He respected that.

"Come with me." She walked tentatively toward the door and stopped with her hand on the handle.

"You don't have to show me."

"I know," she said softly. "But…I want to."

He nodded, understanding that she was finally unlocking the last piece of herself for him, and then she opened the door. She took a deep breath, pushing it all the way open for him. He followed her into the space.

It was perfect. So inherently Andrea that, for a second, it was as if he couldn't breathe. The painting he had bought her hung like a trophy from the wall, but otherwise, the room was covered in canvases. One wall full of modern art was a kaleidoscope of colors. The others were dark and broody. Almost all were black and white with just a few streaks of color here and there. Still more paintings were lying on the table in the center of the room—unfinished and in need of more work.

He could almost see her in here, deciding what to work on each day. Picking up a piece at random and throwing all her thoughts and ideas onto the canvas. They didn't have to be for anyone else. Just her.

And, thus, they were exquisite. Each and every one of them.

She had none of the pressure of showing them to the public for critiques or for the need for approval through a sale. She just had the canvas, paint, and the brush. He loved her even more in that moment. So much, his heart constricted.

"These," she said tentatively, pointing to the bright paintings, "I think were my favorites that I did over the last couple of years…before…well, before the breakup. I tried replicating artists I admired until my work started taking on its own form."

She bit her lip and then drew her gaze to the darkened side of the room. "These, I did while we were apart."

It was like seeing a window into her soul. Those months apart had been brutal, dark, depressing, agonizing. He could see it in every brushstroke. In the dark lines and the dark colors and the depressing dark emptiness of the paintings.

He choked on words.

"I think my new stuff is a compromise," she said, gesturing to the exquisite paintings on the table.

They were a compromise. Halfway between the strict structure and bright colors of the early years and the dark depressing months apart. Happy, whole, united with love. That was what her new work screamed.

And then he knew. He just knew.

Fuck it.

"Run away with me."

"What?" she asked. She was threading her fingers together, as if anxious of what he would think of the pictures. As if he could think anything she had created was less than amazing.

"Run away with me." He took her hand and drew her toward him.

She stuttered into his embrace and looked up at him with wary eyes. "Ha-ha. Okay, Clay."

"No, really, Andrea," he said without preamble, looking square in her eyes. "Marry me."

Andrea stilled and gave a half-laugh. "Clay, come on."

Clay just smiled, sank down onto one knee, and removed the blue Tiffany box from his jacket pocket. Her eyes rounded to the size of saucers.

"No, you come on, Andrea. Run away with me. Marry me."

Her hand flew to her mouth. She gasped in pure shock at what was happening before her. He saw tears brimming in her eyes.

Yeah, there was no way she had seen this coming. Though, frankly, he hadn't seen it happening this way. There was just no other way it could have happened once he was here. She'd shown him a part of her soul. And he wanted her to have his for the rest of their lives. It was only fitting.

"Clay," she breathed. "Oh my God!"

"Is that a yes?" he asked.

"Yes! Are you joking? Of course, yes!"

He laughed and jumped up, sweeping her into his arms. "God, I love you."

"I love you, too. Oh my God, you just proposed."

She held her left hand out, shaking slightly, and he plucked the enormous, way over-the-top diamond out of the box. It was a giant circular diamond set with a double halo of diamonds around the center stone.

The band was a simple thread of diamonds all the way around her finger. And, when he slid it into place, he smiled triumphantly. The diamond took up almost her entire tiny finger.

She really started crying then. "Oh my God, it's gorgeous. This is exactly the ring I would have picked. How did you know?"

"Because I know you, baby," he said, drawing her in for a kiss. "I've always known you. And I've always wanted to spend the rest of my life with you. Now, it's just official."

"We're official," she said in awe. "Oh my God, we're official."

"You just have to do one thing when we get to Chris's big party tonight."

She beamed. "What's that?"

"Tell all of them yourself, so they don't kill me."

"What? Why?"

He laughed and ducked his head. "Well, the party is actually for you, and I was planning on proposing to you there. So, they're all waiting for us."

She started laughing uncontrollably. "You sly little dog! I had no idea. Why didn't you wait?"

"I couldn't wait. The moment was perfect. How could I not let you know I wanted to share the rest of my life with you when you were sharing so much with me?"

"Oh, I do love you!" She threw herself into his arms. "We're getting married!"

Andrea screamed that all over again as soon as they entered the room of her favorite restaurant. She threw her hand out to the gathered audience—Gigi, Brady, Liz, Chris, Ethan, Cash; Jamie and her husband, James; Victoria and her boyfriend, Daniel.

Everyone oohed and ahhed appropriately when she showed the giant diamond around the crowd.

But it was Gigi who came up to Clay in the mayhem and smacked him on his arm. "I put all of this together, and you proposed at home?"

"Thanks, Gigi. Couldn't have done it without your pep talk at the office."

"Damn, I really wanted to see! Tell me everything."

"Ask Andrea. I'm sure she'll want to tell the story a million times."

Gigi rushed forward to get a good look at the ring on Andrea's finger and to ask Andrea to tell what had happened. The guys all sidled up next to him with shots in their hands, clapping him on the back in congratulations, and then they all downed the drinks.

When everyone finally settled down, they had a celebratory dinner. The girls were already scheming, and Clay let them. It was one of the best days of his life. He couldn't have asked for any of it to go better. The girl of his dreams had said yes, and he was with friends and family. He couldn't be happier. He had never thought this day would come, but he was glad now that it had.

Once dinner ended, Clay retrieved his fiancée— *fuck! his fiancée!*—and wished everyone good night. "Let's go this way."

"What's this?" she asked.

"I had a moonlit stroll planned. Thought we could still walk the short path around the place?"

"That sounds wonderful." She wrapped her hand around his arm and started walking through the darkened trail. "The girls are so excited. They wanted to know everything. Liz had just done this, so she went straight into wedding-planner mode, but, damn, I mean, I never thought this would happen. I don't even know what I want."

"Yes, you do," he said easily.

"Maybe I do," she agreed with a grin. "I just…well, we should probably think about a date."

"Indeed."

"What do you think?" she asked.

"I think when it's warm."

"So, probably next spring then?"

He stopped them in their tracks underneath a streetlamp and kissed her. "I was thinking a little sooner."

"But…"

"What about in two weeks?"

"What?" she gasped.

"Why wait?"

Her mouth was agape. "Because…there's so much to plan. And we just got back together a couple months ago. And…"

"And all things that change nothing. I'm completely dedicated to you. You are completely dedicated to me. We already live together. Plus, we're already going to be in Hilton Head."

They'd planned to go on vacation after her gallery opening so that they could have a breather after his grueling work schedule. He might…or might not have had an idea that this would happen, but he obviously hadn't mentioned that to her.

"Yeah, I mean, we *are*, but, Clay, I can't plan a wedding in two weeks!"

"Yes, you can," he told her simply. "Just think. No stress. No worrying about every little detail. Because we both know you'd obsess about it otherwise. Just you and me, our family, and the exchanging of rings on the beach. Run away with me."

Her mouth opened and closed. "You really mean it?"

"I've had a decade with you already. I know I want this. I'm entirely sure. Why wait?"

A slow smile grew on her face, and then she threw her arms around him and kissed him. "I'm going to be a Maxwell in two weeks!"

"Baby, you've been a Maxwell all your life."

Chapter 30

OFF THE MARKET

Clay had thought that having only two weeks to plan a wedding would make his spur-of-the-moment elopement a small, intimate affair. Just he and Andrea on the beach with I dos and a kiss.

Nothing fancy. Nothing extravagant.

Apparently, he had been very wrong.

"Ugh, it looks like it's going to rain," Andrea grumbled from his side.

She was supervising the stringing up of lights and flowers all over the pool area of the Maxwell beach house in Hilton Head. A team had been brought in to fully fit the deck into a proper reception space to Andrea's likings.

"Then, baby," he said, scooping her up for a kiss, "we'll just get married in the rain."

She wrinkled her cute little button nose. "It would ruin everything. Don't bring rain down on our day, Clay."

He laughed. "Nothing could ruin today."

"All right, Andrea," Liz called from the other side of the pool deck. "We have to get you ready. Get your ass in here."

She scurried over toward Liz, and Clay followed.

"Not you," Liz said, smacking him in the chest.

Andrea walked through the house to the awaiting hair and makeup team that had taken over his father's study downstairs. It was hilarious to glimpse a group of men and women with crazy piercings and exaggerated hair dye standing around in his father's hard, cold study.

Clay wrapped his fingers around Liz's hand on his chest and smirked at her. "We need to talk."

"Oh?" She raised an eyebrow.

"I just want you to know that, even though I know you are really, really going to want to…you shouldn't object today."

Liz burst out laughing and snatched her hand back. "I'm already married, you idiot."

"Look, I'm going to be officially off the market. I know it's going to be your last chance, but for Andrea's sake."

"Oh, of course…for Andrea's sake." She pulled him into a fierce hug. "It's really good to have you as a brother."

"You, too…sis."

She groaned and pulled back. "That sounds so weird."

"It really does."

"Good luck out there," she said with a wink before disappearing back into the house.

Brady and Chris showed up a few minutes later after procuring last-minute necessities that Andrea had insisted on. She'd given them a list as soon as they'd arrived, and they'd been gone all morning. Brady handed off the stuff they'd gotten and then pulled out a bottle of scotch.

"It's tradition," Brady said, nodding his head toward a table that would be later filled with whatever treats Andrea had gotten. "It's only fair that we finish this bottle tonight since we didn't get to give you a proper bachelor's party."

"We're pretty upset about that actually," Chris said.

Clay took a shot from Chris. "Sorry to disappoint, guys. A little last minute for those kinds of plans."

"You couldn't have given us three weeks?" Brady joked.

"Now or never," Clay said.

"Hey, hey, hey!" a trill voice called from the doorway.

Clay turned to see Savannah walking out onto the deck all alone.

"Where's mine?"

"You're not old enough," Brady and Clay said at the same time. Then, they both started laughing.

"I'm twenty-one!" she cried.

"Here you go, Savi," Chris said.

He passed her a shot, and she beamed up at him.

"Thanks, Chris."

Brady held his drink up high. "To my brother, who has finally found what he has always been looking for."

"And it was right in front of his face," Savi added with a giggle.

"For the last decade," Chris said.

"Assholes," Clay muttered. Then, he tilted his drink back and let it burn down his throat.

Savannah roughly smacked her brothers on their shoulders. "Both of my brothers are off the market in the same year. Whatever will the women of this poor country do with themselves?"

"They'll live," Brady said.

Clay shrugged. "Don't give a fuck."

"What about you, Savi?" Chris asked.

"Yeah," Clay said, as if realizing for the first time that she really was riding solo. "Where are Tweedledee and Tweedledum?"

"Excuse me?" she asked. She arched her eyebrow and crossed her arms.

"Is my brother Dee or Dum?" Chris asked with humor in his eyes.

"Dum," Brady and Clay said in unison.

Savannah just glared at them. "That's not funny."

"Aw, come on, Sav," Clay said. "At least we made your boyfriend Dee."

"Oh, yes, that makes me feel much better."

"Where are your two suitors anyway?"

Savannah ignored them. "I don't have suitors. This isn't the eighteenth century. I have a boyfriend, who was already going to be out of town this weekend, visiting his family. I couldn't go because I'm the editor at the newspaper, which I'm totally neglecting."

"Don't let Liz hear you say that," Brady said under his breath.

"And Lucas?" Clay asked.

She shrugged. "I don't know why you think I'd know where he is. Ask Chris!"

They all turned to Chris.

"School. He said he wanted to come bang you…"

Savannah's eyes widened. Brady and Clay looked ready to kill someone.

Chris just laughed at their reactions. "I mean…*bug* you, but he couldn't leave."

"I don't know why I put up with any of you!" Savannah muttered.

"Because we're family," Clay said, throwing an arm around Savannah. "You have to love us."

Savannah grumbled, but he knew that she loved him. His family wasn't perfect. But they were his family. They'd gotten through a lot together. And he'd do it all over again if it got him to this spot. Because this was what it was all about.

Love was enough.

Family was enough.

Friends were enough.

And he never wanted to forget that again.

~

Shortly afterward, all their guests—the few that there were—were ushered down to the beach.

Clay stood alone with Brady, his best man, on the pool deck, waiting to head down to the beach.

"You ready?" Brady asked.

"Yeah," Clay said. He swallowed hard, tucked his hands into his pockets, and rocked back and forth. "You ever get cold feet with Liz?"

"I was nervous as hell," Brady admitted.

"No, you weren't!" Clay said. "I was there."

Brady smiled. "I'm very good at controlling my emotions. Part of the job description. But I can assure you, I've not been that frazzled in a while. I was ready to marry her. More than ready, mind you. It's a big step though, and you can't help the nerves. Even if they're excited nerves."

Clay nodded. That was exactly how he was feeling right now. Excited but nervous, but excited…but nervous. His stomach was rolling. He'd truly never anticipated this moment. Now that he was here, he realized how dumb he'd been to think that.

He took a deep breath and released it slowly. He was ready.

The frantic wedding planner Andrea had managed to corral into helping them with the necessities for the day ducked back up the stairs and beckoned them forward. "We're ready for you two."

Clay gulped and then followed her. The beach was stunning. It was a beautiful day with just a few ominous clouds off in the distance over the water. Nothing to worry about. A spectacular archway made of oak driftwood had been set up with blush-colored flowers spiraling through it. Chairs, the color of sand with blush-pink cushions, were before it, already filled with guests—his parents, Savannah, Chris; the rest of the Atwoods, sans Lucas; Gigi, Jamie, Ethan, and Cash.

Clay and Brady stood at the front by the archway where Amelia—a woman Andrea had located on the Internet, who was ordained and lived on Hilton Head Island—stood to marry them.

Amelia shook hands with each of them. "Good to meet you both. I have everything here that your bride sent over," she placed her hand on a soft leather folder. "Just follow along."

"All right. Thanks so much for doing this on short notice," Clay told her. He straightened out the soft-pink bow tie he wore with his navy-blue suit.

"It's really my pleasure."

And then the chatter stopped because Liz, the matron of honor, had just walked down the stairs to an instrumental song played by a violinist. She had a dusty-blue dress, holding pink and white flowers. Clay realized, as she drew closer, she was barefoot. He almost laughed. Of course. He wished he were barefoot instead of in boat shoes.

Liz stopped to the side of Amelia and winked at him.

Then, the music shifted…along with his world.

Andrea appeared like a vision. She had never been more stunning.

He choked on words to describe her magnificence. A blush dress so light pink that it was almost white covered her frame, as if it had been handmade for her frame. It was high fashion meets beach wedding—the duality of which was exactly Andrea. The gown was strapless and flowy with sequins woven intricately into the bust to make her glow lightly in the afternoon sun as the train dragged lightly behind her in the sand. Her hair was down in supermodel soft waves that framed her face and fell down her back. But the best of all was her smile. The all-encompassing magnetic smile.

He'd put that smile on her face.

It was worth a lifetime to see that smile.

Andrea finally reached him. She handed off her enormous bouquet of pink and white peonies with soft green leaves as a finishing touch. Then, she took his hands into hers.

"Oh my God," Andrea breathed.

"You may take your seats," Amelia said. "I am honored to be here today, on such short notice, to bring together these two people who obviously love each other very much. When Andrea reached out to me just two weeks ago to ask me to marry the pair who you see before you today, I was excited to find their love had manifested so fully. Despite their struggles, they stand before you today, prepared to make life's most sacred vow."

Amelia nodded at Andrea. "Repeat after me."

"I, Andrea Billings, take you, Clay Maxwell"—tears started streaming down Andrea's face, and she hiccuped—"to be my husband. My partner in life. And the love of my life."

She swiped at her eyes and beamed up at him. He'd never been happier to see her cry.

He repeated the statement.

All he wanted to do was kiss her. Kiss the breath out of her. But he'd have his moment. Damn, it had never been harder to wait to kiss her.

Amelia coached them through the *to have and to holds*, and then they were moving on to the rings. Brady had them in his pocket, and as he pulled them out, a deep rumble cut through the ceremony. All eyes flickered to the skyline where clouds were rolling in much faster than they had before.

Andrea's lip quivered.

"Through sickness and in health, baby," he whispered to her.

The smile reappeared.

"All right, with that in the background, let's try to keep you dry," Amelia said with a chuckle. "These rings signify an unbreakable bond and union, a circle of love forged together eternally today. Let's start with the groom."

"This ring is my sacred gift," Clay said, repeating after Amelia. He held Andrea's hand in his, and the ring was resting between them. "With my promise that I will always love you, cherish you, and honor you for all the days of my life. And, with this ring, we are wed."

He slipped the ring onto her finger, and her face split into a smile.

Andrea took Clay's ring from Brady, and just as she recited the same words…raindrops fell.

Just a trickle at first and then a downpour. A typical afternoon storm was cutting through their ceremony.

Andrea looked ready to cry as all her hard work was being torn apart by the storm. Then, she looked back up at Clay, who had a huge smile on his face.

"I love you," Andrea cried over the rain.

"I love you, too."

"And, with this ring, we are wed," she said, pushing the ring onto his finger.

"I now pronounce you man and wife. Please, kiss your bride," Amelia said with a laugh.

Without a second thought for what was happening all around him, whether or not people were trying to find shelter or enjoying the rain or even paying attention to them at all, Clay grabbed his *wife* by the back of her head and kissed her like he'd never kissed her before. Their lips met with passion as rain fell all around them, soaking their clothes and coating their faces. But still, he didn't let go. He just continued on until they were both panting and breathless.

"I cannot believe it rained," she said over the yell of the storm.

"I can. It's just like us."

"What?"

"Life-changing and completely unpredictable."

Chapter 31
ANDREA

By the time the afternoon showers had abated, the decorations were destroyed. But, as they walked back up onto the deck and found all their friends and family waiting for them, just as drenched as she and Clay were, she didn't have a care in the world. She was a Maxwell.

"Mr. and Mrs. Clay Maxwell, everybody!" Brady's voice boomed over the crowd.

Everyone cheered at their union, laughing and whistling.

Andrea could barely catch her breath. This had all happened so fast. One minute, she had been lost in a world of anger and depression and guilt, and the next, she was happier than she had ever been in her entire life.

Andrea turned into Clay, and he pulled her in for another wet kiss. She giggled, completely ignoring the way her wedding dress clung to her body. When he released her at last, he hoisted her into his arms with ease.

"Clay," she gasped.

"My wife needs to get out of these clothes, so she doesn't catch a cold," Clay said to the crowd.

Andrea buried her face in his shoulder in horror as catcalls rang out all around them. Clay deftly carried her across the pool deck and into the house. Her dress left water droplets all down the hardwood floor as Clay took her up the stairs and to their room. She had reserved a suite at a nearby hotel for later, but she wasn't complaining about getting out of these clothes right now.

Clay dropped her on her feet once they were inside, and she shivered. She hadn't realized that she was even cold because his words had been ringing through her over and over again. Those beautiful words.

"Your wife," she whispered.

"Well, you are now." His voice was deep and seductive.

God, I love this man.

"I know. I just...I never in a million years, not even in my wildest dreams, thought we would be here today."

One thought had been going through her mind since he had asked her. She just hadn't been able to bring herself to ask him. But she knew she could now.

"I thought you didn't even want to get married," she said softly.

He smiled and slipped his hands down the wet lacy fabric of her gown. "I didn't."

"Oh."

"I wanted to marry you."

Andrea grabbed his face in her hands and dragged his lips down to hers. She was feverish, wanting nothing more than to strip him of all his clothes and really become his wife. Consummate their marriage in all the best ways.

She pulled his bow tie loose and threw it to the ground. His eyes widened with surprise and lust. Yes, she was going to do this right now. No, she didn't care that there were people waiting for them.

He nodded. Completely there with her.

She stripped him out of his remaining sodden clothing, and then he helped her take off the soaked dress. It made a squelching noise at it hit the ground. She would have to care about that later but not right now. She left the expensive garments hastily discarded on the floor, and they both fell into the king-size bed they'd had sex on countless times over the years.

Clay fiddled with her white lace thong that read *Mrs.* in Swarovski crystals when they heard footsteps on the stairs. Heavy footsteps. Lots of them.

"I guess we're not the only ones who wanted to change," Andrea said with a giggle.

He buried his face in her chest and brought her nipple into his mouth. "I guess not."

"Oh, that's not fair."

"Fair?"

He swirled his tongue around the erect nipple and then sucked it into his mouth again. She groaned and wrapped her legs around his waist, dragging him closer.

"Fuck," he grumbled against her body.

Her entire body was aflame, and he was stoking the fire. She couldn't wait. She couldn't drag this out. She just wanted and needed him in that moment.

"Clay, please," she pleaded.

He didn't argue. She was sure he could hear the need in her voice. He removed the last scrap of fabric covering her body. Then, he steadied himself over her and slid inside her.

She moaned and threw her head back. "Oh my God, you've never felt better."

"You like when your husband fucks you?"

She nearly purred. "Oh, yes."

And he did. He started up a fierce rhythm. One that said he'd been thinking about fucking her all day, wanting to do nothing more than take her to the next height again and again.

She threaded her fingers through his short blond hair, pulling harshly. Her lips found his ear, neck, shoulder. She nipped at him, trying to get him closer and closer. Fuck, she loved this man with all of her being.

She had always known. She had been a goner from day one when he kissed her on that beach all those years ago. Been bold enough to take their relationship a step forward. She had loved him even more in college and still more in law school. When it'd felt like everything else around them had fallen apart, they'd still remained strong.

After loving him so completely and feeling ready to move forward, only to be rebutted over and over again, she'd thought they could never fix what was broken between them…but then he'd come back. He'd changed…yet stayed her Clay Maxwell. And this was the *man* that she was making passionate love to. Not the boy she had needed, but the man that she wanted…the one who had shown her the true meaning of love.

As they came together for the first time as husband and wife, sealing their lives together, she knew that she would never be the same. And she was perfectly happy about that.

She had a new family. He was her family. He was her life.

"I love you so much," Clay said into her shoulder, breathing heavily.

"Oh, Clay, I have always loved you." Then, she kissed him.

They took their time with cleaning up and coming down from the high of the day…and their afternoon delight.

They changed into fresh clothes. Clay into a pair of khaki shorts and a button-up. She had set a shorter all lace dress aside for tomorrow, but it would do now.

When she had finally gotten the dress on, Clay took her hand, and they walked back downstairs. Most of the other guests were back out on the deck, clearing off some of the debris from the rain and wiping down the benches so that they could sit down.

The wait staff had brought out dinner as well as an assortment of Parisian macaroons, all in blush pink, pearly white, and dusty blue. Her favorite. The cake was three-tiered even though there were so few guests, but she had insisted. It looked as if it were made of pearls with an artful mosaic of their wedding colors running like a river down one side.

Once everything was cleared off, they sat around the pool, eating and mingling with all their friends. Music played through the poolside surround sound stereo on the deck. She had actually allowed that since it made little sense to have a band for fifteen people. It was one of her few compromises on the wedding.

As "You Are the Best Thing" by Ray LaMontagne filtered in through the speakers, Clay wrapped Andrea up in his arms for their first dance.

After their first dance, Savannah cut in to dance with Clay, and Brady offered to dance with Andrea. Clay twirled his little sister around the dance floor like he had done when they were kids. Savannah was laughing exuberantly.

Brady was an excellent dancer. He practically swept Andrea off her feet. She understood why Liz had fallen for his dancing.

"I'm really happy for you two," Brady said with his charming smile.

"Me, too."

"No, really. You've done wonders for Clay. I never knew if he'd come around."

"Well, all I did was leave," she said with a shrug.

"I'm sure that had to be hard."

She frowned and then remembered it was her wedding day. Life had given her lemons, and she had actually made a kick-ass Arnold Palmer. "It was hard, but it worked out in the end, didn't it?"

"Absolutely. I couldn't have asked for a better sister. You really bring out the best in him."

She chuckled softly. "Thank you, Brady. I'm really happy for you and Liz, too. I know you went through a lot to get to where you are. Way more than Clay and I did."

He shrugged. "It's all on a scale of terrible, I suppose. The important thing is, we each found our way to the people we love."

"Well, I couldn't have done it without you. Thank you for telling me about how Clay was doing while I was away…even when I didn't think I wanted to hear it."

"Always looking out for him, you know. Old habits die hard. And, anyway…we're here today, Mrs. Maxwell."

"Oh, that's the best," she said with a giggle.

After the dancing, Clay and Andrea cut the cake, while champagne was passed around. Brady clinked his fork against his glass to get everyone's attention.

"Since all of you happened to be at my wedding earlier this year, you might remember a certain toast from the groom over there," Brady said.

"Oh no," Clay mumbled.

"Oh, yes," Andrea said with glee.

"And so you all know he had this coming."

Their friends and family laughed.

"Just keep it under an hour!" Clay yelled back.

Brady laughed and nodded. "Fair." He cleared his throat. "Obviously, I've known Clay his entire life. He's my younger brother. For a long time, he was just that annoying kid, following me around. Then, he was that annoying kid who got into Yale. Then, the Supreme Court. Then, Cooper and Nielson. I'd like to say he outgrew the annoying part, but we all know him better than that."

Everyone laughed good-naturedly, and Clay just shook his head.

"That is, until this year. I remember a time during my senior year of college, when I was playing ball at UNC, and Clay came to visit. That was rare. We didn't get along like that back then. I tried to show him a good time. Sorry, Mom and Dad."

Their dad laughed, and their mother just covered her ears, like she hadn't heard what he just said.

"We had a great time that weekend, as brothers. But, even then, I knew something was different about him. I knew Andrea, of course. They've really been together since they were kids even though they didn't officially start dating until college. But it wasn't until that weekend when I realized that Clay really loved her. Call me crazy. Back then, I wasn't exactly a romantic."

Liz nudged him in the side. "Well, thank God I changed that."

"Agreed, baby," he said with a laugh. "The thing is…I don't think Clay knew how much he was head over heels for this girl."

Andrea beamed, and tears glistened in her eyes. When Brady had first told her this story, she had broken down into wretched sobs on the spot. But, now, she could remember it with fondness…knowing Clay had always loved her. And would always love her.

"With anything that's truly great, it takes time, sacrifice, and devotion to maintain. You two have put in the years. You've put in the time. Lord knows, we all saw the sacrifice and devotion over the last year."

Clay smiled back at his brother, who held his glass high.

"I couldn't have asked for anyone better for my brother, anyone who just understood him and loved him for who he was. And, in return, I'm ecstatic to call you my sister. To Clay and Andrea."

Everyone toasted and drank their champagne.

Brady finished his off and then grinned. "And, apparently…to great sex!"

Andrea buried her face in Clay's shoulder.

He just laughed. "Got that covered, man."

"After that horribly embarrassing moment," Andrea said with a laugh, "I want to throw my bouquet!"

Of course, the only unmarried women in the bunch were Savannah, Gigi, and Chris's sixteen-year-old sister, Alice Atwood. Clay groaned as they lined up to try to catch the bouquet. Andrea was sure that he was hoping no one would catch it. He was super protective of the women in his life but especially his little sister.

Andrea tossed the bouquet over her head. It flew in the air, and all three girls reached up to catch the gorgeous peonies. Then, it landed softly into Savannah's hands.

She squealed and jumped up and down. "Mine!" she cried.

Andrea laughed and gave her a hug.

Brady and Clay both held their hands up.

"Now, wait one minute."

"Savi…I don't think…"

"You're too young for any of that."

"Andrea, maybe try one more time."

"Hey!" Savannah snapped. "It's mine! And I'm next anyway, right? We're going in order."

Brady shook his head. "I think I see some serious conversations with this boyfriend of yours in the future."

Savannah rolled her eyes. "What. Ever."

"We should probably cover Tweedledum, too, just as a precaution," Clay teased.

"Whoa now!" Andrea said, breaking them up. "Leave poor Savannah alone. She can be up next without you two interfering in her love life!"

"Thank you, Andrea," Savannah said. "So, butt out, jerks!"

Brady grabbed Savannah around the shoulders, and they were jabbing at each other in good nature.

Andrea shook her head and turned back to Clay just as Gigi walked up. She gave Andrea a huge hug and then one for Clay.

"Congratulations! Both of you! I'm so happy for you."

"Thanks, Gigi," Andrea said.

"I'm so glad you could make it," Clay added.

"Me, too. It's been fun…erm…awkward but fun."

"Awkward?" Andrea asked.

Gigi's eyes darted to Chris's and then back to her in a second.

"Oh, because you slept together?" Clay said.

"Clay!" Gigi snapped. "Will you give it a rest?"

"Well, did you?" Clay asked.

Andrea put her hand to her head. *Tactless.*

"For your information, we didn't. I don't think he's interested in me like that. So, if you could stop the interrogation about it, it might be less awkward…since I guess I'll probably have to be around him a lot more."

Clay held up his hands. "All right, all right."

"But, for the record," Andrea said, taking Gigi's hand, "Chris would be crazy not to be interested in you like that." Sometimes Andrea still have trouble being around Gigi, but the more she interacted with her, the more she realized how misguided she had been. Clay and Gigi were very similar people, and they really were *just* friends.

"Thanks," she said softly. With a small frown, she cut her eyes back over to Chris.

The night wore on. Soon, people were retiring to their respective hotel rooms, and Andrea knew that she and Clay should head back to their own hotel room. But she just wanted to waste the night away here with Clay forever.

Clay's father approached with a tin of cigars.

Clay's eyebrows rose. "For me?"

"Of course for you!" Jeff said with a smile. "Andrea?"

"No, thank you. I'll stick to my champagne."

"Good choice."

The guys lit their cigars, and Andrea watched them—father and son—having their moment. She had always wanted a better relationship for Clay with his father. Since she had sworn off her family, she had taken up the Maxwells as her own. She hated that Clay had never been able to talk to his dad the way she knew he wanted to. He had been intimidated and put off and afraid for so long, thinking Brady was the favorite. But she knew that his father was just reticent with affection. As they stood together, she could see the bond forging now.

"I wanted to give you two this before your mother and I headed to bed for the night," Jeff said, passing over an envelope to Clay and Andrea.

Clay opened the envelope, and when Andrea saw what was inside, her eyes widened as big as saucers.

Inside was the deed to Andrea's parents' beach house. *How the hell did he get that?*

"This is too much," Clay said at once.

"No, it's not. I know you two already bought a house together, but I thought this would be a good addition."

"How?" Andrea asked.

"I bought it years ago," he admitted. "Your mother didn't want to keep it, but…you were family, Andrea, even then. I couldn't let you lose that home, too. I always figured, one day, I would give it to the two of you. And today is that day."

Tears came to her eyes, fresh and hot. She walked forward and hugged Jeff tightly. "Thank you so much. It means more than you'll ever know."

He patted her on the back. "I know, honey. Thank you for making my son so happy."

Clay laughed, as if he were trying to reel in all of his emotions. Andrea leaned back against the railing on the deck and stared at her husband and the father she never had.

"I guess, now, all I have to do is become attorney general to keep you proud of me," Clay said with a false laugh.

"What do you mean?" Jeff asked, taking another deep pull on his cigar.

"You remember," Clay said like he was desperate for his dad to remember…to know what always ate at him.

Oh, how she hurt for him then because it was clear on his father's face that he didn't remember.

"You were right here, in this house, and you said Brady was good enough to become president and that

I'd be an attorney general…because it worked for the Kennedys."

Jeff scratched the back of his head. A habit that both of his sons had acquired from him. "I honestly don't remember that, son. You should know…I'm proud of you, and I always have been. I hope you never thought that you couldn't be whatever you wanted to be. If attorney general is your dream, then you're doing a fine job at getting there. If it's not, then being the best lawyer in D.C. is pretty damn good, too."

Clay opened and closed his mouth. In the matter of one conversation, his father had just shattered every preconceived notion Clay had had about him.

"I thought you preferred Brady," Clay muttered, as if he'd been holding the words in for too long.

"How could a father choose one child over another? I think Brady and I just had more similar interests. You always took after your mother, and I respected that. And, since you always did your own thing, I just felt like you needed my guidance less. Maybe I was wrong for thinking that," Jeff said. He looked down and then back up at his son, as if struggling for the right words. That didn't happen often to a politician. "Clay, I'm sorry if you ever thought that I wasn't proud of you. I've always been proud of you."

"I love you, Dad."

"I love you, too, son."

They clasped hands, and then Jeff went to talk to his wife.

"Are you okay?" she asked carefully.

"Walk with me?"

Andrea nodded and followed him out to the beach. They walked in silence in the star-filled night until they reached their spot, the spot of their first kiss.

After a minute, Clay spoke, "I always thought that my dad really wanted me to be the attorney general. To follow behind Brady. I've been holding on to this dream, and my dad didn't even remember saying it."

"So then, let it go," she said. "Do you want to be the attorney general one day?"

"I don't know," he answered honestly.

"And that's okay," she said, slipping into his arms. "You have me. Let the rest of the world figure itself out as we go. I never knew I'd open an art gallery, and here I am. You can do *anything*, baby. I know it."

Clay kissed her under the moonlight in the exact place where they had first shared a kiss. "How did I get so lucky?"

"We made our own luck."

"That we did, my love. That we did."

Epilogue
FIVE YEARS LATER

"*Zoooom!*"

Clay laughed and chased after his daughter, Cassidy. She was two going on three, and her little legs were racing ahead of him as she tried to escape the dreaded torture of putting on shoes.

"Daddy, flying!"

"All right, baby girl." He scooped her up in his arms and flew her around the room, like an airplane.

She squealed and giggled until he flopped them both down onto her small bed. He scooted her so that she was on his knee, and he started bouncing her up and down.

"Again. Again!"

"No more airplane for now," he said. "First, shoes."

"No shoes. Airplanes, Daddy. Airplanes."

"You sound just like your Uncle Brady," he said with a laugh as he scooped up her hot-pink sparkle shoes off the ground and started fitting them to her feet.

He and Andrea had adopted Cassidy just over a year ago. Andrea had said she wanted to start to have kids right away after the wedding, and Clay had been surprised to find that he did, too. But, after almost three years without any luck, Andrea had come to him to ask about adopting.

They'd both had an interest in working with orphan charities, but adoption was taking it to a whole new level. But, after seeing the kids and adopting Cassidy, he'd known there was no other choice for them. Even if they were able to have kids later, Cassidy was the best thing that had ever happened to them. With her freckled skin, dark curly locks, and big, wide chocolate eyes, she was the cutest little kid he'd ever seen. They were both happy to give a child in need a home, and most days, he completely forgot that they'd even adopted. She was just their little Cassidy Anna Maxwell.

"Honey!" Andrea called from the other room. "Are you two ready?"

"Just about," he called back.

He tied Cassidy's last shoe, tugged her red-white-and-blue Captain America tutu straight, and then smiled at the X-Men shirt she had on. They were all her favorite, and she had insisted on wearing them. What could he say? His little girl was a badass.

He scooped Cassidy up and trotted her down the stairs to the living room. "Here we are."

"Mommy!"

Andrea laughed when she saw Cassidy. "You're taking her to Jefferson's birthday party in that?" she asked about Brady and Liz's son, who was turning three today.

"Yep. It's what she wanted. All the other kids will be jealous."

"They'll be something," she said with a laugh. "Come here, bug."

Cassidy rushed over to her mom and threw her arms around her shoulders. Andrea kissed her all over her face. Cassidy giggled and started making kissy noises of her own.

"Airplanes!"

"No airplane right now. I have some exciting news for you today." Andrea picked her up in her arms and ruffled her unruly curly hair.

Andrea had tried to tame it when they first adopted Cassidy, but it was no use. Clay liked it that way.

"News?" he asked.

"Yep! You want to know, too, bug?"

"Yeah!" she cried.

Andrea handed her back to Clay. "Well, it's a super special surprise. You like surprises, don't you?"

"Tell me! Tell me!"

"Not even your daddy knows!"

Cassidy was bouncing up and down. "What is it, Mommy?"

"Yeah, what is it, Mommy?" Clay asked with a wink.

"Well…" She cleared her throat and then bit her lip. "It looks like you're going to be having a little brother or sister."

Clay's mouth dropped open as Cassidy squealed. "Andrea…" he stammered.

"I know! I found out last week, but I wanted to wait to tell you until I knew for sure."

"Baby, that's incredible. Oh my God!"

He switched Cassidy to his hip and pulled Andrea to them. Together, he and Cassidy hugged her fiercely.

"Group hug!" Andrea said with a laugh.

When he pulled back, he asked with slight trepidation, knowing they had waited a long time for this moment, "You're really sure?"

A tear glistened in her eye, and she nodded. "Yes, I'm really sure."

He put a hand on her stomach and laughed. "This is the best news, baby."

She sniffed and nodded. "God, Clay, I can't believe this is finally happening. We're going to have another baby. A little brother or sister for Cass."

"Now, you listen here, little man," Clay said, pointing at her stomach. "You can't be a girl. I'm already outnumbered."

Andrea laughed and wiped her eyes. "You're ridiculous, Clay Maxwell."

"Mmm…you're ridiculous, Andrea Maxwell." He kissed her hard on the mouth. "But we know who is really ridiculous! Cassidy Maxwell."

He zoomed her around the room. She laughed and laughed until he finally took her out to the car to drive over to Brady and Liz's.

"Do you want to tell them?" Clay asked as he helped Cassidy out of the car.

"Let's just wait until after the party unless Cass says something. I want to make this Jefferson's day."

He nodded, bursting at the seams with joy. He wanted to tell everyone. He wanted to scream it from the rooftops. They'd been trying so hard for so long. Andrea had felt like a failure so many times, even when he'd told her over and over that it didn't matter to him. Because it didn't. He loved her. He wanted her happiness. If it wasn't making her happy, then they didn't need to try. They needed to *practice* but not for conception…just for love.

So, they had adopted Cass and tried not to stress the small stuff. They had other things to worry about. Like Andrea's art gallery taking off beyond her wildest dreams, including opening additional galleries in New York City, Los Angeles, Chicago, and Paris all in a matter of years. She was a sensation. Not just selling others' works, but her own, which had garnered a lot of attention once she had finally revealed them.

Clay and Gigi had abandoned Cooper & Nielson together, deciding to give up corporate law and focus more on what mattered—by opening up their new firm Maxwell & De Rosa. They still worked with big clients who had left Cooper & Nielson with them, but they spent their time on humanitarian cases as well. Made sure they remembered why they were in law…why they loved it—to help people. He wouldn't say that he had completely abandoned his dream of going for attorney general one day if Brady became president, but for now, that dream was on hold for another one.

They walked into Brady's house without knocking on the door and found Brady in the kitchen, pulling dishes out of the refrigerator. A domesticated Brady was one that Clay still couldn't get used to seeing.

"Clay! Andrea!" Liz said as she walked in through the back door. "Little Cass!" She bent down and held her arms out. "Give your Cool Aunt Liz a hug."

Cassidy ran forward into her arms. "Cool Aunt Liz!"

Clay shook his head. "Oh, dear Lord. You have her calling you that?"

"Well, it is true," she said. She squeezed Cassidy tight. "Jefferson is out back. You want to go play?"

"Yeah!" she cried.

They all followed Cassidy out the back door as she rushed toward her cousin. Andrea placed a birthday present on a table for Jefferson, and then it was her turn to be pulled into a hug by Liz. Brady passed Clay a beer as they waited for everyone else to get here.

Liz grabbed a cocktail off the table and took a long drink. "What do you want, Andrea? We have these mixed cocktail things that Brady put together. We have champagne and beer, or I can make you something."

Andrea froze and then shook her head. "Um…nah, I'm not drinking."

Liz looked at her like she had just grown horns. "What? Why not? Come on! You won't have to drive home for hours."

"No. I'm just…not thirsty."

Liz laughed. "What? Are you pregnant?"

There was a long silent pause in which Liz covered her mouth.

"Oh, y'all, I'm so sorry. I didn't mean it like that. I'm so inconsiderate. I know you've been trying. I didn't mean it. Fuck!" Her eyes darted to the kids and back, and then she grimaced. "I mean…"

"It's okay," Clay said with a laugh.

"No, it's not. I don't mean to joke about that kind of stuff. I know it's been hard for y'all."

"No, really," Andrea said with a giddy grin. "It's okay because…I am. I just found out today."

"Oh my God!" Liz shrieked. She pulled Andrea into a hug. "Oh my God! Oh my God! Congratulations!"

Brady reached his hand out, and Clay shook it. "Congrats, man. I'm so happy for y'all."

"Ahhh!" Liz cried. "Tell me everything. When are you due? What names are you thinking? Boy or girl?"

"Boy," Clay said automatically.

Andrea laughed and shook her head. "Uh-uh, honey. She's definitely going to be a girl."

"You'd deserve it, Clay," Liz said with a wink.

He shrugged. "Maybe."

They all laughed.

Everyone else started showing up, and Clay and Andrea couldn't seem to contain their secret. They'd been trying to get pregnant for so long. So much of their time had been devoted to this, and all of their friends and family were so excited for them.

A bet was made immediately on whether or not it was a boy or girl. Clay insisted it was a boy. Almost everyone disagreed with him. Even little Cassidy said she wanted a sister.

Clay just laughed and shrugged. He told everyone they had eight months left before they would find out. He pulled Andrea into his arms and kissed her cheek.

"You know," he whispered into her ear, "I don't mind if it's another girl."

"I know you don't."

"So long as she's healthy, that's all that matters to me."

She squeezed him tight. "Well, she's going to be the middle child, just like you, so you'll have to treat her extra special."

"Middle, eh? We're going to have another?"

"At least one more," she told him with an excited glint in her eyes.

"Well then, I'll have to treat them all extra special, won't I?"

"Yes, you will. We both will. All our little girls."

"Why are you so sure it's a girl?"

She smirked. "Intuition."

Nine months later, they found out Andrea was right.

And right about the next one, too.

And Clay realized that this was life's greatest adventure. Falling in love with Andrea all those years ago on the beach at Hilton Head had turned out to be one of the best decisions of his life. But choosing to love her all these years later and sharing that love with their kids…now, *that* was truly the best decision of his life.

THE END

Stay tuned for Broken Record, *Savannah's stand-alone story in the next book in the Record series.*

Broken Record follows Savannah Maxwell, a driven college journalist with a taste for rebellion against her political family who is torn between her political-oriented boyfriend and the boy she's always wanted…

COMING FALL 2016

PREORDER NOW!

ACKNOWLEDGMENTS

First and foremost, I want to thank my husband, Joel. Despite himself, he loved Clay and truly helped me mold and shape this character. Without him, I might have gone crazy through this entire process. I'm very grateful to have someone so understanding of my career and the men that I create. Also, for taking care of the cutest puppies in the world when I was engrossed in this story.

This book wasn't created in a vacuum nor did it get into readers' hands without the assistance of a group of incredible women. Thank you Rebecca Kimmerling and Katie Miller, who read this book chapter by chapter throughout the entire process. I appreciate all the late nights, the brainstorming sessions, the message after message after message during rewrites and edits, and the continual joy and appreciation for the project. Thank you Polly Matthews for loving my bad boy, even when you didn't think you would, and for giving me your particularly picky input on my guy. My wonderful beta readers—Holly Malgieri and Autumn Review—I couldn't have done this without you! Christy Peckham and Anjee Sapp, I appreciate you giving me another set of eyes and always supporting me!

Thank you for the tireless support of my agent, Kimberly Brower. You helped mold this book, even through the self-publishing process. I appreciate all the content edits, early morning breakfast conversations about marketing, and the innumerable emails back and forth to make sure this was right. Danielle Sanchez, the queen of PR! You know I've gone through hell and back with publicity, and I couldn't be more grateful to have your beautiful face working with me on this project!

To all of the advocates for this book behind the scenes—Jovana Shirley at Unforeseen Editing for editing and formatting (thank you for being so flexible!!!), Sarah Hansen at Okay Creations for the wonderful design that held true to the originals and yet breathed life into the series, Lauren Perry at Perrywinkle Photography for the amazing work with the model for this book and your incredibly wonderful heart! Also, my Linde #squad girls who championed this book from the start! I couldn't have done it without you guys!

And, of course, my readers! Thank you to everyone who read and loved the Record series. Thank you for giving Clay a chance even though he isn't Brady and, as you just read…never *wanted* to be Brady. I love you all so much and hope that you'll stick around and read Savannah's story, *Broken Record*!

ABOUT THE AUTHOR

K.A. Linde is the *USA Today* bestselling author of more than fifteen novels including the Avoiding series and the Record series. She has a master's degree in political science from the University of Georgia, was the head campaign worker for the 2012 presidential campaign at the University of North Carolina at Chapel Hill, and is the current head coach of the Duke University dance team. She currently lives in Chapel Hill, North Carolina, with her husband and two super adorable puppies.

K.A. Linde loves to hear from her readers!

You can contact her at kalinde45@gmail.com or visit her online at one of the following sites:

www.kalinde.com

www.facebook.com/authorkalinde

http://twitter.com/AuthorKALinde